GRACE IN THE SHADOWS

BOOK 2

CHRISTINE DILLON

www.storytellerchristine.com

Grace in the Shadows

Copyright © 2018 by Christine Dillon

All Scripture quotations, are taken from the Holy Bible, New International Version®, NIV®. Copyright ©1973, 1978, 1984, 2011 by Biblica, Inc.™ Used by permission of Zondervan. All rights reserved worldwide. www.zondervan.com The "NIV" and "New International Version" are trademarks registered in the United States Patent and Trademark Office by Biblica, Inc.™

This book is a work of fiction. Names, characters, any resemblance to persons, living or dead, or events is purely coincidental. The characters and incidents are the product of the author's imagination and used fictitiously. Locales and public names are sometimes used for atmospheric purposes.

Cover Design: Lankshear Design.

ISBN: 978-0-6481296-3-9

For Jenny, with whom I've had many adventures. So thankful you're my sister and friend.

In memory of my aunt, Letitia Helen (1942-1976), much loved by those who knew her. She used the last of her strength to introduce someone to Jesus. May I use my last breaths as wisely.

NOTES TO READERS

* Christian authors are told not to put miracles in their stories. This seems like peculiar advice since God is a God of miracles. One of the reasons for this advice is that people don't want to raise the false expectation that God will always work miracles. Sometimes he chooses not to.

The miracles in this story are real stories that happened to people connected to our family. Both stories were more dramatic than I've described, as both people immediately became Christians. There are more details about the real stories in the acknowledgments section at the back of this book.

* This book is an Australian story and thus, mostly uses Australian conventions of grammar, punctuation, and spelling.

PROLOGUE

Late 1960s
Sydney, Australia

*I*t was love at first sight.

And second. And third.

Each memory was a lustrous pink pearl from a necklace she now kept locked away. Out of sight but not entirely out of mind.

The first pearl was their first meeting. She pressed so close to the glass that it fogged, blurring the outline of the pink-wrapped bundle beyond. Years of pestering her mother and now the day had come. She had a baby sister.

Finally.

She hopped on the spot. As though her sister read her mind, the tiny eyes snapped open and the little rosebud mouth opened in a yawn. She liked to think that, even then, her sister was seeking her out through the glass separating them.

The second pearl was the memory of her mother as she cradled the baby close and enclosed her in love. Had Mum held her the same way? Like she was the most precious baby in the whole world? Her sister latched on and sucked. She could almost see her growing.

She hugged her arms around her waist. Did her mum remember she had an almost eleven-year-old daughter, or was she too cocooned with the baby?

She leaned forward. "Do you think I'll ever have a baby?"

Her mother smiled. "Probably—most girls do. But don't grow up too quickly. I want my daughters with me as long as possible."

It was special to be wanted. Like being wrapped in her favourite mohair blanket on a winter's evening.

The third pearl was the first time she'd held her sister. The responsibility lay heavier than the child. Like she held a delicate china figurine.

She gazed down. Oh, the little cutie-pie. Solemn dark blue eyes stared back at her. What did they see? An older sister who already adored her? No kid would ever bully her sister. She'd be a hovering presence. A wall of protection. A hero.

The subsequent years had added more pearls. Creamy, dreamy memories. Times that became her only joys in the struggle wearing her down.

One pearl she remembered far too often. It had been a blazing beauty of an autumn. Bright blue skies, crisp mornings, and breezes which blew the leaves in languid eddies.

Her little sister swished through the fallen leaves, giggling as they crackled underfoot. She stooped down and threw armfuls of leaves into the air. They swirled around her in whirls of red, yellow, and faded brown.

Oh, how she loved this little sister of hers. How could she think of leaving her?

She swooped down and tickled.

"Don't, don't," her sister squealed.

They chased each other around the trees until they were both worn out. A sunbeam sliced through the leafless branches and illuminated the toddler in a warm glow.

"Look, look. The sun is shining right on me." Her sister raised her arms above her head, tilted her face to the sun, and laughed as she twirled.

Pure joy.

Another pearl. Another memory to lock away.

CHAPTER 1

1996

Sydney, Australia

*R*achel opened one eye. The early morning light glowed around the edges of the floor-length curtains. She yawned, rolled over, and thwacked her arm against solid flesh.

He groaned.

"What-d-ya hitting me for?" He propped himself up on one elbow. "Trying to get my attention?"

"Sorry." She wasn't about to tell him she'd forgotten he was there.

He reached over and drew her to him. "Best night of the month." He couldn't come more often, or his wife would get suspicious. She had end-stage lymphoma, and he got away for three days respite.

Rachel curled her lip. *Rachel's respite. Glad to be of service.*

"Can't you come with me to the hotel?" He kissed her shoulder.

"Not possible. I've got an extra shift at work."

"Why does it have to be you?"

Better cover up quick, or she'd be late. She scooted away from him and grabbed her silk robe off the floor.

He lunged for her. "C'mon babe. Don't be cruel."

She batted his hand away. "I can't miss a day."

He pouted his lips. "You work too hard."

Said the man who had a job that allowed him time off work to care for his wife. Working at David Jones wasn't like that. There were plenty of younger women queueing for her job.

Rachel slid the mirrored doors of her wardrobe to the side and took out the hanger with the crisply ironed black dress. Once in the bathroom, she turned the lock.

Hot jets stung her skin as she washed her hair. As she stepped out of the shower she glimpsed herself in the mirror. Did her hips look more rounded? How was that possible with her diet and exercise regime?

She blow-dried her hair and dressed. The diamond earrings had been a gift from a previous partner. She'd kept the diamonds and dumped the guy. He'd been too clingy.

Rachel opened the top drawer of the bathroom cabinet and took out her makeup kit. She squinted at the mirror. Was that a faint line on her neck? A cobweb of fear brushed across her heart. She'd fought hard, but forty was around the corner. Could she keep her job if she began to look old?

With swift, practiced strokes, Rachel covered her face with foundation and added mascara and eyeshadow. The lipstick must wait until after her fruit and coffee. Even without the lipstick, a young version of her mother stared back at her. Would her mother recognise her now? It had been more than twenty years.

Her chest and throat tightened. How could she face her mother? Still unmarried. Sure, there'd been men, but her mother wouldn't be impressed there'd been more than one. For Mum, life was simple. Marriage, children, and stand by your man. That was a laugh. Rachel's first man had jumped ship right when he was most needed.

She'd always intended to write and let her mother know she was safe, but it had never happened. What kind of person was she, that she'd cut herself off from her family? She'd loved them once. At least, she'd loved two out of the three. The other one she was only too glad to never see again.

Rachel dabbed her nose with a tissue, careful not to smudge her makeup. Then she unlocked the bathroom door and strode back into the bedroom, banishing the ghost of her past. She walked on stockinged feet to the kitchen. If she hurried, she could finish breakfast and leave before Mike even got out of bed.

After breakfast, she went back into the bathroom. Mike's footsteps padded across the carpet, and his presence loomed at the door. Ignoring him, she outlined her lips and stretched them for the lipstick. A quick blot. Perfect. One advantage of her job was discounted makeup and plenty of free samples.

Mike came into the bathroom in his towel. He knew better than to delay her now she had her lipstick in place.

He patted her bottom. "Looking hot in that skirt. Tighter than before. Must be the cheesecake last night."

She stifled a harsh retort. She hadn't been mistaken. All she had to do was look at dessert and she gained weight. Could she go to the gym more often? More often, how was that even possible? She practically lived there already.

*T*he train clattered into St James Station, frozen in the 1930s by the yellow and green tiled walls, curled iron balustrades, and wooden handrails.

Once inside the station bathroom, she placed a hand on the wall to steady herself as she slipped off her comfortable shoes and replaced them with high heels. They tortured her feet, but heels were one of the unwritten expectations at work. She peered in the mirror. No lipstick on her teeth, and only one tiny strand of hair out of place. She tucked it back in. Perfect.

Elizabeth Street was awash with people. She turned right into the flow. She wasn't the only one dressed in David Jones black and white. The lack of colour might seem limiting, but as long as employees looked neat and professional, they could follow their own tastes in style. Rachel winced as she remembered her first job. The oil from the fish and chips shop had invaded every pore. If she'd been there any longer, she'd have turned into a blob of grease.

David Jones had been on Elizabeth Street forever. It still had the original sandstone exterior which shoppers from the war years would recognise. Most of the interior was modern, but sometimes Rachel would ride up the original metal cage lifts and imagine the grandeur of past eras.

She entered through the staff entrance and made her way to the beauty department. The basement and ground floor were crammed with the concessions for every major cosmetics brand. The bigger the company, the better the spot, with the biggest brands close to the entrances. She'd started with a small brand in the basement and, with hard work, had moved up to a major, international brand near the main doors. Now she could glimpse natural light instead of being buried underground.

Rachel had thought she was early, but Yvonne was already laying out samples. Perhaps she should have caught the earlier train. Their manager had resigned recently and now the race was on to see who'd be promoted. Yvonne had a chance, but her toadying ways were a little too obvious. Margaret was better liked, but being married with children counted against her. The cosmetics company preferred singleness and ambition, which gave Rachel the advantage. Maybe the company would bring in someone from outside. She hoped not, because she needed the money. Rent in

Sydney was high, and her current man's guilty conscience couldn't be relied upon to prop up her income. She'd learned to budget. A tough lesson for someone with her upbringing.

There was a click of high heels behind her. Rachel spun around.

"Made it," Margaret said, breathless. "Didn't think I would. Billy had a slight fever last night and then screamed about going to Grandma's."

Yes, Rachel did have a chance to get the promotion. If only she had a better education. Perhaps the cosmetics company would allow her to work towards something like a business or marketing degree one evening a week. How many years would that take?

Rachel unlocked the cupboard with the wedding appointment notebook. She rang the first number on the list for tomorrow.

Once the calls were done, she drifted over to the next makeup concession to greet Alice, one of the few friends she'd made at work. They usually had lunch together at least once a week.

"I applied for the manager's job as you suggested," Alice said. "Have you received a response to your application?"

"No," Rachel said. "But it's been less than a week since the closing date."

"I thought they were in a hurry."

"Maybe, but they'll need to narrow the possibilities down to a short-list."

Would her name be on the list?

CHAPTER 2

*E*sther hurried across the car park between the physiotherapy and the accident and emergency departments. The day had started out normally but had deteriorated.

She'd been cleaning her teeth before leaving for work when she'd heard the thud in the kitchen. One look at her grandmother sprawled on the floor, face the colour of wet paper and one leg twisted at an impossible angle, and she'd known. Broken femur.

The ambulance officers had almost needed to knock Naomi out to get her out of the house.

Esther glanced at her watch. She had less than an hour before Mrs Oliver arrived for her back treatment. The nurse had rung to say Naomi would need a total hip replacement. Esther's boss, Sue, had insisted Esther go and visit before the surgery.

Naomi lay still, eyes closed. Her colour was a little better, but her breathing was shallow.

Oh, Gran. Get well. What if she lost her? The statistics weren't good for old people and broken hips. *Stop it.* Gran has as many years as God chooses to give her but losing her would be hard. There'd been too many losses. Her health, her fiancé, her home. Her relationship with her father had been smoothed over, but that was because he didn't know where she lived. What would he do when he found out?

Naomi stirred, sighed, and opened unfocused eyes.

"Rachel—" she murmured.

That was odd. Gran's mind was usually razor sharp. "Gran, it's me. Esther."

Naomi started and her eyes focused. "Of course. Sorry. Wasn't sure where I was."

Was the confusion the result of the pain, the medication, or waking up from a deep sleep? After all, her grandmother was eighty-five. Until today, she'd been as lively as a sparrow.

Worry harshened Esther's voice. "Have the medical staff told you what's happening?"

"That I'll have surgery this afternoon? Don't you worry about me. Betty and Joan had falls and hip surgery, and they're back to normal."

Esther's lips twitched. Trust her grandmother not to make a fuss.

"Isn't it your lunchtime, Esther? Please don't avoid eating because I can't."

"I didn't want you drooling." Esther said.

"Only a rabbit would drool over your kind of lunch."

Esther patted Naomi's hand. "Obviously your humour has survived."

"Looks like I'll be needing it. The doctor said I might be in here for two weeks. Will you be my therapist?"

"I work in outpatients." Besides, the hospital would never allow her to treat her own family. "You'll have a therapist who specialises in rehabilitation but once you're home, I'll crack the whip."

The sides of Naomi's mouth curved up. "You'd better not crack it too hard, or I'll kick you out."

"You know I'm willing to find my own place whenever you want me to."

"Don't you dare." Naomi shook a finger at her. "I've loved having you as a housemate."

It was an unusual arrangement but it worked.

Tears pricked Esther's lashes. People died every day under anaesthesia. Especially old people. Finding that her grandmother was alive had been a blessing to counterbalance all the pain of last year.

"You're quiet, dearie."

"Just thinking Dad would never have thrown me out if he knew it would lead me to you."

"God loves to take the worst things and bring good out of them."

Esther kissed her grandmother's hand. "You were one of the best gifts God gave last year." Finding out Gran loved Jesus was another blessing.

"Thinking is fine, but don't worry about me," Naomi said.

"You know me too well." A band constricted Esther's chest. "You've become so important to me."

"The feeling's mutual, as you well know." Her grandmother blew her a kiss. "Even if something should go wrong, you know we'll meet again."

"But I've just met you. I don't want to lose you." Not when her relationship with the rest of her family was strained or rocky or both. Why, oh why, couldn't she be part of a normal, loving family?

"And you most likely won't, but it might be a while until I can manage around the house."

With Esther's lingering tiredness, they might need help. "The therapists are great. They'll soon have you back in top form." Esther wagged a finger. "Make sure you behave yourself."

Naomi winked. "When do I do anything else?"

Naomi would soon be a ward favourite.

Footsteps crossed the floor to their quiet corner. "Mrs Macdonald, I'm here to give you the pre-medication."

"Isn't the pre-med to make me calm?"

"Something like that," the nurse said. "Most people prefer it."

"I'm not most people. I'm quite calm. Jesus has things firmly under control."

The man raised his eyebrow. How many of his patients talked like this?

"If I don't make it through the anaesthetic, I'll go straight to meet Jesus." Naomi chuckled. "At my age, that's more of a gift than a curse."

He backed away. "The orderly will come soon to take you down to surgery."

Naomi turned back to Esther and smiled weakly. "You taught me a lot last year."

Esther had never considered that her trials might inspire someone else.

"I don't want to be dopey when I'm wheeled into the operating theatre."

Esther suppressed a shudder. Too many reminders of her surgery a year ago. "Let's pray together before you go. Dear Jesus. Thank you that we live in a country with a good medical system and that Gran can be in this particular hospital. Thank you that we, as your followers, have nothing to fear. Amen."

"Come here, dearie, and kiss your old gran before you go."

Esther smoothed her grandmother's hair and kissed her forehead, careful not to lean on the bed and jar her grandmother's hip. "Love you. I'll ask the nurse to call me when you're out of surgery."

If Naomi made it through surgery.

CHAPTER 3

*R*achel had pushed herself tonight. An extra ten star jumps. An extra round of weights. An extra series of burpees. An added half kilogram weight for her triceps. An added kilo for her biceps. This was one battle she was going to win. No, not merely win. She was out to conquer and beat her body into submission. To not give Mike any reason to comment on her weight.

Arms and shoulders. Abs and back. Buttocks and thighs. Her muscles burned. Good. She was working hard.

Half the men in the gym were pretending not to watch her. She ignored them. She wasn't in the market.

Rachel wiped her head and neck with her already sopping towel. She gulped down half a bottle of water, then moved to a room where she unrolled her exercise mat. The mat would get sweaty, but it would be all her own sweat.

Sit-ups, push-ups, squats. Rachel concentrated on her breathing. Forty-six, forty-seven. Her legs burned. Forty-eight, forty-nine, fifty. She straightened and jiggled her legs before picking up the medicine ball. Holding it out in front of her, Rachel lifted her knees and counted her repetitions.

She snatched a quick break to drink, rolled up her mat, and headed for the treadmills.

"What's with all the extra sessions this week?" one of the fitness trainers asked as she passed. "In training for a competition?"

Rachel shook her head.

"Rather you than me. You're wearing me out watching you."

What did he know with his twenty-something body? Hers was on the long downhill slope already, even if the slide wasn't yet visible to anyone without her x-ray eyes. To most people, her legs and abs were taut and her skin evenly tanned. Bottled tans did the job. No way was she letting the sun age her. Her looks were her greatest asset and she paid top dollar to keep them that way.

Good. Her favourite treadmill was available. The one tucked out of the way.

Rachel walked towards it and then stopped. A young woman was sitting cross-legged on the floor, breastfeeding her baby. The last thing Rachel wanted to see. Her stomach knotted. It shouldn't be allowed. This was why she never came to the gym in the mornings, even on her days off. The woman had a piece of material draped over herself, and she wasn't disturbing anyone. Except Rachel. Making a fuss would only lead to questions she didn't want to answer.

Rachel backed up and found another machine. Normally she enjoyed the treadmill, because her mind could float along without counting repetitions. Today, that was dangerous. The breastfeeding woman had unsettled her, and now the hum of the treadmill made her mind slither down the slippery-dip of memory. She clenched her teeth and concentrated on the control panel in front of her.

The treadmill coursed along. Wide circles of sweat soaked Rachel's shorts and shirt. The sweat bands around her forehead and wrists were almost useless.

She stumbled and put her hand out to the bar to support herself. If only she could shut off the passing of time as easily as she could adjust the speed of a treadmill. Had Mike thought the added weight was a good thing, or were his words a warning? Did he already have a younger woman in the wings?

The treadmill timer clicked. Now for a series of faster intervals. She cranked the speed up a notch and increased the incline.

Running outside would be more interesting, but gym machines allowed her to sculpt all her muscles without having to think about it. This upmarket gym had proven to be the best place to find the right kind of male friends. Rich ones. She was too fastidious for sleazy bars.

Her lungs sucked at the air and she swiped the towel across her forehead and cheeks. The best thing about speed intervals were that they left no energy for thinking. Thinking was a bad idea. There were too many alleys she didn't want her mind to wander down. It was better to skate past the entrances than explore.

Her feet pounded along, her speed dictated by the machine. Like her life. Things happened and she reacted. She liked to think she was in control but she wasn't. Life was a never-ending sequence of work, gym, and counting calories. Interspersed with beauty treatments and monthly haircuts.

One of her friends in primary school had owned a mouse. It was amusing to watch it running in its wheel. Running, running, running, but never getting anywhere. Sometimes, with a supreme effort, the mouse would get a little ahead but he'd slip back a millisecond later, more exhausted than ever. What would the mouse think of her treadmill? Of her life? Would he question why she did it?

Rachel adjusted the dials for the rest interval. It wasn't what anyone else would call a rest, but it was no longer a sprint. Rachel took a deep breath and focused on expanding her chest and feeling the muscles in her neck, back, and shoulders.

The slower speed allowed her mind to drift. Today it drifted back to her first boyfriend. She shook her head as though to shake the memories out of her ears. He refused to disappear. Her stomach clenched like someone was wringing out a wet shirt. She must not think about him. Must not think about what happened afterwards.

She took another deep breath and forced her mind past the darkness. Instead, she remembered what happened after he'd gone for good. That was a little safer. Back then, her hair and skin reeked of hot oil and fried onions. There weren't many job options for sixteen-year-olds. His leaving had forced her to think again. Had led to her job at David Jones.

When she'd left home, she'd taken all her clothes. A rich girl's wardrobe wasn't to be sneered at. She tried everything on and sorted them into three piles. Clothes that were keepers, clothes that needed to be adapted, and clothes that were irredeemable. The last pile had made her think. They were too good for rags.

Rachel wiped the sweat off her cheeks and nose.

It hadn't taken her long to work out that there was no point giving quality clothes to second-hand shops in her area. It was the shops in rich areas who would appreciate them. And those were the shops where she found stuff to fill the gaps in her cupboard. For fifty dollars, she'd come away with a whole new mix-and-match wardrobe.

One minute to go. She kept running. Running, running, running. Three, two, one. Made it. She reached forward to slow the machine down for the final cool down. She must have worked off that cheesecake by now. She didn't plan to become one of those bimbos who forced themselves to vomit after meals. She was healthy, not crazy.

Rachel switched the machine off, grabbed the towel, and mopped her head. Whew. She'd pushed it tonight.

Now for a shower and an early night to catch up on beauty sleep. Sleep washed away all the stress toxins in her system.

Tomorrow was a day off. Maybe she'd sleep all day. Allow herself to forget that the tide of time was already lapping hungrily at the base of the cliff.

CHAPTER 4

*N*aomi was out of bed and sitting in a chair. Esther
kissed her forehead. "I've already heard you're a star."

"The physiotherapist was pleased. My frame and I didn't break
any speed records, but we managed to get to the door and back."

"It'll get easier every day. They won't let you go home until you
can walk up the three steps into the house." Esther pulled her chair
close. "How are you coping with the pain?"

"Nothing like childbirth, dear."

Esther stifled a grin. If only all the patients were of her grandmother's generation. "Do you think you can cope with two extra
visitors?"

"It depends what kind."

"Joy and Gina."

Naomi beamed. "They're not visitors they're family but I will
need a catnap before they arrive."

Esther draped a light blanket over Naomi's knees. She'd made it
through surgery, but she looked old and frail. *Lord, I can't bear to lose
any more family.*

She had a meal every week with her mum, and their relationship was better than ever, but she missed the easy relationship she used to have with her dad. She'd been such a daddy's girl. She'd adored him. Strikingly handsome and full of enthusiasm. Sure, he was rarely at home, but when he was, he'd swing her round and say, 'How's my darling today?'

What daughter didn't love to feel treasured by the most important man in her world? Last year had ripped them apart, and her monthly visits home were a strain, but she wasn't giving up. He was still upset at her decision to leave Victory Church.

A spot of saliva dribbled out the corner of Naomi's mouth. Esther's chest tightened. Such a precious woman. How had she lived without her? There'd been no extended family in Esther's life. No grandparents, no cousins, no uncles and aunts. The Macdonalds were a small clan, and Mum was an only child whose parents were long dead.

Maybe the loneliness of her childhood was why Esther had such a longing for an older sister. She'd never longed for a brother or even a younger sister. Only an older sister would do. She hadn't known her hope was futile until she was eight and learned older sisters couldn't be bought at the supermarket.

Naomi snuffled in her sleep. Perhaps she too dreamed of reconciliation. *Lord, bring our family together before it is too late. Give Gran the desires of her heart.*

---

*J*oy entered the room, followed by Gina with a bunch of flowers.

"My, what beautiful flowers," Naomi said. "Esther, could you put them in the vase?"

Esther sprang into action.

"Now, I don't want to talk about myself," Naomi said. "I'll live. What have you been up to?"

Esther, Joy, and Gina had been meeting up regularly since the beginning of the year to encourage each other and pray.

Esther turned to Joy. "Have you had any opportunities to talk about Jesus at the cancer clinic?"

"A few words here and there, but nothing like what I had with you."

Gina laughed. "Well, it's not often that someone lashes out at God right in front of you."

Esther grinned. She'd been furious at God for not healing her. Joy's persistent questions had driven her crazy, but she'd learned she couldn't escape God when he gets to work.

"You know we've been praying I'd have opportunities to tell Bible stories," Gina said. "Well, I've had three. Now Esther won't be the only one sharing her experiences."

"Well done," Joy said. "What did God teach you?"

Gina pursed her lips. "Like you said, when we pray for opportunities, we keep seeing them. I was terrified before I opened my mouth, but the fear was gone once I started."

"You've reminded me that I've stopped praying for opportunities," Esther said. "I miss having my faith stretched."

"Have either of you considered leading a story group at church?" Joy asked.

Esther looked across at Gina. "What do you reckon? Could we do a group with the young workers?"

"I don't see why not. Stuart would be delighted to have someone volunteer to lead the group but what about your energy levels?"

"I think I can manage it if I pace myself. The only issue is that Gran is going to need me in the evenings for the next few months."

"Don't use me as an excuse," Naomi said. "Besides which, why can't our place be the venue?"

"Are you sure?"

"You're not going to host wild parties in my living room."

Esther chuckled. "That's true."

There was a drawn-out pause. Not an awkward pause, but the comfortable pause that happens between good friends.

"I'm blessed," Esther said. "You and Joy have been like sisters to me." Her face heated a little. "When I was younger, I dreamed about having an older sister."

"That's not unusual when someone is an only child," Gina said. "Sort of like an imaginary friend."

"I had a sister," Joy said. "Sometimes I would have preferred the imaginary sort."

Naomi had closed her eyes.

"My sister was completely real to me," Esther said. "I even had a nickname for her. Tickles."

Naomi licked her lips.

Joy held out her hands to them. "Ladies, why don't we pray and leave Naomi to rest?"

Maybe that was why Gran wasn't participating much in the conversation. The anaesthetic must have knocked her around more than she was letting on.

"Gran, do you want to pray with us, or should we leave you and go outside?"

"I'll survive if you're quick. Then you and the nurse can help get me back into bed."

They all held hands. Each prayed first on their own, and then Joy said, "Loving Lord. Thank you for bringing Mrs Mac ... Naomi safely through her surgery."

Coming from China, Joy still struggled with the informality of calling someone older than herself by their first name, but Gran had insisted.

"Help her pain to be manageable tonight so she sleeps well. May she be a light in this hospital for the few days she's here. Amen."

How typical of Joy to focus on the essentials. Not just getting through each day, but taking Jesus wherever they went.

CHAPTER 5

A heavy lead ball settled into Rachel's stomach. Why had she applied for the manager's job? Ten of them had made it through the application stage. Alice hadn't, but she'd still whispered, "Hope you get it." Alice was too nice, and Rachel didn't deserve it. After all, she wasn't averse to clambering over a friend to succeed.

The room was quiet. Nine perfect mannequins frozen on their seats. Asking them to all arrive together seemed a form of torture. Rachel's interview was last. Was there significance in the order? Her stomach curdled and seethed. Dry toast for breakfast would have been better than cereal.

The door to the main office opened and the first interviewee walked out, head held high. Was she confident or faking it? The receptionist's nails clicked on her keyboard. She looked up. "Yvonne."

Rachel gave a ghost of a smile. No point in letting her dislike show and making enemies with someone who might become her boss. David Jones was a cushy job compared with many alternatives, and Rachel had no intention of losing it.

Rachel had to use the bathroom twice during the wait. The second time she freshened her makeup.

She peered at her face. How had she ever ended up looking like this? As a kid, she'd been a long way from physical perfection, she'd just wanted to be normal. To be allowed to make mud pies or jump in puddles. But her wishes didn't matter. Her father had wanted a little doll. Her mother brushed her hair until it shone, tugging it into tight French braids. No wisps were allowed to escape. As a kid she hadn't known what a corset was, but she'd walked as though wearing one under her high-end clothes. She'd learned to say 'please,' 'thank you', and 'excuse me' like her life depended on it.

Her father had beamed whenever people said, "Isn't she a darling?"

Why could she never get her father's voice out of her head? If she wet herself as a toddler, she was told she'd never be a Proverbs 31 woman. If she made a noise in church, she was told the Proverbs 31 woman knew how to behave in public. If she interrupted her father, she was told the Proverbs 31 woman would never interrupt. The Proverbs 31 woman had glided through the sky, glowing like some kind of fairy princess. She was always clean, always tidy, always in control, and never ever a disappointment to her father.

Rachel swallowed the acid in her throat. The Proverbs 31 woman was the opposite of everything she'd been. She'd resented the woman because she could never live up to her standard. Maybe even hated her.

Now her mother was the perfect Proverbs 31 woman, but it was the last thing Rachel had wanted to be when she grew up. Yet here she was. A perfect woman. How had appearance become of prime importance to the kid who'd preferred skipping to dolls and climbing trees to tea parties? Odd how things had turned out.

"*R*achel, please take a seat."

Rachel sat down. She'd experimented with all sorts of sitting postures the night before. Sitting right back in the chair with ankles crossed, knees together and her hands on her lap, would hide her fear and still look professional. She smiled to relax her cheek muscles. Did she exude calm confidence without over-confidence?

"Why don't you take us through your work history?"

That was the problem with CVs. Good interviewers took notice of the details. Would they quiz her on her personal history? If they did, could she present it positively?

"I worked in a restaurant first." Restaurant sounded grander than takeaway shop and it wasn't strictly a lie. There had been some tables for customers who wanted to eat on the spot rather than take their fish and chips home.

"I spent five years at David Jones in Chatswood before I was asked to move to the city store. I've been here ever since."

"But not always working for the same cosmetics company?"

"No. Working for different companies gave me broader experience."

She could handle questions about her current work. She wasn't her father's daughter for nothing. Even though she hadn't finished school, she'd had the best of the best before she left.

She answered a few more predictable questions.

One of the interviewers stared off to the right. Was she even paying attention? The woman's chin dropped and she reached for the CV in front of her and ran her finger down the page.

Should Rachel be worried?

"Your CV mentions your restaurant job. How old were you then?"

"Sixteen." Why had the lady spotted the deliberately vague part of her application?

"You don't mention how many hours you worked."

What could she say?

The woman pierced Rachel with her gaze. "Well, was it full-time or part-time?"

Rachel's mouth went dry. "Full."

The woman glanced down at the form in front of her. "And yet you attended one of the best schools in Sydney."

The woman's badgering reminded Rachel of her father. She almost gagged. She wasn't going to let her father muck this up for her, he'd wrecked enough of her life. Could she somehow spin her reason for leaving school in a positive light?

"Were you expelled?"

"No."

The woman tapped her forefinger on her thigh. A single word answer would never satisfy her.

"I had a difficult relationship with my father." Understatement of the year. "I went to live with my grandmother." Would that satisfy her?

"And?"

Would the woman ever stop probing? A butterfly pinned to a board couldn't feel more uncomfortable. Rachel's palms were clammy. *Don't panic.*

"I went to a local high school for a while, but it wasn't great. I finished Year 10 and decided to take a break and then working proved to be more to my liking."

Had she blown her chances? Had the interviewers noticed the hardness in her voice when she mentioned her father? Little things like attitude could sabotage an interview, especially when there were other good candidates. Why hadn't she thought to bring a handkerchief to wipe the sweat off her palms?

The short interviewer with glasses took over. "What are some of your strengths?"

Safe ground. *Thank goodness.*

She didn't mention what they could see for themselves. It was better left unsaid that cosmetics companies chose staff for their looks and grooming. Cosmetics were about glamour, after all. Her genes, upbringing, and figure gave her a big tick in this department.

"I'm organised and hard working. I have good people skills and repeat customers usually ask for me by name." A private school education had its uses. Rachel listed a few more things she thought they'd want to hear. She was in the swing now.

"And your level of French?"

Yippee. Her French was galloping to the rescue. With most of the top cosmetics brands being French, she thanked her lucky stars that she'd stuck with French and not switched to Latin or German.

"I'm fluent."

"That's rather unusual for an Australian."

"I had excellent teachers and have travelled to France and New Caledonia."

Now was her chance to show she was manager material.

"French has been useful in the past, but an increasing number of our customers are Chinese. I've been considering learning Mandarin."

All three interviewers sat up straight. "And if you were to get the job, what would you like to see happen at your concession?"

She was in charge at last. "First, I'd like to see us do some research." *Don't be vague.* Interviewers like precision. "Research our current customer base to determine what languages are needed. Lots of people speak English as a second language but don't necessarily require our staff to speak their language. Those customers are happy with a greeting, which is easy enough to learn but some languages are more important, because the customers don't speak English fluently. We could start hiring people who speak those languages and advertise the fact."

"How would you see that working?"

"Perhaps a half day a week where a specific language is available for consultations. Say, Chinese on Mondays and Arabic on Tuesdays."

The interviewers asked a few more questions before the interviewer seated in the middle closed the interview. "Thank you, Rachel, we'll get back to you with our decision within a week."

Rachel stood, smoothed her skirt, and left the office. Behind her came the murmur of voices. Being last meant her interview would remain a strong impression. Would it be strong enough?

CHAPTER 6

*E*sther picked up her menu. Tuesday was the best day to meet mum because her father had dinner with his pastoral team before recording his weekly radio broadcast.

Esther ordered the smoked chicken salad, and mum the salmon.

"Aren't you due for your first three-month health check-up?"

Esther nodded. "In two weeks. It's come around too fast."

Mum raised her eyebrows.

"I've spent the last three months trying to forget about cancer, but now I'll have to confront things again."

"What sort of things?"

Esther shifted in her seat. "Everything. Fear, and the feeling my life is totally out of control." Her shoulders tensed. "That all the good eating and exercise in the world couldn't prevent it and it may come back."

Mum clenched her hand.

Oops, not such a tactful answer. What else could they talk about? Too many topics were out of bounds because they tripped over the wires of Mum's loyalty to Dad.

"Mum, what have you been enjoying lately?"

"Sewing. Your father has requested more banners for the church."

He knew crowd pleasers when he saw them. There'd be queues of people wanting to be involved.

The waiter arrived with their salads. Once he'd gone, Mum said, "A few girls from the group you used to lead are being baptised this Sunday. Your father wanted to know if you'd come."

Dad specialised in getting others to communicate for him. He knew she'd find it harder to turn down her mother. Esther sighed. Was this another attempt to entice her back to Victory? Dad seemed to believe that if he could get her through the big double doors, she'd see all she was missing. He'd already offered her a role leading the ministry to young workers. That had been a temptation because it had been on her wish list for three years.

How did he manage to convince himself that their arguments of last year were minor hiccups that could be smoothed over? They were deeper than that. A disagreement about what the Bible said and about the kind of God they served.

"Kathy and Tina already invited me and I plan to be there, although I need to check it's okay with Gran."

"How's she going?"

"Really well. The therapists are happy with her progress." Naomi would be discharged late Friday afternoon so Esther could take her home after work. That would give them a whole weekend to see if Naomi could cope on her own during Esther's work hours.

Since the conversation with Joy and Gina, Esther had dreamed twice about her fantasy sister. The dreams had been vivid, not the typical imaginary friend kind of thing.

"Mum, did we ever have an older girl staying with us when I was a toddler?"

Blanche stopped chewing mid-chew.

"I don't remember her name, but I always called her Tickles."

"I wouldn't forget someone with a name like that," Mum mumbled.

She hadn't exactly answered the question. Was this yet another one of those off-limits subjects? What was it about her family? Last year had brought her and Mum closer but obviously not as close as she'd thought. Esther shrugged. Pushing on Mum's locked doors was a waste of time.

"Mum, are you ever going to come and visit Gran?"

Blanche looked over her shoulder. "Your father wouldn't be happy if he found out."

And that was that. Mum would never dare to do anything that might make Dad unhappy. Even meeting Esther was probably a concession. What if Esther's 'rebellion' spread? Dad seemed content to play at happy families for now, a fantasy maintained by her monthly Saturday lunches back home. Three hours once a month was doable, as they could stick with the safe topics of work, holidays, and hobbies.

By the end of each visit, Esther was nearly exploding in her efforts to avoid dangerous topics like the fact that she lived with her grandmother. Dad had asked her to return home as soon as her hair had grown back, but she wasn't shifting. Naomi's love wasn't conditional. Not like her father's. She'd never again subscribe to the warped view that good health was proof of God's blessing. Any move in the future would be to a space on her own. Or perhaps she and Gina could share a place. Gina was the closest she had to a sister.

———

*V*ictory Church seemed unchanged. The same hearty greetings. The same triumphant music. Even the ushers seemed identical, although it was hard to be sure, as they all avoided looking directly at her. Did they wonder whether she was in or out of favour?

She'd have preferred to sit up the back but her parents would never understand. What was it like for her mother to have to sit in front-row isolation every week? Always on show, like an orchid under a glass dome.

Baptisms had been Esther's favourite Sundays, back when she'd been an integral part of this church and engaged to the youth pastor.

Last year Esther and her father had clashed over his teaching. He proclaimed Jesus as there to bless in all ways—materially, health, work, and family. But Esther's cancer had shown her that God often works in ways that don't look anything like blessing. Her father hadn't appreciated her thoughts on the matter. He'd eventually given her an ultimatum and she'd left home rather than buckle. Some things were too precious to give away.

Mum placed her arm alongside Esther's on the theatre-style seats. Esther's leaving had been hard for her. *Oh Lord, when will you restore harmony in my family?*

The first of those to be baptised came up to the podium. They'd all be in white. It looked impressive. Her father had always had an eye for the dramatic.

In a church this size, there was no way everyone being baptised could speak. As expected, her father had chosen the three most dramatic testimonies. A former drug user, a high school principal who had been an ardent atheist, and a person who'd attempted suicide. A vast contrast to last month's baptisms at her new church. A church-goer who had finally understood the message he'd been hearing for decades and a teenager who had grown up in the church. Less spectacular, but there'd been a sincerity and emotion that was missing here at Victory. Here, sin was almost glamorised.

She shouldn't criticise. It was obvious the new believers were sincere. *Lord, help them to read your word and discern your priorities. Protect them from only listening to what their ears want to hear.*

She'd been praying for Dad for months. From a human point of view, there was no chance of change, but Joy and Naomi kept reminding her God was the God of miracles. She wouldn't quit praying until her dying breath.

All those being baptised made promises to God as one big group. Efficiency was one of her father's trademarks. Now each person walked down the steps into the baptistry and was fully immersed. She preferred full immersion to a mere sprinkling, but did her father favour immersion for theological reasons, or for the dramatic effect?

Each of the five teenagers she'd come to support flashed her a smile as they rose from the water. *Lord, protect them from temptation. Let them love you and your word more than anything else.* She'd heard Nick had continued to follow the Bible study method she'd introduced to the youth group, and she was confident he'd continue the pattern. They might not have a future together but he truly loved God's word. Would he be strong enough to resist her father's influence? *Lord, help him be a man after your heart.*

CHAPTER 7

*E*sther woke with a dull headache and stomach pain. She reached for her Bible. Which verses would speak to her fears? She turned to Psalm 46 and read it aloud.

"God is our refuge and strength, a very present help in trouble. Therefore we will not fear, though the earth should change and though mountains fall into the sea ..."

She read the verses again, praying through each line. The fear coiling and swirling around her heart slowly subsided.

Lord, thank you for reminding me you're in control of everything, even my health. Help me to be like Gran, and seize any opportunities I have to talk about you. The highlight of last year had been sharing Jesus with the people at the clinic. The Holy Spirit provided her with the right words whenever she relied on him, and she missed the joy that had welled up every time she dared to open her mouth. *Help Dr Webster to have made some progress towards you.*

By the time Esther went to work, her heart was centred on Jesus rather than on fear.

*W*hen Esther entered Paul Webster's office, he gave her a big smile which he tried to cover with his hand. Did he think it was inappropriate for a cancer specialist? He'd certainly changed since they'd first met. Back then he'd seemed a cold, silvery-grey kind of guy. All professionalism. No jokes, no laughter, no vulnerability. The pictures on the wall used to be cookie-cutter images. In good taste, but predictable. Now there were two new photos of the underwater world and of exploding stars.

Esther indicated the seascape. "Good to see your office looking less stark."

He grunted. "I bought it after I took the kids scuba diving at Hayman Island last holidays. They seemed to enjoy it."

"They'd be crazy not to." From a parenting view, it was a win on all counts. His children could do something with their father without any need for talking. He'd said the children resented him for his marriage breakup. Maybe now that they were older—fifteen and seventeen, if she remembered correctly—they'd learned to cope with the realities of their life.

Dr Webster glanced down at her file. "Michelle will keep booking you in every three months for this first year. Mostly I'll just check how you're going."

"I had expected blood tests or scans or something."

He chuckled. "People expect these visits to be more whiz-bang, but we don't waste money on unnecessary tests. You'll only have tests if they're clinically indicated."

"Let's hope they're not ever necessary."

"Fingers crossed."

And he'd given her the opportunity she'd prayed for. "You should remember I'm not superstitious." Esther grinned. Now it was her turn to get him back for all his playful attacks on her. "I would have thought a medical man wouldn't trust in fairy tales."

"I knew you wouldn't let me get away with anything. Okay, you pray, and I'll rely on the treatments. Now will you let me get on with my job?" His voice held no rancour. "How tired are you?"

"It's variable. Some weeks I sail along, but I usually crash on the weekends."

"Not much partying then?"

She made a face. "It's success if I can get through the full week at work. I'm grateful to be living with my grandmother. She goes to bed early and hasn't needed help until now."

He looked up. "Have things changed?"

"She broke her hip a few weeks ago."

The occupational therapists had made a home visit before Gran was discharged from hospital and were satisfied with the layout of the house. Esther had needed to move a few small items, as well as the mat in the hallway. They couldn't risk another fall.

"Can you get others to help if need be?"

Joy had taught her how to spot small opportunities to talk about truth. If only Dr Webster would become curious enough to investigate some of his assumptions. "We go to a good church. They've already sent some meals around."

"Lucky you."

Esther opened her mouth, but her mind was blank. She closed it again.

"So you're doing well. It doesn't look like you're gaining weight."

"Is that sometimes a problem?"

"It is, if people are less active than they were." He raised an eyebrow.

"I still cycle to work and swim regularly."

"Great. Keep it up. Have you had any unexplained aches or pains?"

Esther shook her head, and Dr Webster closed her file.

"I know you've been dying to ask me if I've read the books you gave me." She'd given him two books at the end of her radiotherapy in February as a thank you gift, one about the reliability of the Bible and the other about Jesus's resurrection.

Lord, thank you for getting him to raise the topic. "I had wondered."

"Sorry to disappoint you."

Her heart sank.

"I put them in my to-read pile, and they got buried by the books I've been reading for a research paper I'm delivering in June."

What a pity.

"But now they're found again I'll put them somewhere I'm more likely to see them."

Where? The bathroom? But no matter. She must get back to praying for him regularly.

"Please make another appointment with Michelle for three months from now."

Michelle had a busy role as receptionist for the numerous specialists in the centre. Esther had prayed for months during her treatment that they could have a decent conversation about Jesus. It had never happened. Along the way, God had answered Esther's prayers for others. Why had he been slow to answer on Michelle's behalf?

CHAPTER 8

*M*ichelle beamed at her. "Esther, good to see you."

"You have an impressive memory. Or did you have to check?"

"I don't forget people like you."

Esther raised an eyebrow.

"People who are humorous, polite, and actually talk to the staff." Michelle worried her lower lip with her teeth. "This might sound odd, but I remember you because you bring joy with you."

"It doesn't sound odd to me. I am joyful."

Lord, please keep other people away for a while and give me the words. You've promised you would. "Have you ever been curious about why I was joyful?"

"I have, and it baffles me. Most people who come here are angry and fearful. You were like that the first time I met you, but after that, you were more joyful every time." She glanced at the clock on the far wall.

"I'll get out of the way if anyone else needs your attention," Esther said. *Lord, it's been a long week. Give me energy.* She leaned against the counter. "You're right. Everyone starts scared and alone, but cancer proved a blessing because it forced me to confront things I'd have preferred to avoid. It exposed the lies I'd believed."

"What lies?"

"I presumed God would heal me, and I was angry when he didn't." How would Michelle respond to the idea of God in a conversation?

"Having cancer sounds like a good reason to be angry at God."

Lord, help me know what to say.

A childhood story flashed into Esther's mind and she said, "We tend to treat God like a genie in a lamp, as though his job is to grant wishes and give us a smooth ride through life. If that was what God was like, everyone would sign up for his team but we'd sign up for what we could get out of God, not for who he is."

Michelle's eyes remained focused on her.

"Since accepting God for who he is, I've discovered Jesus gives far better gifts than healing."

"Like what?"

That was the right kind of question. "Not at all what we expect. We want healing from whatever plagues us but God tells us, 'You've got a bigger problem. Let's deal with that first'."

"What could be worse than cancer?"

"Could I tell you a brief story?"

"A story? That sounds okay," Michelle said.

Esther cleared her throat. "Jesus came to a town where there was a paralysed man. The man's four friends lifted up his mat and carried him towards Jesus."

Michelle sat motionless. Was she bored or intrigued?

"They couldn't get anywhere near Jesus because of the crowds, but they refused to give up. They took their friend up onto the flat roof, dug right through it, and lowered him down in front of Jesus. Jesus looked at the man and said ... Well, what do you think he said?"

"You're healed."

"That's what everyone was expecting, but Jesus said, 'Son, your sins are forgiven.'"

Michelle narrowed her eyes.

Esther hurried on. "There was a group of religious experts there and they thought, 'Who does Jesus think he is? No one can forgive sin but God alone.' Jesus knew what they were thinking in their hearts. He asked them, "Which is easier? To say to this man, 'Your sins are forgiven,' or to say, 'Get up and walk?' But to let you know I have the power to forgive sin, I say, "Take up your mat and walk."' Immediately, the paralysed man jumped to his feet, rolled up his mat, and went home."

Michelle tilted her head. "So you're saying our greatest problem is sin? I've never thought I was a bad person."

Esther had already had this conversation with others and had learned what to say.

"We define sin in terms of crimes."

"How else can it be defined?"

Another brilliant question and there was still no one nearby. Late afternoon appointments were obviously the way to go.

Michelle was old enough that she'd probably gone to Sunday School.

"Do you remember what the snake said to Eve in the Garden of Eden?"

Michelle nodded.

"Eve's decision led to all the pain and chaos in this world."

Michelle's brow furrowed. "I can't see how eating a piece of fruit is such a big deal."

Lord, give me the right question.

"But why did she eat it?"

"Maybe she felt God was holding out on her by not giving her everything."

Esther never knew what question to ask in advance, but once Michelle responded, God placed an appropriate question in her mind. She'd missed the excitement of working in tandem with God. Her tiredness had disappeared.

"And was God holding out on her?"

Silence made Esther want to jump in with answers, but Joy had taught her to follow Jesus's model and ask questions.

Michelle's mouth formed an 'o.' "God wasn't stingy at all. He'd given them everything except one kind of fruit."

Esther almost cheered. Instinct told her explaining was faster than asking questions, but sometimes instinct was wrong. "So why did Eve want to eat the fruit? Let me quote the snake. 'You will not die. For God knows when you eat it you'll become like him, knowing good and evil.'"

"Is it ..." Michelle cocked her head to one side. "Is it that she wanted to be like God?"

"That's it." Esther smiled, the smile of hearty congratulation. "That attitude is what God means by sin."

"You mean God's view of sin is that we try to be God?"

"And what is God like?" Did Michelle have enough biblical background to answer?

"Well, he created the universe and set it running."

So Michelle did have some background. "And do you think he was good?"

"I'm not sure about now, but I think he was at the beginning."

Esther wanted to defend God, but where would she start? Her mind was blank. *Lord, help. What's most important?*

Within milliseconds the words were in her mind.

"You said Adam and Eve wanted to replace God at the centre of his universe. They wanted to be the sun and for everything to revolve around them. Sin is saying, 'I'm the centre, I'm number one, I'm God.'"

"And that's our real problem?"

"Yes. Not cancer or paralysed legs, but that we don't know God. And worse, don't care to know him. So Jesus came to restore our friendship with God. Once we accept him, then he gives peace and joy."

Michelle stared at her.

"Even if this cancer kills me, I know I'll go to be with Jesus forever." What an incomparable promise. "That's why I'm joyful."

"Perhaps God did another miracle." Michelle twirled a lock of hair. "Normally we'd have been interrupted long ago. You've given me a lot to think about."

Would they ever have another conversation like this? How could she keep Michelle moving forward in her understanding?

"Do you have a modern version of the Bible at home?"

"We have a Bible." Michelle pursed her lips. "But I'm not sure it's modern."

"I'll bring one in next week."

"You don't have an appointment."

"I only work next door. I'll bring it in a bag with your name on the outside. The Bible's a thick book, and that scares some people, so I'll suggest some sections to read. Many people think the Bible is a book of rules but more than half of it is historical stories."

"I'd forgotten about the stories."

Not one interruption. God had answered her prayers at last.

"I'd better not forget to get an appointment. Dr Webster said three months from now but I wanted to ask a favour. Are you able to tell me when Robert Boyle is booked in?"

"Is that the guy you usually talk to when you're here?"

"Yes, I'd prefer to come when there is someone friendly to talk to."

"I'm not supposed to tell you about other clients, but I'll check for you. You've lined up appointments before, and I doubt you have evil intent."

Esther hadn't thought her request might make matters awkward for Michelle. "It's okay if it's not possible."

Michelle frowned and checked the calendar. "You'd have to wait an extra week."

"I doubt a week will be a problem. I'll return in a few days with a Bible."

Michelle looked up to smile at someone approaching behind Esther. "Your stories make me want to read it for myself."

---

*E*sther arrived home drained but on a high. Two wonderful conversations. Why was it that she could talk so easily with everyone but her own family? Dad was virtually impossible nowadays and even Mum had secrets.

Esther chopped up some broccoli and popped it in a saucepan. She'd just have time to change out of her work clothes and lay the table. She set the slow cooker going every morning so that most of the meal was done when she arrived home.

Naomi leaned on the counter to get the cutlery out of the drawer. She insisted on helping even if she couldn't yet carry much to the table.

Esther gnawed her lip. Did Gran have secrets too?

"Gran, do you remember the conversation at the hospital with Joy and Gina?"

"There were quite a few conversations."

Was Gran being evasive? She'd never seemed anything other than open and honest up until now.

"I've been having vivid dreams about an older sister. When I mentioned them to Mum, she clammed up."

Naomi fiddled with the forks on the counter. "Childlessness is a touchy subject with your mum."

"We weren't talking about childlessness."

"Well, talking about sisters hurts her. Your mum always longed for a big family."

Had Mum had miscarriages? Or a child that died? If that was the case, why hadn't anyone said anything?

Esther clenched her fists behind her back. She wasn't a child. Why did her parents treat her like one? And why did Naomi seem to be in cahoots? She wasn't going to push the issue today, but the topic wasn't over yet. Not by a long way.

CHAPTER 9

*R*achel was due to head north for a short holiday at Port Macquarie in two days. She'd rented a studio looking out on the beach. An extravagance, but one she deserved after the disappointment of missing out on the promotion. It had gone to an outsider, a woman who used to work in the Paris head office.

How long had it been since she'd holidayed alone? She needed to escape the glitter of glass, the brilliance of man-made colours, and the scents designed to attract attention. Better to luxuriate in the shine of sun on sea, the blues and greens of the natural world, the scent of sand and surf. Beyond that, she needed to walk barefoot and feel the coarse sand between her toes instead of the hurt of high heels. Her stomach fluttered in anticipation.

Two more shifts. Could she make it?

Alice, eyes down, buffed the main counter at the adjacent concession as though she wanted to dig a hole in the glass. What was with that? Seconds later, she rushed past Rachel in the direction of the bathrooms.

It happened five more times before lunch. Alice was never gone long but she always came back looking pale, her eyes smudgy. Was she pregnant? Her third child was already eight. Not that Rachel paid attention to any talk about children. Anything to keep Alice from pulling out photos and gushing.

Was this why she'd avoided friendships with women all these years? Women stuck their noses into sensitive nooks and crannies. Women got weepy and Rachel didn't do weepy. She'd not cried in more than twenty years. Not since that day. And she had no intention of starting now. Tears were weak, and weakness would have destroyed her.

Alice was the closest Rachel had to a friend. She hadn't caught on to Rachel's habitual tactics of keeping things polite, superficial, distant. Alice kept on being friendly no matter what Rachel did— and sometimes she'd been plain rude. It drove Rachel crazy, but how could she be cruel to someone so determinedly nice?

Alice even made cakes for her birthday. The first year Alice came in with the mound of deliciousness, a big lump had threatened to choke Rachel. How had Alice known that carrot cake with sour cream icing had once been one of her favourites? Alice showered her with homemade gifts—journals, photo frames, fudge. Gifts from a home where money was stretched. Each gift threatened to blow the valve cranked shut in Rachel's heart.

Now she avoided coming to work on her birthday. Her co-workers thought it was so she could celebrate. Little did they know, it was to avoid celebrating. To avoid simple gifts that reminded her of the only place she'd ever felt at home. To avoid the memories buried down a deep mine shaft, along with the memories of how often she'd gone and stared at the door of that home.

The door wasn't anything special. A painted door with a brass knocker, but behind the door was home. A place of warmth and welcome. A place of acceptance and peace. A place she could have stayed if she'd been smart but somehow her teenage heart couldn't handle love and security. Hadn't been worthy of it.

So she'd run.

Sometimes she hadn't been able to stop herself going back and looking at the house, as though the essence of the place could be sucked through the air and in through her pores.

Rachel closed the register drawer with a snap, rolled her shoulders, and tilted her neck side to side. If only today were busier, she'd have less time for old memories. She glanced over at Alice. A slow business day was probably a good thing from Alice's point of view. Alice looked like a ghost having an off day.

Alice looked right and then left, and sidled over to Rachel. "Can we go to Hyde Park for lunch instead of Pitt Street?" She sniffed. "I need to talk to someone."

Great. That's what Rachel had been afraid of but she couldn't say no, not after all the years of kindness. Maybe Alice would be able to keep her mind on work if she got whatever it was out of her system.

---

*A*lice scurried, head down, across the black and white stripes of the crossing and into the park. Rachel followed as fast as she could, even though her heart wasn't in it. Would she have to pretend enthusiasm for something that gave her no joy? Or sadness about something she'd prefer not to know?

They meandered. Whenever there was an empty seat or spot under a tree, Alice would look around and move on. Was she trying to find a deserted corner? Hyde Park on a sunny day wasn't the place for isolation.

Rachel's feet ached. She would have changed her shoes if she'd known she'd spend her lunchtime traipsing to and fro. Alice tugged her arm.

"Here will do." She sat down on the park seat with her back to anyone nearby. Then she pulled out her lunch and gnawed on a carrot stick like a nervous rabbit about to bolt down its hole.

Rachel followed her lead and unpacked her own salad. Maybe they'd run out of time. That would be a relief. Why couldn't Alice pay for a counsellor and spare her being sprayed with excess emotions?

They sat in silence. Alice ate only enough to sustain a tiny mouse. Every so often, her lip would tremble and her eyes well with tears.

Rachel lost patience. "You shouldn't have come in today. You're obviously unwell. Are you pregnant?"

"No!" Alice gave one harsh wail and put her head down so her hair covered her face. Her shoulders shook in sync with her sobs.

Not a pregnancy then. Had someone died?

Rachel looked round. The people closest to them had their heads down as though studying for a PhD in breadcrumbs. Rachel reached into her bag for clean tissues. She pushed two into Alice's hand and awkwardly patted her shoulder. Over-the-top emotion was not her thing. She couldn't walk away, but what was she supposed to do?

Alice blew her nose with one tissue and dabbed her eyes with the other. "It's a horrible, horrible day." She hiccupped. "I had a miscarriage yesterday."

Rachel's stomach heaved. No, not that. Anything but that. She closed her eyes to steady the nausea. She had to say something, but what?

"S-sorry to hear that." It was a platitude, but better than saying, 'Get me out of here!'

Alice stared at her, her face mottled and streaked with black tear lines. Rachel handed over another tissue.

"I know miscarriages aren't unusual, but knowing that doesn't help." Alice teared up again.

Alice had three healthy children. Rachel had nothing. She swallowed the bile in her throat. Was Alice puzzled by her lack of words?

Alice gazed at Rachel, her eyes pools of misery, loss, and grief. Why did she have to look like that? Why couldn't she shrug her shoulders and move on?

And why couldn't Rachel say the kinds of words Alice needed?

Alice hung her head again. Big tears plopped one by one onto the lid of her lunch container. The tissues were already sodden. Rachel handed over the rest of the packet.

"We were so happy. I'd already told all of our family." Alice hiccupped loudly and covered her mouth with her hand.

Loss upon loss. The world was a brutal place. How come Alice was still so easily bruised? Rachel had toughened up years ago. Now she was strong as steel, tough as leather, and dry as a desert.

Where had that last thought come from? In her childhood, she might have assumed God was talking to her. But now? Looking at the mess of the world, she'd concluded either there wasn't a God, or he didn't care about the world he'd made. He certainly wouldn't care for someone like her.

Alice was still burbling on, as though her inner confusion was leaking out. "I even told the kids ... why oh why did I say anything so early?"

"Don't beat yourself up. Sometimes these things happen." The emptiness of the platitudes tasted metallic on Rachel's tongue.

Alice's puppy eyes melted again.

Well done, Rachel. Well done. What kind of friend was she that this was all she could offer?

A tide of guilt swirled in Rachel's heart, burning. Why couldn't she empathise with Alice? Was it because she'd refused to allow herself to grieve all those years ago? Was that why she was so dry inside?

Rachel mentally tightened the valve on the pipe of her emotions. The past was long gone. Dead and buried. It must not drag down the present.

CHAPTER 10

*E*sther, Gina, and five young women gathered in Naomi's living room. Esther handed around tea in her grandmother's Royal Doulton cups. The crackle of a fire accompanied the sipping and munching of Gina's Anzac biscuits.

"We're going to try a new method of looking at Luke tonight," Esther said. Joy had suggested starting with the Old Testament, but Esther had stuck with Luke, since she was currently studying it. "We're going to use a Bible storytelling method."

The group members exchanged glances.

"We'll choose certain sections and learn them well enough to tell others before we discuss them."

Gina spoke up. "We'll try it tonight and see what you think."

Esther smiled at Gina. Esther's enthusiasm meant she sometimes skipped necessary explanations, but Gina was more sensitive to people's feelings.

"And in case you think stories are just for kids—as I did," Esther said, "this is a method for adults. Gina will do an introduction before I tell the story."

Gina looked around the group. "Almost exactly two thousand

years ago, between four and six BC, an angel appeared to a teenager called Mary."

The two of them had wrestled with which Old Testament prophecies and context needed to be included. Joy had suggested they root the introduction in history. Real people, real time, real place.

"What do you think it must have been like for Mary and Joseph? A young couple, pregnant before marriage, in a highly conservative society."

"For a start, no one is going to believe they saw an angel," Trish said. "It all sounds too convenient to be true."

"They'll all be gossiping about Mary and Joseph," Carol said. "Their reputations are ruined, and their parents and families are ashamed."

Gina let each group member express an opinion, then indicated Esther. "Over to you."

Esther cleared her throat. "Gran came out of hospital last Friday and with all the extra work to do around here, I haven't had the time to learn the story, so I'm going to be learning with you."

She opened her Bible, and some of the group members grabbed theirs. "Please don't open your Bibles."

Several of the ladies halted mid-action.

"I know it sounds strange for your Bible study leader to tell you not to open your Bibles. Don't rush off to Stuart yet."

They giggled at the mention of their pastor's name.

"I'll read the passage to you. Listen closely, because afterwards, you're going to whisper the story to yourself as best you can. After that we'll repeat the process." Esther glanced across at Gina for reassurance.

Gina gave a tiny nod. "It's all a bit unfamiliar, but you'll get it."

Esther and Nick used to work as a team like this at Victory Church. Gina couldn't replace a fiancé, but perhaps she could be the sister Esther had longed for. More like a twin because there were only a few months between them.

"While they were still there, Mary gave birth to her firstborn, a son." Esther read the passage slowly and with expression all the way to the final line. "When the shepherds had seen him, they spread the word concerning what had been told them about this child, and all who heard it were amazed at what the shepherds said to them."

"I've spotted one problem already," Gina said. "The passage begins with 'While they were still there.' It's vague about who 'they' are and where 'there' was. I think we should start with, 'while Mary and Joseph were still in Bethlehem.'"

"Good idea," Esther said. "Everyone, spread out and whisper the story to yourself. Tell it as accurately as possible in your own words."

"There's no way I can do it after hearing it once."

"You'll be hearing it more than once," Esther said.

"My story is going to be full of gaping holes," Trish said.

"Mine will too," Esther said. "But we'll know where the gaps are, and that will make us listen more carefully to the next reading."

Soon the room was filled with whispers. Some of them sat still, but others used plenty of gestures.

"How did you go?" Esther asked once everyone was quiet.

Carol groaned. "I only remembered a third."

"You'll improve," Gina said.

"As a pastor's daughter, I've heard this story every year of my life," Esther said. "I thought I knew it, but I struggled to get half right."

"Yes, there's a vast difference between hearing it, and knowing it well enough to tell it accurately. Esther, shall I read it this time?" Gina reread the passage and they practiced twice more.

"Okay, let's all find a partner and tell our full story to the other person," Esther said.

"Mine isn't ready yet," Irene said.

"Well, make your partner go first so you get to hear it again."

Several women chuckled.

Esther and Gina paired themselves up with other group members.

Once they'd finished, Trish said, "I'm puzzled why we've spent two-thirds of our time learning a story. There's barely any time to discuss it."

There was always one bold enough to ask the question everyone was thinking.

"That's a question I've asked in the past," Esther said. "It does feel like a waste of time, and I always feel an internal pressure to get on with the discussion."

Several of the group nodded.

"Last year, when I was having chemotherapy, I told stories to a Roman Catholic lady. I prepared a new one every day, so I had to work hard every evening. I read the Bible out loud to myself. When I felt reasonably confident, I told the story to my grandmother and we discussed it. I soon worked out, the better I learned the story, the more I gained from it."

Esther leaned over and picked up some coloured cards. She held them out. "Pick a card."

Everyone selected a card.

"Each card has a number on it. Before we start, there are some simple rules." Esther held up her index finger. "First, the answers can only come from within the story or introduction. Second, everyone must answer every question. Third, every answer must be different, and finally, your answer can't be more than two sentences. Got it?"

They revised the four rules again before Esther said, "Now, who has the first question card?"

"I've got it," Gina said. "What do you like most about this story?"

Esther had been confident this question would be easy enough, and soon they were onto the next. "Who has question two?"

"What questions might someone have about this story?" Irene said.

There was silence.

"To ask in another way, what questions would your non-Christian friends have?" Gina said.

Esther smiled her thanks across to Gina.

"Most would say something like, 'Go on. Stop pulling our leg. Virgins getting pregnant? An unlikely story'," Trish said.

"Who was David, and why was Bethlehem called his town?" Gina asked.

"What do angels look like, and why are people always afraid when they see them?"

"Why aren't you answering the questions?" Trish huffed.

"Did anyone else notice we weren't answering questions?" Gina said. "Can anyone think why we might do that?"

Judy, the shyest group member answered, "Is it to make us think?"

"Yes, and to go home thinking," Gina said. "Another reason is that we want you to learn to turn to the Bible and rely on the Holy Spirit to teach you." She looked round the group. "There are lots of other reasons, but you can work them out over the next few weeks. Now, who has the next question card?"

It didn't take long to discuss what they learned about people through the characters in the story, and what they learned about God.

"The final two questions are our application questions," Esther said. "Having heard this story, what are you going to do in response to it this week?"

One of the group members said, "I've never said anything to my workmates about Jesus. I doubt they even know I'm a Christian so I'm going to pray this changes."

A few of the others were also convicted by how the shepherds immediately went out to tell everyone what they'd seen and heard.

"That leads right into the final question," Gina said. "Who has question six?"

"I do," Trish said. "Who would you like to tell the story to this week?"

Each one shared a person's name and they prayed for them.

They were still discussing what they'd learned when they headed out the door to go home. Esther closed the door behind them. The evening had gone better than she'd expected. Of course, a lot of that was due to Gina. She was a star. Exactly the kind of person she'd have chosen for a sister. If choosing was possible.

But that was the problem. You couldn't choose your family, and hers was driving her crazy. She wouldn't quit praying that God would do some miracles between them, but she was going to concentrate on serving God. God would never let her down, and there was satisfaction in leading people to Jesus or encouraging them to mature. Much, much easier than family.

CHAPTER 11

The breathing was harsh in Rachel's ears. How could such a little child move so fast? Rachel panted, her chest tight. She must keep the child in sight.

The child looked over her shoulder. Face sad and eyes accusing. "Murderer," she mouthed.

"No!" Rachel cried out, and tripped.

"Murderer." Other voices joined in. Rachel thumped her fists into the ground. She knew what was coming.

"Murderer," the voices said in louder unison. It became a chant. "Murderer, murderer, murderer ..." There was no escape. No pity.

Rachel looked up at the girl. Stretched her hand towards her, begging for mercy. The child shimmered and was suddenly bathed in a ray of sunshine. She twirled, arms raised above her head and laughter ringing out. Then she shrank and faded. The last image was always the eyes. The eyes that looked so like her sister's.

Rachel rolled over in the double bed and groaned. She squinted towards the curtained window. No light showed around the edges. The nightmare was always the same. She'd had nightmares since that horrible day. The day she'd become a murderer.

Back then, the nightmare had come every night. She'd lost weight and struggled to get out of bed in the morning. Inch by tenuous inch, she'd clawed back from the brink. The nightmare dropped down to once a week, then less and less often. Nowadays she only had to grapple with it occasionally.

Until last week.

Now her nightmare was back with a vengeance. Every night.

Could Alice's grief have triggered something in her subconscious? Coming to Port Macquarie was supposed to be a much needed rest, but keeping her demons at bay was proving a full-time job. Rachel had barely slept since she'd arrived. Now the throb of a headache started at the base of her skull and fanned out until it stabbed the back of her eyes. She closed them.

It didn't help.

Each stab was an accusation, dragging her back to that terrible weekend.

She'd been seventeen.

Mid 1970s

*L*iving with her father was hell. Always expected to be perfect and never tarnish his reputation.

She'd only stayed at home as long as she did because she loved her mother and her sister. Especially her sister. Her mother meant well, but couldn't stand up to her husband.

That last day, Rachel snapped. "I detest your Proverbs 31 woman. I never, ever want to be like her."

At seventeen, she was as far as possible from the perfection her father demanded. Pregnant and in deep trouble.

She'd imagined how scary it would be on her own. Her imagination didn't come close. So she'd bought the pills and done the deed. She'd had no choice.

"These pills and six hours of vigorous exercise should sort out your problem."

She'd been taught not to swallow things given by strangers, but she'd never been this desperate. Never so determined to smother her conscience. Never been ready to do something illegal.

Hand sweating, Rachel handed over the money in a paper bag and took the dark glass bottle. No label. No warnings. No hint of the death inside. What if this went wrong?

She didn't sleep all night. At daybreak, she tipped the first of the pills into her shaking hand.

Society told her she had rights. The fetus was only a clump of cells. A thing. An it.

She knew better.

She must not know. Or think. Or feel.

Nor consider the life she was taking. It was the fetus's life or hers.

Fetus or baby? She dug her nails into her palms. She must not think. Her conscience had to be suffocated or it would rise from the dead. That wasn't something she could afford.

Rachel popped the pills into her mouth and swigged a mouthful of water. The taste of guilt burned all the way down.

Now for the vigorous exercise. Six hours? She was fit, but six hours would be tough after the stress of the last weeks.

Rachel ran down the internal steps of her apartment building, then climbed them two by two. Would this be vigorous enough? She was scared to go too far from her apartment in case she fainted. The last thing she needed was to be taken to a hospital and interrogated by a doctor on the lookout for people like her. This was her personal business. Everyone else could keep their nose out of it.

Down and up she went. Down and up. Down and up. A mindless rhythm. Every so often she did squats and push-ups.

Thirty minutes in, she was sweating. By the end of ninety, she needed a towel to keep from dripping all over the carpeted stairs.

She dropped into a squat and pushed out her legs so that she could do a push-up. *Repeat. Don't think. Keep going.*

The first nausea and backache hit sometime around the three-hour mark. She pushed on.

It was no longer anything like normal cramping.

At four hours, she retreated to the bathroom and threw up. The acrid smell of vomit pierced the fog in her mind.

She must not think. She sat on the toilet and fixated on the black spot of mould on the wall. *Don't think.*

She rocked back and forth.

Wave after wave of cramps beat at her. Smashing into her belly like tidal waves. She damped down a moan as sweat cascaded down her face and body. Her legs trembled.

At last the bleeding started. Too late to stop it now. Too late for anything but go through the pain and never allow this to happen again.

She must not consider the life she had taken. Must not think. Must not feel.

Dare not.

Port Macquarie, 1996

*R*achel's headache throbbed, despite the darkened room.

She'd justified her decision back then, but even as she lay bleeding, she'd known that Gran would never have turned her away. Her pride had gotten in the way. She hadn't wanted Gran to see her shame and failure.

Rachel reached for her painkillers. No use trying to get back to sleep. She'd head for the beach and see what exhaustion could do to help her rest.

As she slipped her shoes on, she remembered the child's accusing eyes. Her relationship with Kevin only survived another month. A corpse lay between them.

Love, convenience, and desire died soon after.

CHAPTER 12

*E*sther collected her chicken salad from the staffroom fridge and went out the back door of the physiotherapy department. She took a plastic chair from the stack and joined a group of four therapists. Such a glorious spring day shouldn't be wasted inside.

"What are you doing on the weekend?"

That was the standard question in a group of Australians who worked together. Even the answers were predictable. Parties and the outdoors for singles, attending sport and videos for the families.

"And you, Esther?"

"Mostly at home with my grandmother. I'll tackle the garden if the weather stays fine."

"You need to get a life," the newest employee said.

Esther shrugged. "I'm recovering from cancer. By the weekend, I'm barely hanging in there."

The therapist flushed. "Sorry, I didn't know. Your grandmother is lucky to have a live-in carer."

"Esther might be the lucky one," Brenda said. "Her grandmother has been my gold-star patient of the year."

Esther grinned. "I'll have to tell her you remember her."

"She was spunky, never complained, and always said things worth saying." Brenda grinned. "Do you think she'd be willing to adopt another grandchild?"

"She has a ton of adopted grandchildren at our church." *Lord, please lead this conversation somewhere.*

There was an awkward pause. Why was it people believed only negative reports about churches? Her new church might be small in comparison with Victory, but it was full of people who genuinely loved and followed Jesus. "I've been going to Gran's church for less than a year, but it's already like a family to me."

Two of the therapists grunted and changed the subject to the latest movie.

Making conversation here was hard going. There was such a limited range of topics. Fortunately, Esther had Thursdays to look forward to. Talking with Joy was like a hearty meal instead of snacking on junk food.

Esther finished her meal and did her best to join in the chat, but she hadn't been to see a movie since she and Nick had broken up. Gran didn't even have a TV. It had been hard to adjust at first, but after nine months of talking, music, and craft, she no longer intended to own a TV. The six o'clock news on the radio was more than enough to keep up with world and local happenings.

"I ate too much," Brenda said.

Esther hadn't noticed.

"Esther, do you want to go for a quick walk?"

Esther had never talked with Brenda one-to-one before. Was she only a convenient walking companion, or did Brenda have some other purpose?

"Sure. I'll pop my stuff away and meet you out front."

The streets around the hospital were mostly ordinary

suburban homes. Perfumed gardenias, cascades of vibrant purple wisteria, and the last of the sweet-smelling freesias filled the gardens.

They walked in silence, the kind of silence that suggested Brenda had something on her heart. Was it something important? *Lord, give her courage.*

"I'd heard something about your grandmother before I met her that made me think she might be a little odd."

"What do you mean?"

"I'd been on a date with one of the anaesthetists. He said that your grandma refused the pre-med, which he found unusual. Just before they anaesthetised her, she said, 'Now, young man, there is no need to fear for me. If I don't make it through the anaesthetic, I'll only go straight to be with Jesus.'"

Esther always wanted to rush in and explain, but Joy kept saying, 'Use questions not explanations.' She'd give it a go. "What was it about those words that made you wary?"

Brenda glanced over at Esther. "You won't be offended, will you?"

Esther shook her head.

"Your grandmother sounded so sure of what would happen if she died. The only people I've known like that were intense and … weird." Brenda tapped her head. "You know. Trapped in a time warp, wearing funny clothes, and forcing you to turn or burn."

Where had Brenda encountered such people? "And what did you think after you met my grandmother?"

"That's why I wanted to talk to you. She was not pushy at all. She did talk about Jesus, but in a natural way. As though he was her best friend."

"Haven't you ever heard anyone talk about Jesus in that way?" Gran would be thrilled her broken hip had led to this conversation.

Brenda snickered. "My dad is a strong atheist. Scepticism for breakfast, lunch, and tea."

Lord, now what can I say? "Do you know why he was like that?" Esther said the first thing that popped into her head.

"I picked up hints here and there. Something about his grand-parents being from some closed group. I can't remember their name."

Joy was right. Asking questions rather than making statements kept the conversation humming. Esther considered possible groups. "Would it have been the Exclusive Brethren?"

"Maybe. His dad escaped. No one told them when their grand-parents died, so they missed the funeral. Dad said it didn't matter, as they wouldn't have been allowed to go."

There were many different ways this conversation could go depending on what Brenda asked or said. *Lord, help.* Maybe if she could connect with her testimony somehow.

"I can understand why your father rejected his grandparents' views. So many people twist the Bible to suit themselves." Esther swallowed. "Did you notice any changes in me last year?"

Brenda pursed her lips. "You got more relaxed about cancer, but I assumed you'd merely adjusted to the process."

Perhaps Esther should have shared more last year, but she hadn't wanted to say negative things about Nick or her father.

"Not exactly. In fact, the further into chemo I went, the more challenges there were." *Lord, give me wisdom about what to share and what not to.* "I also grew up believing some wrong things about the Bible."

They turned the corner. Only two more blocks to go.

"I ignored parts of the Bible that talked about how tough it could be to follow Jesus and concentrated on all the positives. I didn't notice my bias until cancer blasted all my silly ideas to pieces."

Was anything she was saying making sense? Was Brenda even listening?

"I was angry at God for allowing me to have cancer, and chock-full of doubt. My old church wasn't any help. They told me the cancer would disappear if I did things like not eating and praying certain kinds of prayers."

"Was that why you skipped lots of lunches last year? I thought you were on some sort of crazy cleansing diet."

Esther cringed inside. Who else had been watching, and what conclusions had they drawn?

"It was foolish, and I was confused and angry. A woman I met asked me all sorts of confronting questions about the Bible. After I calmed down, I set out to prove her wrong."

"And did you?"

"Nope." Esther chuckled. "After I read the Bible properly, I discovered she was correct on every count."

Brenda grunted. "Dad always said the Bible was a bunch of fairy tales designed to trick kids and old ladies."

"Well, I'm neither a kid nor an old lady, and I believe every word."

Brenda's eyes widened. "Every word?"

"Yes." Joy swirled through Esther's heart.

"You seem normal, and your grandmother was amazing. Maybe there is something there."

"You can read the Bible and find out for yourself."

Brenda stopped walking and took a step back. "The Bible's huge, and I was never good at Shakespeare at school."

Esther laughed. "That's what most people think. The King James Bible uses Shakespearean language, but there are many modern versions." What could she say to make the Bible sound worth reading? "More than half the Bible is stories—well, historical accounts." She didn't want Brenda to think 'stories' meant made up.

"Stories sounds okay," Brenda said.

"You know the stranger I mentioned? She's now one of my best friends and has taught me about telling some of the key stories from the Bible and discussing them. Would that style suit you?"

Brenda gnawed her lip.

Oops, she'd been too enthusiastic. "Why don't we try once? Then you can decide if you want to hear more."

Brenda's shoulders relaxed. "Once would be fine."

Esther restrained herself from skipping back to work. The whole conversation had been a miracle. God had provided every word she needed.

But when was he going to do miracles for her family?

CHAPTER 13

*R*achel tossed in the bed and moaned.

Holiday. What a joke.

A week of endless nightmares.

Some nights she got the murder scene. Other nights she got the scene with Kevin the day she told him about her pregnancy.

He'd tossed the dregs of his coffee into the sink. "How could you be so incompetent? I gave you all the stuff you needed. It was your job to make sure nothing happened."

In the nightmare, she saw herself blink back tears and wrap her arms across her stomach. She'd been nauseous for weeks but hoped it was a stomach bug. False hope. She'd known. Deep down, she'd known.

There would be a price, a high price for her mistake. Kevin wouldn't support a baby, and a baby couldn't be hidden. Bye bye to regular work.

No job meant no home. No home meant being on the street and the street had no mercy. She had expensive tastes. A lifetime of filthy linen, second-hand clothes, and dirt made her shudder with revulsion. No way.

Kevin might not have been the man of her dreams, but at least he paid something towards her rent. It could have been worse. He'd been relatively kind. When they'd met at the gym she'd told him she was eighteen. It made him feel better.

Only a flimsy fifty-dollar note stood between her and the street. She knew what Kevin demanded but could she pay the price?

Even in the nightmare, she saw herself with her arms cradled around her belly and rocking, rocking, rocking.

On the worst nights, her nightmares spiralled into a whirlpool, circling, repeating, merging with each other.

Rachel woke, trembling and crying in the dark. Her whole body knotted with tension and her headache pounded like the bass drum in a marching band.

Deep breathing, hot baths, massage, aromatherapy, sleeping pills —nothing made the slightest difference. Nothing offered peace. It was as if an ulcer had opened, a meteoric crater oozing the guilt she'd thought was gone, back into her blood.

Rachel rolled over and sat up. The mirror on the dressing table reflected a stranger. Sick, haggard, old. Black bags hung under her eyes. Her mouth tasted foul and her tongue furry. Ready for a star-ring role in a horror movie.

A pulse beat above her right eye. An accompaniment to her thoughts. *Do it, do it, do it.*

The message was clear, an echo of the undercurrent in all the nightmares. *There's only one escape. Do it. There's only one way to be free. Do it. End the nightmares. Do it.*

Her gut twisted. A dark poison of despair filled her veins. *Do it.*

She surged to her feet with sudden energy, packed her meagre belongings, locked the door, and left the key where she'd been instructed. *Do it* pulsed through her blood.

She got into the car on automatic pilot, snapped in the belt, and headed back towards Sydney. *Do it, do it, do it* hissed the wheels.

*R*achel changed gears and her Mini hugged the tight corner. Two curves to go and she'd had a perfect run. There was no one behind her. No one to stop her.

Do it, do it, do it.

She changed down her gears for the last curve and slid smoothly around.

Now for the downhill. The quality of her driving no longer mattered.

The next corner would do. That is, if the road was deserted. She had no intention of taking anyone with her.

The voice throbbed again in her ears. *Murderer, murderer, murderer.* She shook her head to clear the voice, but it was no use. There was only one way to be free.

The second corner was approaching. Her speed was higher than sensible, and she skidded a little. *Careful.* Crashing into the embankment wouldn't achieve her purpose. Now the third corner was behind her.

She narrowed her eyes and focused on her target. The road was clear and the corner was on her side. She gunned her car, jammed her hand on the horn, and sped straight for the edge. It would soon be over.

At the last second, she closed her eyes.

---

*R*achel had expected an explosive bang as she hit the protective rail and then a long tumble.

Bang!

Instead of tumbling like she'd imagined, there was the squeal of tyres and violent shuddering. Then absolute silence.

Had she somehow died without being aware of it?

She cracked open her eyes to the blinding light of an Australian morning. The car was stationary on the edge of the road. Unbelievable. Even more unbelievable, she was pointing uphill, parallel to the edge of the cliff.

Rachel loosened her death grip on the steering wheel. Why was she here? Was she hallucinating? She pinched her left forearm. Ouch! Not dead then.

It made no sense. Her body should be lying shattered far below and her soul gone to wherever souls went. She'd hoped for oblivion. Freedom from the nightmares and relentless accusations. Yet she was here, planted safely on the shoulder of the road.

Rachel held her hands in front of her. They quivered like she had hypothermia.

Rachel fumbled with the seatbelt. It took three goes before it released with a slithering zing. She opened the door and rolled out. The heat of the road burned through the knees of her jeans. More proof she was alive.

She grabbed the edge of the door and hauled herself upright. No cars. One hand on the roof, Rachel staggered towards the back of the car. What possible explanation could there be for her still being here?

She squinted along the bottom of the car. Everything at the back appeared normal.

Nothing on the left side of the car and not a single scrape or dent along the whole length of the railing. Rachel continued around to the right-front tyre. Little ribbons of rubber fluttered from the wheel rim. A blowout. She fell to her knees and threw up.

The bitter taste of her vomit was the taste of failure. She couldn't even kill herself. She leaned her forehead against the warm metal of the car. Tears welled up, poured down her cheeks, and fell to the ground with tiny plops. Her nose ran and she had nothing but the back of her hand to wipe it with.

"Are you having a spot of bother?"

Rachel jumped like she'd been electrocuted. She swung her head towards the tail of the car. A blurry-edged man in late middle-age peered at her. Rachel stood up and put her dirty hands behind her back.

A white ute was parked behind hers and a hazard triangle had been set on the road. He stepped aside, and she caught a glimpse of a woman inside.

"My wife's not been well."

Rachel was too shell-shocked to care who he was, but his voice was kind and concerned. Grandfatherly.

"I'll grab my tools and get that tyre changed for you." He moved back towards his car.

She heard the splash of water as he washed away her vomit. Rachel leaned on the back of her car and shook. She wrapped her arms around her body.

His boots crunched back across the gravel to his car. He returned with a plaid picnic blanket. "Wrap that around you."

Once she was properly wrapped up, he got out her spare tyre.

He didn't make any comments. He didn't ask any questions. He simply got on with the job.

Rachel slid down the car and sat on the ground with her head down, a churning blackness in her head. Who'd ever heard of a blowout on the edge of a cliff?

The car jolted as the wheel nuts were removed. Rachel bent her legs up further and leaned her head on her knees. Did she fall asleep, or did her brain simply shut down?

"Miss?"

She jumped.

"The wheel is on, but it needs more air."

"Keep forgetting to put air in the spare," she mumbled.

"Are you alright? You haven't been drinking, have you?"

"No, not drinking." The stranger didn't need to know her business.

"Blowouts can be dangerous. You could easily have gone over the edge."

She didn't tell him that had been the point. The blowout had saved her life. She wasn't sure she wanted it saved, but she didn't have the energy to go up the mountain and try again. A lethargy flooded every limb. If only she could curl up and go to sleep right on the edge of the road.

He left her again. The other car's door creaked and voices murmured. He came back with a fold-out stool and a basket. He set up the stool for himself and rummaged in the basket. Liquid gurgled and he offered her a mug of lukewarm tea. "Sorry it's not hot, but it's sweet. Drink up."

She was too tired to say that she didn't like sweet tea. She wrapped both hands around the mug and attempted to get the tea in her mouth. Her teeth clattered against the china and she spilled some of it down her front. Once she'd had half the cup he started to feed her. A chocolate chip cookie, a smooshed muesli bar, and a handful of peanuts and sultanas.

It was easier to do what he wanted than to reject what was offered.

"Okay, now finish the tea."

What did he do in real life? Whatever it was, he was used to being in charge.

Somewhere nearby a currawong carolled, and two feathered streaks of scarlet screeched overhead.

"That's better. I'm glad my wife didn't eat all her snacks earlier. God must have known we'd need them."

She should have guessed. Her do-gooder was another religious nut. How did she attract them?

"There's a repair shop in the town at the bottom of the hill. We need to get that tyre filled properly. Do you think you can manage to drive? I'll drive behind you with my hazard lights on."

There'd be no chance of driving off the edge with him following, even if she still felt like it.

The man stayed by her side until she was buckled back in.

"Okay, I'll go and watch the road until you do your U-turn. Then drive slowly and steadily without any sudden turns. It's not far." He closed her door and headed back to his car.

He followed her all the way to the garage like a mother hen with a single chick. How long had it been since she'd felt this safe?

Once the tyre was properly filled up and the others had been checked, he came over again. "I don't like to say this to a lady, but you're not looking too well. Do you think it might be safer to book into a local motel and sleep for a couple of hours?"

"I need to work tomorrow."

"How far are you going?"

"Sydney, near Chatswood."

He looked at his watch. "It's still early. You could sleep for six hours and still make it comfortably."

Rachel sighed. Now that she was alive, she didn't want to smash someone else up. "Umm ..."

"Let me see if there's somewhere suitable."

He was gone before she could stop him and a few minutes later he returned.

"There's a motel around the corner. I've already given them a call, and they've got a quiet room with a good lock on the door."

He was behaving more and more like a grandfather. Soon he'd be patting her on the head and buying her ice cream.

Once again, he followed her along the road. Then he paid for her room, waved goodbye, and was gone.

She'd never even asked his name.

CHAPTER 14

On Monday morning, Rachel woke to bright sunshine. She'd slept six hours at the motel. Slept like the dead, which was ironic. No nightmares, no waking up to trembling and tears, no headache. Then she'd driven home without incident, eaten some scrambled eggs on toast, and slept another ten hours.

The woman in her mirror this morning looked totally different to the woman of yesterday. There was nothing visible to say she'd been right to the edge. Nothing visible to let others know she was only here today because of a tyre blowout. Nothing visible of the new scars on her heart.

David Jones hadn't changed at all. Why had she expected it would? The new manager started in a week, but today everything was normal.

Alice drifted over to Rachel's counter at mid-morning. "Things are a little better, although there were times I wanted to end everything." She dabbed her eye. "But I wouldn't do that to my husband or the children."

Well, Rachel had no children or anyone else to care, yet here she was. Not at all where she'd planned to be.

A potential customer drifted in their direction. Rachel unglued herself from the counter, pasted on a smile, and grabbed a perfume bottle. "Would you like a sample of our latest fragrance?"

There was no more chance to talk to Alice until three o'clock.

"I haven't asked you about your holiday yet," Alice said. "What did you get up to?"

Should she tell Alice the truth? Nope, that wouldn't do. "Oh, walks on the beach and swims and such. Nothing special."

"Sounds like what I need. No responsibilities for a while."

Rachel flicked an imaginary speck of dust off the counter. Alice was such a trusting person she couldn't spot evasion. The valve on Rachel's heart had been closed tight for so long it was probably rusted shut.

"You're going to think me strange," Alice said. "I woke up early on Sunday morning, worrying about you."

"Worrying about me?" Why would Alice waste her time?

Alice flushed. "I had an impression you were in some kind of trouble. Maybe even in danger."

Now what was going on? Rachel had thought the weirdness of yesterday was behind her.

"Did anything happen early yesterday morning?"

Would this conversation end more quickly if she brushed Alice off or if she said something?

"You must have the second sight." Rachel kept her tone casual. "I did have a car tyre blowout right on the edge of a cliff."

"What?" Alice sucked in air. "Seriously? You nearly went over the cliff?"

"Well, I would have." Rachel wasn't going to mention that she had intended to. "But the blowout spun me around instead of sending me over the edge."

"I knew it. I just knew it." Alice blushed. "I prayed for your safety."

Where were all these religious fanatics coming from? "I didn't know you prayed."

"I don't do it nearly enough, but it seems to be all I've been doing the last ten days."

Alice had never shown any symptoms of being a Christian before. If she had, Rachel would have won a gold medal for a sprint in the opposite direction.

"I think you've experienced a miracle," Alice said.

"It was no such thing."

"I think it was. You needed a miracle and God woke me up to pray for you. You're here, aren't you?"

And she wouldn't be here if the blowout hadn't happened. She'd have been lying smashed and burned at the bottom of a ravine but it couldn't have been God. She didn't believe in God. Certainly not in a God who cared about people like her. God, if he existed, cared about people like Alice. Nice people. People who obeyed him. Who liked him. Not people like her.

"No matter what you say, I believe you saw a miracle." Alice's eyes shone.

"We'll have to agree to disagree. I believe it was a coincidence."

"There's one way you could prove it," Alice said, her cheeks flushed. "Ask for another miracle."

Alice had got to be kidding. "Even if God exists, I don't think he can be expected to do miracles to convince sceptics."

"Why not? The Bible is full of sceptics."

Rachel snorted. "Okay. I'll do it, but I'll make it highly unlikely."

Alice nibbled her nail.

Rachel closed her eyes. What could she ask? Something so unlikely that it could never be mistaken for a coincidence. She pictured the huge ground floor of David Jones. What would be outrageous enough to make a total mockery of this challenge? She giggled. "Okay. Got it."

Alice glanced around. Was she beginning to doubt? Well, good. She ought to. This challenge should silence her forever.

"Well, what have you come up with?"

"I'm not going to say it out loud. Someone might overhear, or you might go and get someone to do it."

"But how will I know you're not tricking me?"

"Okay, okay, I'll write it down." Rachel found some scrap paper and scrawled a sentence. "I don't have an envelope, but I'll fold it up and put it back in my purse." She put it in the zippered compartment and put the purse back in the cupboard. "And that's that. Let's get back to work."

"But what did you write and how will we know?"

"Alice, this was your idea. I would never have thought to test a God I neither believe in nor trust but now I've thrown down the challenge." Rachel looked at her watch. "And your God has fifty-nine minutes to deliver."

"I made a mistake, and I apologise."

"Well, it's too late now." Rachel squinted at her watch. "In fifty-eight minutes, I will be free of ever thinking about God again. You'd be smart to follow my lead."

She shouldn't have thrown out that last dig. A tear slid down Alice's cheek.

Rachel smiled grimly and looked for a customer. She'd sort out this God thing once and for all.

A stream of customers kept her busy. Every so often, she surreptitiously checked her watch. Forty minutes, thirty. She sold more makeup and booked in two customers for wedding consultations the following week.

Twenty minutes. Ten.

Rachel snorted contemptuously. Freedom from superstitious myths was around the corner. She shouldn't laugh, because over at her counter, Alice was wilting. It wasn't kind to crush her.

Although Alice should be thanking her. What kind of modern woman was held captive by ancient lies?

Eight minutes. Five.

Rachel had her head down when she heard a gasp, some laughter, and a burst of excited chatter. She scanned the ground floor. Twenty metres away, a middle-aged man had his hands firmly planted on the floor. Could he have done what it looked like he had? No way. She wasn't going to react. Not yet. Her self-talk didn't stop her heart rate speeding up.

She walked across to Alice. "What did I miss?"

Alice narrowed her eyes. "You weren't responsible for that, were you?"

"For what?"

"That man did a handstand right in the middle of main aisle." She giggled. "It was perfect. His legs were straight up in the air for ages."

Impossible.

Rachel looked at the clock. Just before her deadline. She whirled around. "How did you do it?"

"Do what?"

"Did you go and get the paper out of my bag?"

"Of course not. What do you take me for?" Alice clapped her hands together. "Was that your test? Was it?"

"Two parts of it, but he looks too young to fulfil the third part."

"What do you mean too young?" Alice bobbed up and down like a toddler pumped full of sugar. "What age did you set?"

"Fifty."

Alice stopped bouncing and her shoulders slumped. "You're right. He doesn't look fifty but I'll go and ask. Some people look younger than their age."

"I don't think we'll get a chance to find out his age."

Two security guards arrived and crossed warily towards the

man as though they expected him to launch into a series of cart-wheels, or start singing opera.

There was some discussion before the two guards escorted the man away from their area. Alice jerked into action as though to follow them. Rachel grabbed her arm.

"Leave it. If your God is real, he needs to sort things out without your help."

The stranger stopped mid-stride and spoke to his escorts. All three turned around and headed for the main doors. Rachel held her breath. Now what?

They were almost past where Rachel was standing when the man veered towards her. The closest security guard grabbed his arm. He said something, and the guard let him go.

The stranger walked right up to Rachel. "I'm feeling like a fruit loop, but I have a message for you."

Was it her or Alice who gasped?

"Go home."

"I don't have a home."

"Of course you have a home," Alice said in her ear.

"I don't think he means that home." Rachel turned to the man. "What home do you mean?"

"The one with the maroon door and the rounded brass door knocker in the centre."

Rachel's arms goose-bumped. Who was this man?

The security man behind him cleared his throat, and the stranger turned to leave.

"Sir." Rachel's voice squeaked. "Can I ask how old you are?"

He didn't hesitate. "I turned fifty yesterday."

CHAPTER 15

*T*oday should have been Esther's first wedding anniversary. Instead, she'd spent this day last year recovering from her first round of chemo. Memories stabbed her and throbbed. She lay on her right side. Then on her left. Finally, she turned onto her back. She plumped up the pillow under her head, but the problem wasn't the pillow. It was the memories.

Victory Church wasn't the typical family-style church. It was a megachurch, and her father had insisted on a megawedding. Mum had laboured over five bridesmaid dresses, and the catering was to have been first-rate. Her wedding dress must still be in the back of the cupboard at her parents' place. How beautiful it had made her look.

Esther flipped onto her stomach. Would sleep ever come?

Maybe she could escape the memories if she did a few stretches and deep breaths.

How long did she lie and stare towards the ceiling? Now she was thirsty.

And the more she ignored her thirst, the thirstier she became. Did she have the energy to get up for a drink? The grandfather clock in the hall struck ten, then eleven, then the half hour. Esther groaned, swung her legs over the side of the bed, and stood. She'd get a drink from the front bathroom so she wouldn't disturb Gran.

The house was silent apart from the ticking of the clock. She took exaggerated care with each step.

Creak.

She'd forgotten the noisy floorboard. Esther winced and took another quick step forward. As she was about to enter the bathroom, there was a noise at the front door.

She froze with her hand on her chest, heartbeat accelerating. What was that? Was the wind rattling the outside screen? Had a jumbo-sized moth flown into the door? She waited, holding her breath, before slowly exhaling. Perhaps she'd imagined the noise.

Tap.

There it was again. And with it came another noise. A muffled sob. Was someone crying and would it be safe to open the door? Esther stood motionless, hovering between fight and flight.

At the back of the house, Gran's toilet flushed. Two people might be better than one. Esther bounced on the creaky floorboard as she walked towards Gran's room.

"Esther, is that you?" came a quavery voice.

"Yes, Gran." She pushed open the door and whispered loudly, "I think there's someone at the front door."

"At this hour?"

"It sounded like someone crying."

"Then we'd better go and look."

"Do you think it's safe?" Gran wouldn't be any help if there was a lunatic on the loose.

"The screen's locked, so we'll be able to see who it is."

As they walked up the hall, Esther's hands were clammy, but Gran appeared calm. Esther switched on the front verandah light and opened the door. A dark bundle was visible through the screen. It twitched.

A woman was on the ground, curled in a fetal position. She looked up, her face streaked with tears.

"Rachel? Is that you?" Gran asked.

The woman cried harder.

Gran unlocked the screen with a click. "You'll have to scoot back so I can open the door."

The woman rolled over onto her hands and knees and moved backwards. Once the door was open, Naomi attempted to haul the woman inside. Esther helped. Otherwise Gran would undo all the good work on her hip, or have a stroke. Whatever was going on, clearly the woman would be staying.

"Esther, would you go and put the kettle on?" Gran asked.

The woman jerked her head up and stared at Esther. The blood drained from her face and she clutched her stomach.

What was going on? Esther's face had never provoked such a response before. She bolted down the hallway to the kitchen. A haven from weeping, murmuring women and late-night mysteries.

Esther clicked on the kitchen light and the electric kettle. A million questions exploded like popcorn. Who was the woman? How did Gran know her? What might Gran want for their guest? A full meal, or a snack? Perhaps fruit would be a good compromise. Esther took the chopping board from its hook and sliced an apple, a pear, and an orange.

The murmuring in the hall stopped and Gran came into the kitchen with the woman trailing behind her.

"Rachel will be staying the night. We'll make up another bed." Gran and the woman seated themselves. "Rachel, do you need something to eat and drink?"

The mystery woman had warm milk and a banana. Then an enormous sandwich and more fruit. Perhaps she hadn't eaten for a while. Esther made up a bed in the study while their guest had a shower. When the woman came out of the bathroom, she was wearing a nightie Naomi had loaned.

Now she reminded Esther of someone. There was something about her eyes. Something about the angle of her chin. Neither Gran nor the stranger were volunteering any information.

---

*E*sther was woken the next morning by the clatter of a pan in the kitchen. She scrambled out of bed.

Gran didn't seem surprised to see her. "You're wondering what's going on?"

"You don't have to tell me if it's none of my business."

"Rachel gave me permission to speak on her behalf."

Who was Rachel, and why had she been allowed to stay?

"I'll go out into the sunroom, if you'll bring our tea," Gran said. "I don't think Rachel will be up for a while. She's clearly worn out."

Esther brought the tea.

"Where should I start?" Gran said.

"First of all, who's Rachel?"

Naomi raised her eyebrows nearly to her hairline. "Do you truly not know?"

"How would I know?" Esther had never seen her before, so why did Gran expect her to know?

"She's your sister."

"Sister? I don't have a sister." Esther jerked and hit her elbow on the arm of her chair. Searing pain and pins and needles ran along her forearm, and tea slopped over the edge of her cup into the saucer.

"You must know about her, or why have you been talking about her lately?"

"I thought that was something I made up." Esther's chest tightened and she turned to stare at Gran. "And you let me believe she wasn't real."

Gran dropped her eyes. "I wasn't sure what to do. I assumed you knew about Rachel."

"Wasn't it obvious I didn't?" She'd never spoken angrily to Gran before but right now she didn't care. Why had Gran kept her in the dark? Why would anyone do that? "I wouldn't have been asking if I had remembered. After all, I couldn't even tell you the girl's name."

"Yes, that puzzled me." Gran leaned her head back.

Gran wasn't going to avoid this conversation. There had been too much avoiding for far too long.

"Why didn't you tell me about Rachel?"

Gran sat up straight. "I've been trying to straighten out my own thoughts. Was it because you never mentioned her, so I assumed it was a deep hurt in your own heart? Or did I lay it aside because you had so many other issues to deal with? Or is it that I'm so used to not talking about Rachel?" A tear glistened on Naomi's cheek. "I pray for her every day, but I'm not sure I expected her to ever turn up."

"It feels like everyone has lied to me."

Gran reached out her hand but Esther avoided the touch. She wasn't ready to be nice.

"I dreamed about a girl. I asked Mum about my dreams not long ago, and she sidestepped the topic. I don't understand how she could do that. Didn't I have the right to know I had a sister?"

"I think you're being tough on your mother without knowing the full story."

"Tough?" Esther's voice rose. "What kind of parent would keep such a secret from me?" A hot rush of blood swept through her. "And Dad. He lied to me. He told me Rachel had been a missionary kid."

Gran's eyes narrowed. "What are you talking about?"

"Years ago, I asked Dad about the older girl who had lived with us. He told me she was the daughter of a missionary friend. Said she'd gone home and wouldn't be back." But even that information had to be dragged out of him.

"This is beyond belief." Gran said. "Are you saying your parents have never mentioned Rachel?"

"I never heard any mention of a sister." A bitter anger burned in Esther throat. "How could they keep her from me? How … how could they deprive me of the one thing I longed for?"

Both women sat in silence. There was so much to make sense of.

A sister. How could she not have known?

Esther turned to look at Naomi. She seemed to have shrunk in the last hour. This was hitting her hard as well.

"So what is the full story? Are you going to tell me, or do I have to live in the dark forever?" Esther winced at her tone of voice. Why was she lashing out at Gran? Her father was the one she wanted to pummel.

"Let me think …" Gran murmured. "Rachel is ten years older than you and left home at nearly fifteen. You'd have been four. It is possible, I suppose, for a four-year-old to forget someone."

"I didn't forget. Not really. Sure, I forgot her real name, and I was confused about her age but Dad lied. That's why I'm angry. Dad lied. Why would he do that? Why would my own father lie to me?"

Gran frowned. "I'm ashamed of my son. Ashamed he went that far." She sat for several moments. "But I can understand why he wouldn't want to talk about it."

"I don't, and I don't understand why you didn't say anything either."

Naomi flinched.

"I'm sorry, Gran. I shouldn't be attacking you for something Mum and Dad did. You did give me a hint. You called me Rachel the day I arrived, and again before your surgery." Esther took a deep breath to steady her voice. "Why didn't you say more?"

"I think I was trying to adjust to the fact you were here. I was puzzled about why you never asked me about Rachel, but it wasn't my story to tell. She stayed here after she ran away from home."

"Here? She lived with you?"

"For a while. Then she left. She kept in contact for the first few months, and I made sure your mother knew she was safe but then things went silent. I've had no calls, no letters, no news, nothing for over twenty years. Sometimes I've thought she was dead." Gran's mouth became a tight, straight line. "Scanning death notices has become an automatic reflex. I worried she'd changed her name or moved out of the state or even overseas. I've prayed every day for her, like I've prayed every day for you and your parents."

Having heard Gran pray, Esther could picture her labouring on their behalf, year after year, without seeing any answers. Maybe one day she'd have the same tenacity.

Gran took a mouthful of her tea. "I'll tell you the little I know, but we'll have to pray Rachel has the courage to tell us the rest."

Esther shook her head. "I still can't believe it. I have a sister. A sister. Maybe it will sink in if I say it often enough."

"I told you at the end of last year about the only time I saw your mother after your parents' wedding. Shortly after we prayed together, she became pregnant. I didn't know anything about it until I saw Rachel's birth notice in the paper." Gran dabbed the corner of her eye. "So many wasted years. Totally unnecessary and heartbreaking."

"I wish Mum had kept in contact with you."

"I'm guessing she feared your father finding out she'd been here. It's not surprising that someone with her family background would avoid conflict. Has she told you anything about her family?"

"Only recently." And only when Esther's cancer had forced the revelations out of Mum's tightly locked heart. "I know her father was an alcoholic and her mother died of cancer. She hasn't shared much, except that she was glad to escape and marry Dad."

"Maybe one day she'll have the courage to work through her

childhood issues. Some things I only heard from Rachel, and she was an angry teenager, but I do know Rachel adored you."

"If she adored me, why did she leave?" The angry words sizzled on Esther's tongue.

"According to Rachel, she left because she hated your father and his god. She'd heard all her life that I was a horrible hag, so she ran this way."

Maybe Esther and her sister had something in common after all. They'd both run in the same direction. "Why didn't she stay?"

"I don't know. Maybe she'll tell us herself."

"Can't you make a guess, Gran?" This conversation mustn't end here. She wanted to know more, she had to know more.

"I've thought long and hard about it and Rachel might disagree." Gran shifted in her seat. "Maybe having rejected the fake god, Rachel could no longer handle the real one. I never hid the fact that I followed Jesus."

"Did she go to church with you?"

"I made her. She didn't appreciate it. Perhaps it would have been wiser not to talk about Jesus at all. She was more broken than I'd realised." Gran blew her nose. "I woke up one morning, and Rachel was gone. All she left was a note. I put an ad in several newspapers to let her know I would always welcome her back."

The thought of her sister alone on Sydney's streets was terrifying. Better to wait until Rachel talked than to imagine the worst. "So you have no idea where she has been all these years?"

"No, and I'm not going to ask her," Gran said. "I'm going to pray every day and wait until she is ready to speak. It might take months, but let's trust the Lord to deal with her pain."

Esther's stomach rumbled.

"Better get breakfast first," Gran said. "I don't think I'll go to church today. One of us needs to be here when Rachel wakes up."

"Why don't we both stay home? I'll ring Gina and she can pass on our apologies."

"*I*'ve remembered a few things that mystified me at home," Esther said as they prepared breakfast. "When Nick and I were preparing for the wedding, Dad said things like, 'Nothing is too good for our only daughter.' Mum looked hurt and left the room."

"Mmm," Gran said as she retrieved the plates from the cupboard.

"You also said something when you told me about your past. You talked about Mum's pregnancy and said, 'That baby was lost to her.' Your wording was odd, and I thought you'd got your timeline confused, or that Mum had a miscarriage but that wasn't what you meant at all."

"Your mother hasn't had it easy." Gran clicked her tongue. "Imagine not being able to mention Rachel at home."

Was that why Mum had always been so aloof? Because of deep hurt and loneliness? "Do you think we could invite her here?"

"I hope so. One day, but Rachel needs to set the pace. We don't want her to feel she must do certain things to gain our acceptance."

CHAPTER 16

*E*sther and Naomi barely saw Rachel that first Sunday. They ate breakfast. Esther did the dishes. She tidied the kitchen. She went to check if any clothes needed washing. Nope. Then she looked at her watch. It was only ten o'clock. All she wanted to do was talk to her sister.

But the study door remained firmly closed. What was Rachel doing in there? When would she come out?

Esther grabbed a book and sat on the verandah in the sunshine. She read one page and then read it again. And again. Nothing penetrated. She closed the book and stared at the sky. Even the clouds moved like they were on a go-slow strike. Her watch said ten-thirty. *Grrrr.* She'd have gone to church if she'd known Rachel intended to stay in her room all day. Church would have offered some distraction.

At twelve, Naomi instructed her to carry a tray to Rachel's door.

She hung around, hoping Rachel would swing the door open and welcome her inside but nothing happened. No sounds of anyone moving inside. No door opening. No one coming out, throwing their arms around her and telling her how she'd been missed.

Was there a person with a beating heart behind the door?

Esther returned to the kitchen to eat lunch with her grandmother.

Was Rachel going to sleep all day?

After lunch, she washed the dishes. The day was getting repetitive. Then she tried tidying her room. It was a waste of time. She ended up leaning back and staring at the wall with her face frozen in a half-smile.

A sister. A sister. How unbelievably wonderful. An amazing out-of-the-box gift. She'd never expected to have her childhood wish granted, but the longing never left her. The longing had a life of its own, apart from logic. It couldn't die when the memories of the older girl she'd adored remained so strong.

To think that that girl had been Rachel.

Esther had trailed behind the older girl everywhere. Into her room, into the kitchen, into the garden. The girl had filled her days with songs, tickles, and laughter. Esther had called the girl Tickles so often she'd forgotten her real name, but she remembered the warm hugs. Maybe those hugs meant more because Esther's parents didn't do hugs. Not with her and not with each other, or at least not when she'd ever been with them.

She did remember the disappearance. It was as if Tickles had been snatched up to heaven like Elijah. Nothing left behind. No clothes, no books, and no goodbyes or explanations. Something about the whole atmosphere of the house had kept Esther mute for weeks. Her parents whispered behind closed doors, and Esther had crouched outside, straining to hear.

"Where's Tickles gone?" she asked one day. Mum had bolted out of the room, and Dad's anger had terrified her. She'd never dared to ask again.

Esther had cried night after night for weeks. What had she done wrong to make the girl go away? She'd begged God to bring her back, even vowing to give up lollies and ice cream for a whole year. Nothing had worked. After that, Esther had refused to pray for a long, long time.

A sunbeam came through the window. Yes, Rachel had been like that sunbeam. Dancing, laughter and warmth. Where had the laughter gone? Maybe Rachel was tired now. Sometime soon they'd be able to get to know each other as adults. Gina had been a great friend, even a sister substitute, but nothing could beat the real thing.

A sister. Something Esther had fantasised about all her life. Looking back, an older-sister-shaped hole had opened in her heart right after Rachel disappeared. Sometimes the longing was in the background, but it surged to the surface whenever she confronted a significant life event. The loss of her first tooth, when she'd wanted to know about the tooth fairy. The first day of high school, when she'd stood all alone on the train platform wondering why her parents sent her to a private school three stations down the track when all her friends went to the excellent school nearer home. The occasions she'd clashed with Dad over boyfriends. He'd been right about two of them, but she regretted the third.

Older sisters existed to forge the way ahead of their younger siblings. Older sisters listened and had wisdom to share. They were there to wrap their younger siblings in sympathy if needed, or congratulate their accomplishments. Her parents weren't the type to effuse. Effuse, what an understatement. Mum might have wanted to sometimes, but Dad always behaved as though accomplishments were expected of a Macdonald. She'd vowed that one day he'd do something more.

Last year, she'd seemed on track, with awards at work and a fiancé he approved of, but it had all come crashing down. Even last year might have been better with an older sister.

Esther sighed. If only Rachel would come out and talk to her.

Her anger at her grandmother was fading, and it was hard to be angry at Mum. How could you be angry at someone for being afraid of their husband? Maybe one day she could even forgive her father.

***

At three-thirty, Esther went and made a cup of tea for her grandmother. The biscuit container was almost empty. She'd do some baking. Her grandmother liked Anzac biscuits and shortbread. They could be made in big batches and frozen. Baking might keep her mind off that closed door.

When was it ever going to open? The day was nearly over and she still hadn't talked to Rachel. They had a lot to catch up on. Now the impossible had happened, she didn't want to waste a single millisecond.

When Naomi was settled with a book and a rug on the back verandah, Esther went back to the kitchen. She had always gravitated to the kitchen when Mum was baking. Maybe she could entice Rachel out of her room. She mixed the oats, sugar, flour, and coconut, then added the melted butter and golden syrup. Her hands were busy, but her ear was alert for any sound from Rachel's room. *Come on, Rachel. Come out and talk to me.*

The door was still shut when she and Naomi ate their simple evening meal.

At the end of the meal, Naomi peered at her over the top of her glasses. "You've been fidgeting all through the meal. What's eating at you?"

"Now I have a sister, I want to talk to her."

"Honey, she might not want to talk to us."

"But we're her family."

"People change a lot in twenty years. Look at how you've changed in the last year."

Esther shook her head. "But it doesn't change the fact that we're family."

"No, it doesn't, and the fact that she's come here shows us that. By the looks of her last night, she might be at breaking point. We'll have to pray and be patient."

Pray and be patient. Esther would pray, but it would be for action on Rachel's part. Not patience. Esther didn't want patience. Not after all these years.

Rachel still hadn't appeared when Esther left for work in the morning. She could barely wait to get home in the evening, but again Rachel didn't appear. By Wednesday evening, Esther had begun to wonder if she'd only imagined a sister.

By Thursday, Esther was almost worried. "Gran, have you seen Rachel at all this week?"

"Not much. I think she's sleeping."

"That can't be a healthy sign."

"Mind your own business, dear. If she needs to sleep, then I intend to allow her to do it. She'll come out when she's ready."

Esther groaned. "And when will that be?"

"I have no idea, but you can't call her a difficult houseguest."

It was easy for Naomi to say. She didn't have to cook the meals or do the extra cleaning. Doing extra work for Gran was fine. After all, she was recovering from surgery and was grateful for everything but cooking for an invisible woman wasn't so easy. And cooking for an invisible woman who looked like staying that way was worse.

CHAPTER 17

*E*sther hurried towards the park bench where she and Joy usually met, midway between the hospital and the cancer clinic. Which piece of news should she share first? Brenda? Or Rachel?

Brenda would be less complicated.

"You know how I've been praying about my workmates? Well, God has answered at last," Esther said as they sat down and got out their lunches.

"You always sound astonished."

"I know, I know. I shouldn't be, but every answer to prayer is like a totally new miracle out of nowhere."

"So what has happened?" Joy ate a mouthful.

Esther told her about Brenda. "And we're going to go for a walk on Monday lunchtimes."

"Which stories are you planning to tell?"

Talking about Brenda first was harder than she'd expected. The news about Rachel was ready to burst out of her like a cork from a bottle.

"She's only agreed to listen to one. I'd better start at the beginning, as she has no church background at all."

Joy finished her mouthful. "Always a wise idea."

Esther made a face. "You suggested it for the church group, and I ignored you but you were right. We've had to add Old Testament background to the stories to help them understand."

Joy wasn't the kind of woman to say, 'I told you so.' In that, Joy was more like a sister than Rachel looked like ever being. A pain shot through her. How could she have a friendship with someone who barricaded herself in her room?

"And you're hoping Brenda will want to hear more?"

"I'm doing more than hoping, I'm praying. Hard." It was a joy to get back to prayer. Since radiotherapy, every crumb of energy had been directed at getting through work. "I've revised Genesis 3."

"With the earlier chapters as the introduction?"

Esther had mapped out a set of stories to share with Brenda. It was one way to avoid pessimism about Rachel. She'd aim for four stories from the Old Testament and five from the New. She handed her list to Joy.

Joy ran her finger down the page. "Good choices."

"I must have had a good teacher." Esther winked.

Joy put away her lunch box. "It's great that you have this chance with Brenda, but I'll pray you find others who are interested. That you might be able to have a group."

"A group? I'd prefer to start with one, but I will start praying for another person."

Joy laughed. "I'll pray for God to do more than you even think to ask."

"You always make me dream bigger than my small ambitions. Could we pray for Brenda and my workmates?"

"And let's also pray for Michelle, Dr Webster, and your other friend at the cancer clinic."

They bowed their heads. Joy never failed to spur her on. Life was full of work, caring for Gran, church, and getting the rest she still needed. Praying and sharing Jesus slipped off the agenda too easily. And she hadn't counted on having someone else to care for. How long would that continue?

Joy lingered in leisurely praise as though standing in front of a masterpiece in the Louvre but Esther couldn't linger today. She was about to burst.

"Amen," Joy eventually said, then looked at Esther with a raised eyebrow.

"Sorry. I couldn't concentrate." Esther grabbed Joy's shoulder. "You're not going to believe it. I have a sister."

"But you're an only child."

"That's what I thought too. She ran away when I was a small child."

Joy scrunched up her nose. "And your parents and Naomi never mentioned her?"

"My grandmother assumed I knew, and Mum and Dad kept it secret." Esther clenched her fists.

"Well, that's unexpected," Joy said. "How's it working out?"

"Not at all like what I imagined." Esther frowned. "I've dreamed so long of having an older sister, but Rachel doesn't seem interested in being a sister."

"What do you mean?"

"She won't even talk to me. All she does is stay in her room and sleep."

"You'd better tell me everything."

Esther looked at her watch. "Won't you be late?"

"When you've worked as hard as I have all these years without any sick leave, you earn some trust. My boss knows I'll work the full number of hours."

Esther poured out the story of Rachel's arrival and all Naomi had told her.

"Hmm," Joy said when Esther finished. "So you spent all your life dreaming about an older sister, and now Rachel is ignoring you?"

"Yes, and it's driving me out of my mind."

"What have I told you in the past about waiting for God's timing?"

"I'm tired, Joy. It's not my grandmother's fault, but she's only able to shower and dress herself. She can't do housework of any sort. And Rachel doesn't help. She doesn't cook. She doesn't wash dishes. She doesn't clean the bathroom."

When was Rachel going to realise that Esther wasn't her slave? Esther was barely coping. Some days it felt like she was holding onto a cliff edge with her fingernails. If Rachel didn't start contributing to the household soon, Esther was going to crack like a raw egg. And cracked eggs were messy.

No wonder her prayer and Bible reading had gone out the window. Every night she collapsed into bed and passed out. Why couldn't Joy simply empathise with her?

"And Gran's garden is growing more and more like a jungle. It was her pride and joy, and now it's an eyesore. The neighbours probably think I'm a neglectful granddaughter."

"It sounds to me like you've got Martha syndrome."

Esther had always had sympathy for Martha. How irritating it must have been to see Mary sitting there, chatting to Jesus, when there was so much to do. After all, Jesus was special. You didn't want to give him cheese on toast. And everywhere he went, twelve hungry disciples followed.

Esther sighed loudly. "No one wants to be a Martha, but someone has to do something or you end up living in a pigsty."

"Yes, but how else could Martha have handled her frustration?"

Frustration. Why did Joy use that precise word? Could she see Esther was edging too close to erupting?

Joy sat quietly. She wouldn't contribute anything until Esther said something first.

"Could Martha have sent out for the equivalent of first century takeaways?"

"Possibly. Or got help from the neighbours. Money didn't seem to be an issue for the family. What else?"

Esther must focus. She still had to get back to the department, put away her lunch things, and wash her hands before her first afternoon client arrived. "Maybe she could have recruited the disciples to help but they might have been more of a hindrance than a help."

"True."

"I know. She could have done a deal with Mary and seen if she would agree to a half-half arrangement so that Martha could listen to Jesus too."

"Any other ideas?"

What was Joy getting at? She'd keep probing until Esther thought hard but thinking was wearisome today.

"Jesus fed thousands with a few fish and pieces of bread," Joy said.

Esther thought for a while and then said, "Maybe Martha would be embarrassed to ask him to use his power for a personal miracle."

"Most of us are like Martha. We forget God is our heavenly Father. He cares about the small things, including our tiredness and frustration. The best thing she could have done was to come to Jesus and say, 'I would love to talk with you, but there is also a hungry household to feed. Lord, what should I do?'"

Joy made it sound simple. Why couldn't Joy be more sympathetic? Sometimes Esther wanted to whinge. She should have known Joy wouldn't let her get away with it.

Esther gathered up her lunch things. Esther had never troubled her father with the minutiae of life. She'd learned self-reliance early because he had no patience with a child's clumsiness or carelessness. Had he been even worse with Rachel? Maybe one day she'd find out, if and when Rachel decided to speak.

Joy stood up and gave her a quick hug. "You might be over-protecting Naomi. She's an adult and a wise one. Do her the courtesy of allowing her to come up with some solutions. She broke her hip, not her head."

CHAPTER 18

*R*achel woke in the dark.
Mopoke. Mopoke.

The bird called from somewhere in the garden. What time was it? She turned over and squinted at the luminous hands of the clock on the bedside table. Quarter past two.

How many days had she been sleeping? She forced her mind back. After the man had told her to go home, Alice had walked her to the train because she couldn't stop trembling. She'd gone home. Had it been two or was it three days at home? She couldn't remember. It might have been four. She'd sat in the dark, hugging her knees to her chest, and cried. And cried. And cried, like the plug on some vast subterranean lake had been pulled out. How could one body contain so many tears?

Then she'd collapsed.

Rachel turned over. The darkness pressed in around her, hemming her in. She had a sudden vision of being buried alive. Her heart jump-started into a sprint. Her blankets seemed to wrap around her. She kicked out and hit the wall. Ouch. She struggled to free herself from her blankets. What was happening to her? Why all these silly imaginings?

The wind rustled the leaves and something tapped her window. She started and drew the blankets over her head again. Silly. There was no one outside. It was only the topmost twigs of a bush.

Her body ached from top to toe, and her eyes stung. She took a deep breath, stretched, and focused on relaxing every muscle starting from her ankles.

---

*S*omething rattled and thumped down the hallway outside her room. Then stopped.

"Rachel." Two soft knocks. "It's me."

Gran.

Rachel rubbed her eyes. Was it morning? The light glowed around the edges of her window. Probably after ten.

Two more knocks. "Rachel."

Gran would keep knocking until she got a response.

"Come in."

The door opened and Gran pushed the trolley into the room. Rachel's nose twitched. Bacon. A smell of temptation. Her stomach rumbled.

"You've barely eaten since you arrived."

She'd had no appetite for anything but sleep for days. Was today Thursday or Friday? Or even Monday? The days blurred together in the soggy sump of her mind. There were too many choices laid out. What should she eat and which utensil should she use? Even such small decisions were beyond her.

Naomi dragged a chair across, sat down, and laid a cool hand on her forehead. "No fever. That's good."

She wasn't sick. Not in the normal way. Sometime during the day before she arrived here, she'd rung work and claimed two weeks of sick leave. There was a decision to be made about going back. Decisions. The word sent palpitations of panic through her.

"Sit up, dear. I'm not going to feed you unless you misbehave." Naomi winked at her.

A month ago, Rachel would have resented being bossed. Today it was a relief. She sat up and rearranged her pillows against the headboard.

Naomi handed her a spoon, and a bowl of muesli with fresh fruit and yoghurt. Rachel took the first mouthful. Sweet and sour mixed together. It tasted good. She ate another mouthful.

"That's right. Keep eating. You were looking peaky, and I have no intention of allowing you to turn yourself into a skeleton."

If Esther had been pushing her, Rachel would have thrown the bowl at her, but Gran was okay.

Soon after Rachel had arrived at Gran's, she'd run into Esther on one of the only occasions she left her bedroom. Esther planted herself in the middle of the hallway.

"Hello," Esther had said, looking Rachel in the eye.

Esther's eyes were the problem. The rest of her had changed beyond recognition but the eyes were the same. The same eyes Rachel had seen in a hundred nightmares. Full of hurt. Full of condemnation.

Rachel had clutched her stomach and dashed for the bathroom. She'd huddled on the ground, shaking. Waiting for the creak of the floor as Esther gave up and walked away. Why was Esther even here? Surely someone her age should be married or have her own home. Odd but not odd enough for her to ask questions. That would be entirely too much effort, and she didn't want to start liking her. Keeping Esther at a distance was safer.

Once the muesli was finished, Naomi handed her a glass of milk and waited for her to drink it. Then at last she could eat the bacon and eggs. It must be thirty years since she'd eaten bacon. Her taste buds did a little dance of delight at the crispy perfection.

"That wasn't too hard, was it?"

Rachel smiled weakly. "Thank you."

"Do you think you could manage a shower? Perhaps wash your hair?"

Her legs shook at the thought, but staying in bed was worse. A shower and a change of sheets were suddenly the most important thing in the world.

"Can I strip the bed?" Rachel asked.

"Of course. Let me get out of your way."

Gran struggled to her feet and pushed the breakfast trolley out the door. "I'll come back and put clean sheets on the chair while you're in the shower. Toss the old set in the laundry basket."

Surely she could manage one small task. Rachel swung her feet out of bed. The room whirled. She closed her eyes and waited. Cracked open one eye, then the other. She gingerly stood up and turned around to pull the blankets off the bed and throw them on the floor. Then stripped the sheets and took them along to the bathroom.

After the shower, she dressed, changed the linen, and sagged back onto the bed. It was the longest she'd been out of bed since she'd arrived, whenever that was.

There had been a glow of satisfaction in merely changing the sheets. She needed that glow. She was going to aim to do one task a day. No matter how unimportant. That should be possible. Shouldn't it?

Tomorrow was still a workday. She'd checked. Tomorrow she'd ring David Jones and resign. It was easier than any of the alternatives like admitting she needed more sick leave. Something had broken inside her. Something she had no idea how to fix.

CHAPTER 19

The first person Esther saw in the cancer clinic was Rob Boyle. He jumped out of his seat and bounded towards her. "My afternoon suddenly got a whole lot better. Go and announce your arrival at the reception desk, and I'll save you a seat."

Esther grinned. "See you in a jiffy."

Michelle saw her and ticked off her name. "Dr Webster is running late."

Good. She'd been praying all week she could talk with Rob.

"I thought I'd never see you again," he said. "Visits aren't fun when you don't know anyone."

"I feel the same so I checked when you were coming next."

He chuckled. "I bet that was against the rules."

"Michelle made an exception. Don't you dare get her into trouble."

"Don't hit me. I won't tell, I promise." Rob held up his hands.

Esther laughed. "How have you been?"

"Not too bad. Even my energy is coming back. I have one more six-month check-up, then one more after another year."

"Lucky you. My initial diagnosis was worse than yours. They'll probably keep checking for longer. This is only my second three-month visit." *Lord, give me a question to get a significant conversation going.* Nothing came into her head.

"What have been some of the best things for you, post-cancer?" Rob asked.

Getting him to ask the questions is even better. "Maybe you'd better go first. I need to collect my thoughts."

"I've had a new appreciation of my family," Rob said. "I used to get annoyed if the kids were mucking up, but now I'm less uptight. I'm grateful to be alive to hear them, even if they're arguing."

"Maybe society would be a happier place if everyone had to go through chemo."

Rob chuckled. "You must be slipping. You didn't mention Jesus once in your answer."

"I don't want to overdo it."

"Jesus is part of who you are. I don't understand it and think it's a little weird, but apart from that you're a lot of fun."

Esther raised an eyebrow. "You think Christians are boring?"

"And they're not?"

"Not the ones I know best. Even breaking her hip hasn't damp-ened my grandmother's spark and spunk. And the people at the church I go to are terrific. They have their faults of course, but they're a real family. When Gran came out of hospital, they fell over themselves to provide us with food. I didn't have to cook for two weeks."

"I can see why you're enthusiastic, but didn't you say that your dad has all sorts of whacko views about the Bible?"

"Sadly, they're not whacko in the sense of being unusual. Far too many people treat God like he's some sort of giant genie in the sky."

"And he isn't?"

She didn't know where to start. A quarter of an hour every six months couldn't possibly unravel the tangled skeins in his mind. "Have you ever heard the story of the Prodigal Son?"

"Sounds familiar. I probably heard it back in the day when I was forced to go to Sunday School."

She'd apologised previously that he'd felt forced. Could she say enough to trigger past memories yet leave him curious to find out more?

"A father had two sons. The youngest one demanded his inheritance early. Once he had it, he went to the city and blew everything on wine, women, and song."

Rob smirked. "Sounds like my kind of guy."

"Hopefully you'll never end up where he did, feeding pigs and eating their swill. That was as low as you could go for a Jewish boy."

"Good point."

"One day the son thought, 'What am I doing here? Even my father's servants have better food than this.' When he was still a long way from home, his father saw him, ran towards him and threw his arms around him. The son said, 'Father, I have sinned against heaven and against you. I am no longer worthy to be called your son, but let me be a servant.' The father called out to his servants, 'Bring the best robe, let's kill a calf and celebrate. For my son who was lost is found. He was dead but now he's alive again.'"

A door opened. "Robert, please."

Why was there never enough time? "God isn't some genie. He's a loving Father waiting for his children to come home."

"I know I haven't bothered to read what you suggested in the past, but I will make it a priority. Make sure your appointment in six months matches mine."

Esther had talked over with Joy why God only allowed her such short conversations with some people. She'd prayed for Rob, Dr Webster, and Michelle the receptionist on and off for nine months. She'd like to see more progress.

Joy had been straight to the point, as usual. "Esther, can God be trusted to bring other Christians into their lives?" Esther knew the answer but wanted to be more than one link in the chain. She wanted to be there for the best part.

"God knows what he is doing," Joy had said. "Are you willing to be a minor link if that is what God wants?"

Esther couldn't say anything other than yes, but it wasn't the way she wanted things to be.

"Esther." She was jerked alert by the nurse calling her name. She stood and headed into Dr Webster's office and sat down without a word.

"What, no greeting today?" Dr Webster said.

"Sorry. I was distracted by a conversation I just had." Esther sat up straight.

"Let me guess. You were talking about Jesus."

Esther's eyes widened. "You do know me well."

"You're one of the few people who has ever given me a thank you book. And yes, before you ask, I have finished one of them."

My goodness. While she was frustrated by Rob, God had been working in someone else's life. "Which one?"

"The one about whether the New Testament is history. The author made some valid points. Enough for me to promise I'll read the other one, but don't get too excited."

It was hard not to. Hearing he'd finally read one would motivate her to pray more.

Esther made her next two appointments with Michelle to ensure that she could meet Rob again. As she was about to ask if Michelle had received the Bible she'd left for her, the phone rang. Esther waited. Michelle put down the phone and Esther opened her mouth. She had to close it again as the phone rang again, and again.

While she was talking, Michelle tucked the phone between her ear and shoulder and mimed a book opening and closing. Then she put up her thumb. Did she mean that she was reading the Bible?

How far had she got through the reading programme Esther had suggested? Looked like she'd have to come back again to find out. Meanwhile she had plenty to pray about and distract her from the ongoing disappointment with Rachel.

It had been nearly two weeks since Rachel had arrived.

She ate, she showered, she slept.

She ate, she showered, she slept.

Most of the time Esther only saw Rachel's back as she scurried into the bathroom. At Naomi's request, she'd bought Rachel another two sets of pyjamas and some casual clothes to wear around. They'd buy more later when, and if, Rachel was ever up to shopping with her. Did she have clothes or money of her own?

Rachel had driven to their place that first night with only the clothes she was wearing. Had she even intended to stay? If Esther hadn't been awake, they might never have known that Rachel had been at the door. Why had she come? What was the use of her being there if she never talked to them?

Rachel was a burden. A burden who lounged around, not lifting one finger to help. Sure, Rachel was tired, but they still had no idea what had happened to bring her to this state. The sleeping beauty hadn't bothered to enlighten them.

Esther wasn't totally insensitive. Obviously something had brought Rachel to a state of collapse, but did it compare to cancer, a mastectomy, chemo, and radiotherapy? Not to mention a cancelled wedding and being thrown out of home. Yet she was still a functioning and useful member of the household.

Why wasn't Rachel?

CHAPTER 20

"*R*achel, I miss having my hanging baskets of flowers," Naomi said.

Rachel raised her gaze from her lunch. Seven baskets around the verandah trailed dry leaves and stems. She hadn't noticed them yesterday when she finally emerged from her room to eat lunch with her grandmother.

How could she have slept so long? Yesterday, she'd realised she had to get out or go stir-crazy. The shady verandah looking out on the patch of lawn and garden had beckoned her.

"Esther has already bought the new petunias to go in the baskets, but I'd like to have them done before she comes home. Would you help me?"

How could she say no? Gran hadn't placed a single demand on her. Not like that cute toddler who'd grown into a demanding adult, brimful of expectation. Rachel was too tired for expectations.

"I'm not sure I know what to do."

Gran stood up. "I'll guide you through the process, but I can't do the lifting and carrying."

Rachel flexed her biceps. "I'll provide the brawn if you'll provide the brain."

"Deal. If you clear the lunch things, I'll gather my wits together."

Rachel cleared the table and carried everything into the kitchen. She even washed the few dishes. Goodness, she'd been slack. Was it a month since she'd arrived? It was like her brain had switched off as she stepped over the threshold. Sleep, sleep, and more sleep. A whole month without exercise, a whole month without responsibilities. Best of all, a whole month without nightmares. Not a single one since the last day in Port Macquarie.

Since the day she'd finally gotten out of bed, Rachel had succeeded in doing one small task a day. She'd resigned from work. She might regret it later, but right now she was too tired to care. Would they rehire her if she recovered? If the city store didn't allow her back, Chatswood might.

Rachel walked back to the verandah. Naomi had already covered the table with newspaper and found a trowel.

"Okay, the first thing is to take each pot down and dump the soil and dry plants into the right-hand compost bin near the back fence."

Rachel took down the hanging baskets. She should be able to get the first task done in three trips.

"Take this." Naomi popped a small trowel in the top of one of the baskets. "It will help you scrape each liner out properly. There's a bucket down there. We'll need half a bucket of the compost from the bin on the left."

Rachel completed the first tasks.

"I think Esther left the plants in trays outside the back of the garage. There should be twenty-eight plants, four for each basket."

Sure enough, a crowd of purple, pink, and white sat waiting. Rachel carried each tray up to the verandah.

Naomi continued her instructions until seven baskets swung in the breeze.

Rachel put her hands on her hips, took a deep breath, and looked around the garden. Many of the bushes were straggly, and weeds grew alongside the flowers.

Oh, to see the garden like it used to be. When the man at David Jones had said, 'Go home', this was the place she'd thought of. The garden had been part of the sense of home. Thinking of a regular job cramped her stomach and sent tingles of panic down her legs, but perhaps she could help Gran in some way. To say thank you.

"Gran, would you tell me what to do if I wanted to do some work in the garden tomorrow?"

"Could I ever. The worst thing about breaking my hip has been watching my garden turn into a jungle. If something isn't done soon, we'll be devoured."

Rachel smiled. She'd smiled so seldom this year, she almost heard her lips creak. There hadn't been anything to smile about for far too long.

"I'll see what I can do to fight it."

*E*sther walked up the back steps that evening. What was that smell of damp earth? She looked around and then up. Gran had repotted the petunias. She was supposed to have left that task for her. How had she managed?

She went into the house. "Gran?"

"I'm in the kitchen."

A week ago, Gran had started preparing the vegetables ready for Esther to cook. It was one less thing she had to do. When was Rachel going to pull her weight?

Esther kissed Gran's velvety cheek. "I thought I told you not to do the repotting."

"I didn't do it."

Had someone from church come to visit?

"Rachel did it."

Esther's jaw dropped open. After being a total slug for a month, Rachel appeared and did the fun job. Who wouldn't prefer playing with flowers to cleaning, scrubbing, and cooking?

"I told you she'd eventually come out. She was never a lazy kid." Gran julienned some carrots. "She's had lunch with me twice, and I asked her to help."

And why was Rachel willing to talk to Gran and not her? It wasn't as if Esther had ever hurt her. She could understand Rachel being angry at their father, but why should Esther be punished for his sins? Why was she still being shunned?

CHAPTER 21

*R*achel waited until she heard Esther's car back out of the driveway before she joined Naomi for breakfast the next morning. Now there'd be no need to talk to Esther.

"Gran, do you have a hat I can borrow?" she asked after she finished her last mouthful of toast.

"Hat, gloves, and tools are all in the gardening shed. Where are you going to start?"

Rachel gestured out the window. "Wouldn't the front be best? That's the part that's visible from the street."

"Esther and I did do the pruning at the end of the season, but all the garden beds need weeding and the lawn needs mowing."

Rachel blew out a gusty breath. "I've never used a lawn mower."

"It's not that difficult. I bought an electric one years ago as it's lighter and easier to use. I don't think you'll have any problems, but come and get me before you start."

Rachel stretched up towards the ceiling and did a few bends and lunges to limber up. "I had a look yesterday. I'll start with the bed along the front fence."

"The weeds should come out by their roots if you loosen the ground around them."

Subtle instruction there, Gran. She might be inexperienced, but she did know weeds needed to come out by their roots.

"I'll ask if I have any problems." Rachel took their dishes to the kitchen, washed up, and headed towards the door. "Am I likely to find spiders?"

"Well, it is Sydney. That's why I buy the thickest leather gloves."

Rachel shivered. "Funnel-web spiders give me the creeps."

"Keep your eyes open, and use the big fork."

Rachel went to the garden shed and found the big hat and long gloves behind the door. She knocked them out against the bench, in case there were any unwanted visitors inside. The tools were all hanging neatly on hooks. She selected the big fork and some smaller trowels, and went along the drive to the front garden.

When she was small she'd loved trailing behind her parents' gardener. He'd always had far more patience than her father.

Rachel thrust the fork straight down into the soil and put the arch of her foot on it. She'd seen the gardener do it a thousand times. The fork sank lower into the ground. What was she doing wrong?

The front window slid open. She should have known Gran would watch. Was it that obvious she was an incompetent gardener?

"Put the fork in at an angle and aim to take the top three or four inches of soil. Then wriggle it from side to side."

Rachel did as she was told. It worked. She bent down and pulled out the weeds.

"If you fork a whole section and then weed it, you won't have to bend as much," Naomi said.

Rachel grinned. How long would she have an instructor?

She'd better listen to her Gran's tips. If she wrecked her back, Esther would probably stand back and watch her suffer. She wouldn't blame her. How was Esther to know she was a trigger for unwanted memories? Rachel barely understood it herself.

Soon Rachel was in a rhythm. Loosen a square metre of earth and weed it. The rich smell of well-composted earth filled her nostrils. Pale pink worms were visible in every forkful. The more worms, the better. That's what the gardener had said, all those years ago.

She'd be stiff tomorrow after a month without exercise. Exercise hadn't seemed important recently. After a month of sleep, she no longer felt like over-stretched toffee. Could she get back to running this week? She'd cancelled her gym membership and couldn't afford it until she had a regular salary once again.

Rachel stood, placed her hands on her lower back, and arched backwards. The bright blue sky was full of puffy white clouds. How long since she'd even noticed the sky? In all those years working at David Jones and taking lunch breaks outside, she'd had to sit on park benches or café seats. Straight skirts and high heels didn't allow her to lie on the grass and watch the clouds. Cloud-watching had been something the ten-year-old version of herself had loved. A cloud like a horse's head drifted across the sky, dissolving around the edges until it became a shapeless blob.

Rachel shook herself. Today wasn't for dawdling. Perhaps one day soon.

She dumped the first load of weeds in the bin. Dark earth now framed each bush.

---

*R*achel used her shoulder to rub the sweat near her ear.
"Are you ready for a cup of tea?" Gran called from inside.

"Perfect timing. I'll tidy up first."

Rachel carried the tools round to the back verandah and lined them up against the wall. She'd mow the lawn after a break. How hard could it be?

Gran handed her a cup of tea and a piece of fruit cake. Rachel stretched her legs out and took a sip. It tasted like heaven. Two hours in the garden, and her taste buds had woken up.

After morning tea, Gran showed her how to run the electric lawn mower. With a purring hum, it was off. The sun warmed Rachel's back, and the fresh green smell tickled her nose. She looked behind her. Who would have thought that she'd find cutting neat swathes so satisfying?

Gran was a treasure. What other lady in her mid-eighties would cope graciously with two adult grandchildren moving in with her? The lawnmower purred down the next section. What was it about her grandmother that she appreciated? Perhaps it was she never sensed Gran expected anything from her. Esther, on the other hand … she was something else entirely.

Ever since the night she'd arrived, Esther's every glance, every posture, every word communicated that Rachel was failing to behave like a sister ought to behave. How long would it be before her sister started lashing her with the sisterly equivalent of the Proverbs 31 woman? Rachel massaged the sudden pain in her stomach.

Why couldn't Esther be more like Gran? Without Esther, she'd be completely content, but Esther was living here and growing impatient. What did she want? Gifts and giggles? Tea and shopping? Hugs and kisses like some little kid? Deep and meaningful conversations? When would Esther grow up? Didn't Esther understand Rachel had no reserves of love to give? They'd dried up long ago.

A white cockatoo screeched behind her, and Rachel jumped.

Would Esther be pleased that she'd started doing some gardening? There was no way to know. Rachel had spent the last month avoiding her. She hadn't wanted to talk to anyone, let alone an almost stranger with judgmental eyes. And then there was the whole thing about Esther's eyes giving her flashbacks to her nightmares and making her want to vomit. A 'quack' would have a bucketful of psychobabble to explain it.

Avoiding Esther suited Rachel. How long would Esther keep judging her and finding her wanting? But talking to Esther would please Gran, and pleasing Gran was a way to say thank you for the haven she'd provided. Why was it easier to work to please someone without expectations than someone with them?

Rachel groaned softly. That was what she was afraid of.

Expectations.

The word itself draped a heavy shawl of stones round her shoulders. Mike and the other men had had expectations. Alice had had expectations but they'd been easier to keep at arm's length. A sister was harder. If her sister had any of the tenacity of the toddler Rachel remembered, she'd be hard to shake off. Those pudgy little legs had pounded after Rachel wherever she'd gone.

Why couldn't Esther accept her for who she was now? Rachel didn't want to move out, but for the last few days she'd begun to long to return to her own space before the lease ran out. Free of the need for conversation. Free of the need for more than the minimum of housework. Free to do exactly what she wanted without feeling a failure but until she got a job, she didn't have the money to pay for that freedom.

Rachel emptied the grass from the mower catcher into the big bin ready to add to the compost. She thumped the catcher against the edge. Well, no matter what Esther expected or how many times Esther pestered her to go out on a 'sister date,' she was going to be disappointed. Rachel didn't have the emotional capacity to be a friend, let alone a sister. Esther would have to grow up and discover that real life wasn't anything like a happily-ever-after fairy tale.

CHAPTER 22

"*E*sther, are you ready to go for a walk?" Brenda asked.

Esther jumped. She'd been praying all week, but she'd also prepared her heart for disappointment. There were too many possible obstacles. Like Brenda feeling embarrassed because a nosy therapist asked why she'd started walking with Esther.

Esther took off her name badge, grabbed her water bottle, and they set off.

"I should go walking during lunch more often. I don't get nearly as much exercise as you do, Esther."

"And I don't have three young children to keep me busy." Why did her heart always race before she talked about Jesus? Was it normal?

"They are a handful, but it's easier now the oldest two are at school."

Esther was tempted to chit-chat, but lunch breaks were short. How could she get to the story? That was always the hardest part. *Lord, help me.*

"Look at that plant," Brenda said. "I always think it looks like a red spider."

A wattlebird swooped down and inserted its beak into the flowers.

Thank you for the lead-in, Lord. "Yes, grevilleas are fascinating. Have you ever wondered why there's such a variety of plants and birds?"

"There, you did it," Brenda giggled. "I could see you were sweating. You could have just asked if I was ready for the story."

Now it was Esther's turn to laugh. "I should have let you teach me. I'm still learning, and starting is the hardest part."

"So start."

"I normally do a brief introduction first." Did she sound as dorky as she felt? "I want to ask you two questions. First, where did the world and all its incredible variety come from? And second, why is this beautiful world in such a mess?"

Brenda was silent. Was she thinking or disinterested?

"The second question is pretty hard for a rehabilitation therapist to avoid," Brenda said. "I go home depressed some days but your grandmother wasn't depressing at all. She was relaxed about her future and full of joy. I ended up telling her a lot more about myself than I usually do."

"She's a good listener."

"It's not just that. You can sense she cares."

"She does."

"Do the introduction, or we'll run out of time."

Esther took a deep breath. "The God of the Bible is introduced as a Spirit hovering over the chaotic waters of a dark universe." She'd never started the introduction like that before. "God said, 'Let there be light' and there was." Esther summarised the days of creation, using the gardens around them to illustrate.

"Finally God said, 'Let us make mankind in our own image.' He made Adam first, out of the dirt, then made Eve out of Adam's rib." Sometimes Esther mentioned the details and sometimes she didn't. "Then God told them to rule over the earth, multiply, and fill the earth. On the seventh day, God rested because he had completed his work of creation."

"This part is familiar."

"God told Adam he could do anything in the world except eat from the fruit of the tree of the knowledge of good and evil. If he ate it, he would die. Back then, Adam and Eve were naked but they felt no shame."

"I'm already bursting with questions," Brenda said.

"Can you wait until after I've told the story?"

"Okay. I'll be good." Brenda covered her mouth with her hand.

Esther had practiced this story with Naomi and Gina. Gina was already telling this story to some of her friends. In a few weeks, they were going to train their Bible study group to tell it too. It would give them a break from Luke and get the ladies passing on something they were learning.

"The snake was the craftiest of all the animals God had made. He said to the woman, 'Did God really say you can't eat any fruit in the garden?' 'We can eat fruit,' the woman said. 'Just not the fruit in the centre of the garden. If we eat it or even touch it, we will die.'"

Esther loved the next line. It was her chance to be more dramatic. "The snake said, 'You will not die. God knows when you eat the fruit you will become like God, knowing the difference between good and evil.'" Esther slowed her words down to emphasise the last phrase.

Brenda didn't interrupt again and Esther kept telling the story. "And God said to the snake, 'Cursed are you among all the creatures of the earth. You will crawl on your belly. There will be enmity between you and the woman's descendants. You will strike his heel, and he will strike your head.'" Esther paused. "And that's the end of today's story."

"But not the real end?" Brenda said.

"No, but you can read some of it at home."

She hadn't known what to expect from Brenda. Had her father's anti-Christian attitude meant he'd withdrawn her from school scripture classes? What would he say if he found out his daughter was listening to the Bible at work? But why should it matter? Brenda was now a married woman.

"Will I find it in those little red Bibles they gave out at school? My husband still has one."

"That's probably a New Testament but I'll bring in a full Bible for you. Adam and Eve are in the first book of the Bible—Genesis."

Brenda blushed. "If you bring one, could you put it in a bag?"

Brenda's reaction wasn't surprising. Most Australians were antagonistic towards the Bible, and it was hard for anyone to admit they read it. Cancer had shown Esther fearing God was preferable to fearing what others thought.

"I always thought they ate an apple," Brenda said.

Esther grinned. "Lots of people think that. Probably because artists drew a reddish fruit and we interpreted it as an apple. Anything else?"

"I don't understand why God allowed the snake and the fruit to be there in the first place. And I don't understand why eating a fruit was such a big deal with such far reaching consequences. It was just a piece of fruit. They weren't murdering anyone." Brenda stopped walking and turned towards Esther. "What's with the nakedness thing? And the striking heel thing?" She grimaced. "Sorry to have so many questions."

"Don't be sorry. Questions mean you're thinking." Joy had taught her not to answer questions, but what if this was their only chance to talk about the Bible? *Lord, give me wisdom.*

"You're asking good questions. Why don't we discuss the two you think are most important?" She'd prayed Brenda would have lots of questions. Why couldn't she talk to Rachel like this?

Brenda tilted her head. "Why did God put the fruit in the garden?" She scrunched up her nose. "And why was eating it such a big deal?"

Esther had discussed both these questions with Joy, Gina, and Naomi. Each woman had answered from different angles. Which would most help Brenda?

"I discussed the issue of why God put the snake and the fruit in the garden with my grandmother."

At the mention of Naomi, a hint of a smile played at the corner of Brenda's mouth. Did she still have a grandmother of her own?

"If there had been no forbidden fruit, then the world would have been a place without freedom, and that's not good." Esther's forehead furrowed. "Freedom needs its opposite to shine. God wanted people to freely choose to listen, to love and worship him. He didn't want them doing it because they had no choice."

Brenda didn't respond.

"The illustration my grandmother used was a marriage. Imagine two husbands. The first husband is forced by someone to say, 'I love you' to his wife at eight every morning." Esther gestured with her right hand. "The second husband also says 'I love you' to his wife at eight every morning, but no one is coercing him. The words and timing are the same in both cases, but how would a wife feel about the two different scenarios?"

"The second wife is more likely to believe her husband means the words."

"It's the same with God. He valued our freedom enough that he was willing to risk us misusing it." How could Esther give a hint that there were more stories? Would Brenda want to hear more? "There was a high price for God giving us freedom."

"What was the big deal about the fruit?"

"I heard someone else answer this question, and what they said made sense to me. I'm not sure the important thing was the fruit. It was the attitude."

They'd reached the hospital car park. Esther stopped and held up four fingers. "This time we have four scenarios. Imagine you and I live in a kingdom one thousand years ago. They have different laws to modern Australia. In case one, a child hits another child. What might be the local response?"

"Maybe a small reprimand."

"Case two. Imagine an adult hits another adult." Esther held up another finger.

Brenda stared at the ground. "Maybe a stronger rebuke or a fine?"

Esther held up a third finger. "What if someone hits a policeman?"

"He'd get locked up."

"And if someone hits the king."

"If this was a thousand years ago," Brenda said, "they'd have had their head cut off or been hung, drawn, and quartered."

"Probably. Now, say that in each case the force of the hit is the same. We could say the action or the sin is the same but what's different?"

Brenda cocked her head to one side. "That's easy. The status of the victim."

Esther had practiced the illustration out loud last night to make sure it didn't come out jumbled. "No illustration is perfect, but I hope I've communicated that disobeying God is far more serious than disobeying someone else."

Brenda looked at her watch. "We'd better dash, but I'm going to go home and think about things. I still have heaps of questions. I noticed something interesting. The story never uses Adam and Eve's names—it just calls them man and woman. Do you think that might be important?"

"I've never noticed that. Thanks for giving me something to think about."

They walked quickly towards the department. "I'll bring you the Bible, and you can read Genesis for yourself."

"I do feel I need to look at this properly."

A good first step. God's word was more than able to convince her it was true. "It's important not to reject something until you understand it."

"Mmm."

"Adam and Eve's story is the first in a series of nine."

Brenda looked across at her. "Nine sounds like a lot, but I'd be happy to do this again next week."

"Sure." Esther kept her voice steady. Now was not the time to do cartwheels. God could be trusted to grow Brenda's interest week by week. And preparing stories for Brenda would keep her mind off her sister. Anything that did that was a bonus.

CHAPTER 23

*A*nother Tuesday evening. Another meal with her mother. Another meal when Esther must not mention Rachel. How long could this go on?

The waiter brought their orders and set them on the table. When Rachel first turned up, Esther had been terrified to even meet Mum in case she said something she shouldn't. She'd said as little as possible about anything. It wasn't a success. Mum had wanted to know if anything was wrong.

Then she'd overcompensated by being too chatty. That had led to more awkward 'what's wrong' questions. Could she finally reach the perfect balance? What if she asked questions that ensured her mum did most of the talking?

"Tell me what Dad's been preaching on lately," Esther said.

Blanche raised her eyebrows.

Great. Wrong approach again. Mum knew she struggled with her father's teaching. She should have thought ahead and prepared the right kind of questions.

"We're doing a series on heroes of the Old Testament ..."

Phew. Mum had taken her question at face value. Esther started eating and made encouraging sounds every now and again.

Mum continued, "And your father is thinking of writing a book …" That was not unexpected. His radio audience was extensive, and the publisher probably begged him to write.

Blanche kept talking. It was almost soporific. Esther was bone weary. Full-time work, then home to cooking and cleaning. She no longer needed to worry about the gardening, although it would make a huge difference if Rachel would do some of the housework. Esther still hadn't talked to Gran. She didn't want to place any more burdens on Gran. She was still far from her energetic self.

"I'm not sure you're listening." Mum peered at her. "Something's going on. You're not unwell, are you?"

"I'm fine."

"Have you got a new boyfriend?"

"No. I wouldn't have the energy."

Mum was like a dog digging for a bone. How long before the truth was dragged out of her? She had to say something fast. Maybe a vague truth would distract her.

"I do have an issue that's bothering me, but it isn't something I can share right now."

"Sometimes sharing secrets helps."

Esther choked on her food. It was beyond belief. Wasn't this the same woman who hadn't mentioned her oldest daughter in more than twenty years? What right did she have to keep a sister hidden from her? If Esther had known Rachel existed, she would have searched for her until she found her. There might not now be such an insurmountable gap between them.

"You and Dad were married a long time before I was born. Why so long?" A pulse pounded in Esther's neck. Would Mum even answer?

Blanche looked down at her plate. "I had trouble getting pregnant," she mumbled.

Esther had avoided issues too often herself not to recognise what Mum was doing. She was sick of being Miss Nice and letting her family get away with life-exploding secrets. It was more than time for answers.

"And?"

Blanche shifted in her seat and kept her voice low. "And I had several miscarriages."

"Why haven't you told me about this before?"

"Your father doesn't like me to talk about it. Says he doesn't want me to get depressed."

Esther doubted Mum's emotional well-being was Dad's main concern. He was more likely nervous about other people asking awkward questions, like why God hadn't protected his family from pain.

Watching Mum squirm was no fun, but neither were secrets.

"Mum, we avoid too many topics in our family. You and Dad work together to keep me from getting close to anything you think might blow up." She sighed. "I don't want a family like that. I want a family that tells the truth."

"Sometimes the truth hurts."

"The secrets are hurting me more." She wanted to ask about Rachel, but didn't have the courage. Maybe she wasn't any better than Mum.

Esther glanced at the clock on the wall. She hated the feeling of relief that another meal was nearly over. Why should Rachel's arrival poison her relationship with Mum? It was time, more than time, to get everything out into the open.

Would a picnic achieve her goal? There was at least one major problem. Half of it was solvable, but how was she going to manage the other half?

CHAPTER 24

$\mathcal{I}$t had taken days to get Rachel to agree to go on a picnic. Esther had only succeeded after she'd recruited Gran to urge Rachel to make the effort.

Now Rachel was seated in the exact spot Esther wanted her, at a picnic table with her back to the car park.

The car Esther had been waiting for pulled in. Punctuality from that quarter had never been in doubt.

"What's the special occasion?" Blanche said as she walked towards them. "And who's your friend?"

Rachel went rigid, her eyes wide.

Esther's stomach clenched. She'd been convinced this was the right way to do things. Neutral ground with no one around.

Rachel still hadn't moved. Blanche walked around to stand near Esther. She looked towards Rachel, but Rachel had her head down. She was trembling.

"Good morning," Blanche said, polite as always.

Rachel still had her head down. What if she never lifted it? Esther hadn't expected her sister to be uncooperative. Couldn't Rachel see she was trying to help?

"Esther?" Mum put down her bag on the table and turned to her.

What could Esther say?

Rachel looked up, her face blotchy.

Blanche gasped and clutched her chest. "Ra … Rachel?" Her voice a mere whisper.

"I'm sorry, Mum. This was not my idea of how we would meet." Rachel kicked Esther under the picnic table. Esther sucked in a cry.

Now Blanche was shaking. A great choking howl erupted from her, a scarcely human sound. Blanche clutched the edge of the table, gasping. Then she staggered towards her car like a dizzy drunk. She dropped the car keys twice before getting the back door open and disappearing. Her muffled howls continued.

"How dare you, you interfering idiot?" Rachel said.

"I didn't think it would be like this." Esther wrapped her arms around her body.

"Did you think at all?"

Esther cowered at the disdain in Rachel's voice.

"Mum hasn't seen me for twenty-five years. You can't suddenly spring me on her."

"I thought she'd be delighted to see you."

"Whatever you've been doing, it can't be called thinking."

What right did Rachel have to attack her? "All I wanted was to have my family back."

"And rushing things has probably destroyed it forever."

"You never seem to care about our family."

"I care!" Rachel pounded the table.

"Well, I haven't noticed you caring for anyone other than yourself."

"That's rich coming from you," Rachel said. "Wandering around like a martyr because you've had to look after Gran and me for six weeks."

How dare she? After all Esther had done.

"Mum's the innocent party in all this." Rachel stabbed her finger towards Esther. "I would never hurt her like you've done."

"At least I tried."

"You tried alright." Rachel sniffed. "For your information, Gran and I have been talking together about how to tell Mum I'm alive."

"Why didn't you let me know? You've left me out of everything."

"You might not have noticed, Miss Judgmental, but I wasn't in a fit state to do anything when I first arrived."

Of course she'd noticed. Esther wasn't blind, but she was no closer to understanding why Rachel had been in such a state of collapse. Had her husband died? Had someone been murdered? Esther had no more clues than she'd had the first day Rachel had turned up. "You're my sister. I want to know what you're thinking."

"Well, I'm not the sister you've been dreaming of."

A sliver of cold steel sliced through Esther's heart. She'd been afraid this was Rachel's attitude. "You were once."

"That was long, long ago. Your life might have enabled you to live in la-la land, but mine hasn't. In my life, the princess turns into a frog when she kisses the prince." Rachel's mouth twisted. "Or the prince is pierced by thorns and dies before he reaches Sleeping Beauty."

So that was what Rachel thought of her. That she was a little kid who'd never grown up.

Rachel indicated over her shoulder. "You'd better go and clear up the mess you've made. Give me your keys. I'm going home." She stomped off, slammed the car door, and screeched out of the car park.

Esther put her elbows on the picnic table and propped her head in her hands. A great weariness draped over her. Since her cancer, Saturdays needed long, slow starts. She'd had high hopes about today, so it hadn't been hard to get out of bed and prepare their picnic. Now she'd blown it by rushing ahead.

Esther gathered up the basket of celebratory food. Celebration.

What a joke. Now she had a sister who despised her and a crying mother to deal with. Mum almost never cried. The last time was the day she'd told them she had cancer.

Blanche was face down on the back seat of the car. A pile of scrunched up tissues littered the floor. Esther tried the door. It was locked. She tapped on the window. "Mum?" Was Esther going to be stuck outside, begging to be let in?

She tapped again and her mother unlocked the doors without raising her head. Esther put the picnic basket onto the front seat and went around to the furthest door. She opened it and put a hand on her mother's shoulder.

"Mum."

Blanche didn't respond.

Esther gave her a little shake. "Mum?"

Blanche lifted her head. Her face was streaked with mascara. "How could you? How could you do that?"

Now everyone was mad at her. "You might not believe it, but I was trying to help."

"Help?" Blanche's elegant eyebrows rose towards her hairline. "Springing a shock on me like that."

"I thought it was better here than in a more crowded place. I knew you wouldn't come to Gran's."

Blanche pushed herself up and sat on the far side of the car. Esther slid into the section of seat she'd vacated.

"You could have sent me a letter or something, or come home and told me when we were alone."

Esther hadn't even thought of those two options. Even if she had, she would probably have dismissed them. She'd wanted a Prodigal Son homecoming celebration. The only problem was that the two main actors hadn't played their parts.

CHAPTER 25

"*E*sther, is that you?" Naomi called as Esther walked up the back steps.

"Yes, Gran." The miserable day was about to get a whole lot worse.

"Rachel's locked herself in her room. What is going on?"

No escape. If only she could lock life out too. "I tried to get Mum and Rachel together."

Naomi gasped. "Honey, why didn't you wait? Rachel and I were working on it."

"But neither of you said anything to me." If only they had, this whole disaster could have been avoided.

Naomi patted the seat next to her. "I've been letting Rachel set the pace."

"And I got frustrated and messed everything up." Esther sat down.

"Is your mother okay?"

"I don't know." Esther sniffed. "We talked for a while and she drove me home, but she didn't say a word as she drove." What a hideous day. It would be a relief to get it off her chest. Gran was the best listener in the family. She wouldn't be angry, only sad. Sometimes sad was worse than mad. Esther poured out the story.

"I wish you'd talked things over with me first. Rachel was beginning to make progress. She was talking about searching for work."

That was unexpected. Rachel had been doing the gardening, although Esther hadn't expected her to stick with it. Rachel and dirt seemed incompatible but the more Rachel had worked in the garden, the more she'd relaxed. Like the early flowers that come up in the spring. A shoot of green, then the curled bud, unwinding and smiling up towards the sun. Rachel was a long way from blooming, but she had been moving in the right direction. Would today's disaster act like a late frost, nipping the buds and destroying their beauty?

"Whatever Rachel thinks, I did consider lots of options, and the park seemed best."

"Dearie, did you pray about it?" Naomi asked.

Of course she'd prayed about it. What kind of question was that?

"When I was younger, I often prayed as if God was there to rubber-stamp my plans."

Ouch.

"I didn't wait for God's timing."

Esther loved having Gran and Joy around, but sometimes their questions were knife-thrusts. Gran's suspicion was too near the truth. Her prayers had been rushed. Rachel's rejection and indifference made her fume. So different to the sister she'd imagined.

"Why is Rachel so cold and distant?"

"I imagine she's been hurt, and badly." Naomi closed her eyes. "A teenager doesn't survive on her own without significant cost. We'll have to be patient until she trusts us enough to tell us what's locked in her heart."

"But we're family. She should trust us."

"You've got a short memory."

"We're not Dad," Esther said.

"No, but we remind her of the pain."

Esther sighed. "Why can't she just be a sister?"

Naomi reached across and took Esther's hand. "I think you're looking in the wrong places for a sister's love. There's nothing wrong with wanting a sister, but Rachel might never be able to be that to you. I pray every day for healing, but she's not yet ready to turn to the only one who can heal." Naomi kissed Esther's hand. "You need to focus your longings on Jesus. He's the one we should desire. No object or person or accomplishment will ever fill our hearts."

And until Rachel had come along, Esther had thought she'd turned to Jesus to fill the longings. Now she wasn't sure. She wasn't sure of anything.

Naomi patted Esther's hand. "Don't despair, honey. Your mistakes can't derail God's plans. You and I aren't big enough to do that."

***

*A*fter lunch and a sleep, Esther tried to pray. She really did but nothing came out right. She wanted to pray for Rachel, but couldn't.

Why, why, why hadn't Esther talked to Gran about her frustrations? Was it because Gran had let her down once? Was she still angry at her?

No. Gran was one person she was no longer annoyed at. Now was the time to go and apologise to her for how she'd treated her. Get one relationship in this mixed up family back to harmony. A hug would be welcome too.

Was that a car stopping outside their front fence? Who would be visiting them? She'd better tidy up in case she had to greet them at the door. Esther jumped to her feet, changed her blouse, and grabbed a brush.

The doorbell never rang. The car must have been for next door. Oh well, she'd go and apologise to Gran. On the way out of her bedroom she glanced at the front door. There were two envelopes stuffed under it. They hadn't been there when she'd come in.

She walked down the hall and stooped down. 'Rachel' was written on the first and 'Esther' on the second, in her mum's copperplate handwriting. So she hadn't been mistaken about the visitor, but Mum hadn't stayed. Would she ever dare to cross the threshold?

Esther took hers to her room. As she expected, Mum was trying to smooth things over. She wrote a note in return.

---

*R*achel heard her grandmother's unmistakeable tread come down the hall. She knocked on the door.

"Rachel, are you there? I've got dinner for you."

Rachel got up, opened the door, and took the tray out of Naomi's hand. "I'm assuming Esther made it home."

"Yes, and we had a good talk. Your mother pushed this under the door sometime this afternoon."

"Thanks, Gran." Rachel took the envelope and placed it on her desk. "You know I'm not annoyed at you, don't you?"

"Yes, but I'm hoping you won't stay annoyed at Esther either. Holding grudges never helped anyone."

Rachel grimaced. "I know, I know. Forgiveness and all that."

"It's a good way to live." Naomi turned to go. "I'm out here knitting if you want to come and talk."

Rachel closed the door. Her anger had fizzled out. Esther had achieved one good thing—their mother now knew she was alive. The meeting wasn't at all like Rachel had envisioned, but next time might be easier. And if her mother was writing, she must be past the first bump in the road.

Rachel took the letter off the desk, eased open the envelope, and smoothed down the expensive paper.

DEAREST PRECIOUS, PRECIOUS RACHEL,

She swallowed the lump in her throat. How could her mother use those endearments? Would she write that if she knew how she'd spent the last years?

PLEASE DON'T LET MY REACTION TO SEEING YOU SCARE YOU. IT WAS A SHOCK. I'VE SOMETIMES WONDERED IF YOU WERE DEAD OR IF I HAD IMAGINED YOU. I LOVE YOU MORE THAN I CAN SAY.

Rachel's lip quivered. Her mother wasn't such a bad person. She meant well, but she allowed her husband to dominate her. If Rachel hadn't hated her father and his god, she'd have contacted her mother years ago.

GIVE ME A FEW DAYS TO ADJUST TO YOUR REAPPEARANCE, THEN I'D LOVE YOU TO CONTACT ME. IF YOU CAN'T COPE, I'M WILLING TO WAIT BUT PLEASE STAY IN TOUCH. I COULDN'T BEAR TO LOSE CONTACT AGAIN.

Rachel would contact her. It was the mature thing to do, and it seemed pointless to reject Mum because she couldn't stand Dad but she needed to get out of this house. Not that she objected to Gran—she was a darling, despite the Jesus twaddle that she used to spout. Thankfully she hadn't done any of that this time. It was Esther who was the problem. Seeing Esther brought back all the feelings of condemnation. Rachel couldn't live with it. All she'd done was what every other modern woman would have done.

Esther wasn't horrible. She probably had lots of friends, but her sister was such a goody two shoes she was sure to condemn her for the way she'd lived. And if Rachel shared about her baby? Even Gran might kick her out for that. No, the only way was to get a job, earn some money, and find another, cheaper, place to live. Put some distance between them.

Rachel turned her mum's letter over.

P.S. I won't say anything to your father unless you allow me to. It will be a hard secret to keep.

Look at the pressure the secret had placed on Esther. Like water in a kettle, even someone as patient as her mother would eventually reach boiling point.

CHAPTER 26

*R*achel pulled into the parking lot at yet another garden centre. It was the tenth for the day. Who was she kidding? Why had she thought a former cosmetics consultant could ever get into the nursery business?

She'd walked around each nursery first. Three of them were visibly rundown, so she hadn't bothered asking for a job. The other six had either told her there was no work or scanned her CV and asked why she'd left her previous job.

"I wanted a total change," hadn't been enough to gain an interview.

This was the last stop. If she couldn't get a job here, she'd have to go back to David Jones. She couldn't bear living with Esther and her fantasy of a perfect family much longer. If a woman of nearly thirty could be so naive as to pull a stunt like the reconciliation attempt, who knew what she'd try next.

Rachel glanced in the mirror. Maybe the lipstick had been a mistake, but she felt naked without makeup. She grabbed her bag off the passenger seat, took out a tissue, and scrubbed her lips.

Perhaps a casual braid or ponytail would be better than having her hair down.

Rachel took a deep breath. One more try before she'd admit defeat with this new line of work.

Rachel walked around first. She didn't want to work at a dilapidated nursery ... not that she could afford to be choosy. She couldn't return to being shut up inside. No way. She wanted the broad sweep of sky, bird calls, and the clean smell of earth. She must succeed.

Her shoes crunched on the sanded paths. Native plants to her right, fruit trees towards the back fence, and flowering plants in neat rows, each labelled with its name and care instructions. The whole area was surrounded by a thick, perfectly trimmed hedge. A fountain tinkled somewhere in the background. There was something homely about this place, but would there be anything here for her? With her luck up to this point, not a chance.

Rachel turned back to the main entry and display area. The displays could use some work, although a new employee would hardly get a say. She waited until all the customers had moved towards the café and then walked up to the young guy at the counter. His name tag said 'Colin.'

Rachel took another deep breath. "I was hoping to speak to the boss."

"He's out on an errand."

Not again. "How long will he be away?"

"Not sure."

"Could I leave my name and phone number?"

Colin looked her up and down. Had removing the lipstick and putting her hair up been a good or bad idea?

"I don't think there are any vacancies."

An icy hailstone of disappointment clogged Rachel's throat. She wrote her name and phone number in neat handwriting and added, 'hard worker looking for a job.' Pathetic, but it might be the only chance she would get. Leaving her CV wouldn't help.

Her feet ached to match her heart. What a waste of a day. This whole area of Sydney was crammed with nurseries, and she couldn't find a single job. What was wrong with her?

As she turned to trudge back to her car, the smell of fresh baked goodness stopped her. Surely she deserved a little treat. A hot cup of coffee and a scone might cheer her up.

As Rachel finished her last mouthful of coffee, a silver-haired man burst through the main entrance and rushed to the counter, gesticulating towards the car park.

Had he run into someone's parked car? She stood and walked out of the café.

"Excuse me, ma'am." It was the silver-haired man.

Normally she'd have been insulted by the old-fashioned title, but the way he said it was warm and respectful.

"I believe you were looking for me."

So this was the boss. A tiny flicker of hope danced inside. Why would he approach her unless he planned to interview her?

She nodded.

"I'm Dirk Klopper. Come to my office, and we can talk."

Rachel followed him in a daze. He sat down behind a paper-covered desk. His slight South African accent reminded her of someone, but she couldn't recall who. Plenty of South Africans migrated to Australia.

"Tell me what kind of job you're looking for."

"Anything that gets me outside."

He asked her a few more questions, which she answered as best she could.

"What did you do at the department store?"

This was the question that had been sabotaging her prospects all day. "Worked at a cosmetics counter."

He didn't blink. He didn't point out that was different to a garden centre. He didn't show her the door. He didn't seem at all interested in her lack of gardening experience. Like it was irrelevant. What was going on?

"What skills did your old job give you?"

This sounded like a genuine job interview. Had her changed look helped after all? "I've interacted with a wide range of people from all different backgrounds."

"What else?"

It was always hard to list her strengths. Almost boastful. "I'm organised, reliable, hard-working, and punctual." She wasn't going to mention her abilities with design, in case the guy took offence. She wasn't trained in design, it was something she'd inherited.

"Have you got a reference?"

"Several. And a CV." Rachel unzipped her bag and handed over a copy. He took no notice of the CV but scanned the references. "Well, these are complimentary. Your boss mentions they were sorry to lose you and you were in line for promotion."

Was he asking a question? What could she say? That she'd had a breakdown and attempted suicide after years of nightmares.

"That all seems in order." He glanced at the CV. "Rachel, welcome to the team. When can you start?"

Rachel stared at him with her mouth open. "Umm, any time you want."

"Can you start tomorrow? Or the next day?"

She blinked. "Yes."

The salary was less than her previous job, but she'd known it would be.

"What am I to call you?" Rachel asked.

"Some of them call me boss, but Dirk will do." He opened a cupboard. "Go and try these overalls on. They should be about your size."

They fit perfectly.

She went back to his office. "Dirk, they fit but ..." She blushed, fearing to expose her ignorance. "What shall I wear on my feet?"

"I'll loan you a pair of gumboots."

Why had he hired her? He'd barely looked at her CV. It was as if he'd decided to hire her before she said anything but that was impossible. And why did his voice seem familiar? She had a good memory for faces, and she was sure she'd never seen his before.

Mysterious. Exceedingly mysterious but not mysterious enough for her to refuse the job.

CHAPTER 27

$\mathcal{E}$sther spoke to Joy as they sat down in the hospital garden. "I've had a miserable week. I messed up with Rachel. The only good thing is that she's found herself a job and starts tomorrow."

"What will she be doing?"

"Working in a garden centre. I never thought she'd apply for a dirty, sweaty job."

"Perhaps you don't know your sister as well as you think you do."

"I don't know her at all." Thinking of Rachel tied her gut in knots. "She won't let me get to know her, and it's been driving me crazy. Not to mention she's of little help at home."

"So you've been frustrated?"

Frustrated seemed too small a word. Sometimes she'd think things were okay, but an eruption of frustration would show her the magma churning beneath the surface. "You were right last time. I should have talked to someone."

"What happened?"

Esther's face heated. She'd been pleased about how she'd

handled last year, yet she'd behaved like an immature kid in recent weeks. Joy never made her feel like a fool. She was the best kind of friend and certainly a better sister than Rachel looked like ever being.

Joy kept quiet as Esther related what had happened with her mother. Joy was a woman who knew when to speak and when not to.

"I should have waited but I didn't, and I've been beating myself up ever since."

"And what did your grandmother say?"

"She basically told me to pray more, be patient, and wait for God's timing." The one thing last year should have taught Esther was to pray about everything, but she'd grown overconfident.

"Good advice."

"Yes, but not easy to do."

Joy looked off into the distance. "I've got a—"

"A story to tell me," Esther finished.

"Am I that predictable?" Joy laughed and held up her hand. "No, don't say anything. I know I'm story mad, but it's because they've taught me almost everything I know."

Esther crossed her legs.

"God told Abraham to leave his family and his country, and God gave them a series of promises. Big promises. He was going to bless them and make them a great nation and a blessing to others. After half a century without children they must have been ecstatic to hear they were going to become a nation. They knew that meant a son." Joy scratched her ear. "This incident happens when Abraham is eighty-five."

What relevance did this story have to her situation?

"Sarah came to her husband and said, 'God hasn't allowed me to have any children. Here's my Egyptian maidservant. Sleep with her. Perhaps I can start a family through her.'"

"Abraham agreed, and Sarah gave him Hagar to be his wife. He slept with her, and before long, she was pregnant. Once she knew she was pregnant, she looked down on Sarah."

Whatever Joy's reason for choosing this story, Esther wasn't in the mood for it. If it was anyone else, she'd be tempted to block them out, but Joy was impossible to block.

"Then Sarah came to Abraham and said, 'Everything I'm suffering is your fault.'" Joy used a querulous voice. "I gave you this woman to be your wife, and now she knows she's pregnant, she looks down on me. May God judge between you and me.'"

Esther still had no clue what this story had to do with her.

"'She's your servant,' Abraham said. 'Do with her what you want.' Then Sarah abused Hagar and Hagar ran away into the wilderness."

Joy cracked her knuckles. "You don't know why I've chosen this one, do you?"

Esther shook her head.

"I'm tempted to let you go away and think about it for a few days."

"Please don't." Esther grabbed Joy's arm. "I don't want any more frustration in my life."

"I'll retell it like I usually do, but I'll give you a clue. Think about what Abraham and Sarah did wrong."

As Joy retold it, Esther's brow furrowed. What deep meaning was Joy seeing? There had to be something.

"You're going to have to help me." Esther looked across at Joy.

"Think. What did Sarah do wrong?"

She could do this. "She came up with a scheme to get a child and scolded her husband when she didn't like the results."

"What else?"

"She abused Hagar, who then ran away."

"And?"

Esther put her head to the side. It didn't help. "I can't think of anything more about Sarah, but Abraham is passive. He's similar to

Mum and even Rachel. They don't see that some kinds of harmony are fake. Real harmony takes work."

"You're rushing in too early with applications. What did Abraham do wrong?"

Esther visualised the scenes in her head. "He goes along with all Sarah's suggestions, and lets her abuse Hagar, even though she is pregnant with his child."

Joy sat silent. It was obvious she still expected more.

"Abraham doesn't lead," Esther said.

"Follow that thought."

"Ask me another question."

"Perhaps, instead of focusing on what Abraham and Sarah did, focus on what they didn't do."

Esther stared at Joy. How did that help?

Joy cleared her throat. "God had promised Abraham he'd be the father of a great nation. What didn't they do that they should have done?"

Esther's mind was still an empty cavern.

"What was his job as leader?"

"Oh." Esther's eyebrows rose. "He should have gone and asked God."

"Yes, and what do you think God would have told them?"

"Wait. I know what I'm doing." Esther stared at Joy. A glimmer of understanding flickered through the synapses of her mind. "Are you trying to say I should have waited for God's timing to arrange the meeting between my mother and Rachel?"

"I think the issue is deeper than that, but I'm not sure you're ready to hear it."

What did Joy mean? She used to love story times with Joy, but they'd been uncomfortable lately. Esther wasn't in the mood for lectures. Perhaps calling it a lecture was too harsh, but she'd wanted Joy to pat her on the back and tell her she was doing all the right things.

"Go away and think about this story. Pray about it. Ask yourself why Sarah came up with the plan in the first place, and what this said about her view of God."

It sounded like too much work. Esther needed all her energy for praying Rachel would change. Was there any way to get Rachel to open up and treat her like a sister instead of a stranger?

CHAPTER 28

"Good morning, Rachel. I'll start you off with Josh in weeding and repotting." Dirk walked her down the path. "You might be tempted to look down on Josh, but I want you to see him with the eyes of your heart."

What was wrong with Josh? Was he the strong silent type or a chatterer? The shed and screened-off area were right at the back of the property. As they entered the shed, a broad-shouldered man pushed a wheelbarrow inside. He gave a huge smile and waved excitedly. Bit unusual. Then he set the wheelbarrow down and lumbered over.

"Is this the lady you told me about?" Josh turned his head to look at her. "What's your name?"

"Rachel. What's yours?"

He puffed out his chest. "Joshua Strong and Courageous Smith." He cupped a hand round one side of his mouth and said in an undertone, "Of course, my name isn't really Strong and Courageous, but that's what Mr Dirk calls me."

Dirk smiled. "I'll leave you in Josh's capable hands. He's our weeding and repotting expert."

Josh stood at attention.

"You'll work here this week, but I'll rotate you round all the areas until we find your specialities." Dirk slapped Josh on the back. "Take good care of her."

"Yes, boss." He saluted. "You can depend on me."

"I know I can. Remember, Rachel isn't used to this kind of work. Give her lots of breaks and make sure she drinks enough water." Dirk headed back to the main entrance.

Rachel had no idea how to work with someone like Josh.

"Now, Miss Rachel …"

"You don't need to call me Miss Rachel. Rachel will do."

"Mum said I must be polite to people older than myself."

"How old are you?"

"Twenty-two."

A wave of nausea swept through her. Her child would have been twenty-two.

"You're pretty, but you're not twenty-two," Josh said in a matter-of-fact tone.

Normally she'd have been annoyed to be called pretty, but there was no innuendo behind Josh's statement.

"Why don't you tell me what to do," Rachel said.

He handed her a new pair of gloves. "Those are for you to wear at work. Your hands will be soft, but they'll get harder. All these pots need to be weeded. You use this tool." He handed her a trowel. "And make sure you dig up the roots." He looked at her sternly. "If you don't dig up those naughty roots, we have to do the job again."

"Got that."

"I'll stand over that side of the bench and you on this side." Josh stood next to her and measured her against himself. "I think you might need a box to stand on." He went over to the side of the shed and pulled out a five-centimetre wooden step, which he put in place and jumped on. "That's right now." He went around to the other side of the table. "Watch me."

They got to work. He worked like a machine. Loosening the soil around the base of the plant. Pulling out the weeds. Putting the pot on the trolley at the top end of the table.

Rachel couldn't compete with the speed of his stubby fingers. Every now and then, he looked across at her and grunted, "Good job, Miss Rachel."

"You should have a drink, Miss Rachel," Josh said after they'd been working for an hour or so. "Mr Dirk says we need to stop and have a good stretch." He stretched up his arms.

Rachel checked over her shoulder and followed suit. Working with Josh was restful, but she had loads of questions. Would Josh mind her asking them?

The first trolley was full. Josh pulled it out to the main path and set an empty trolley in place.

"What happens to the plants next?"

"Sam and Dave will come and get them with the four-wheeler. They're no good at weeding or repotting, but they're good and strong for moving things."

"Are they like you?"

He squinted at her. "What do you mean? Course they're like me. You're the only lady here now Mrs Dirk has stopped coming."

She had been asking if they had Down syndrome as well, but it wasn't a question she could ask outright. She'd know soon enough.

"Is it okay for you to talk while you work?"

"Why wouldn't it be? I work just as fast whether I talk or not. Although I'm super fast when I sing." He chortled. "But don't worry. I only sing on special occasions."

"What's a special occasion?"

"I don't know. My heart tells me and I can't help singing."

Singing had once made her come alive. She could sing alto or soprano, and the high-school choir mistress switched her around. Then came the day when she'd given Rachel the soprano solo in a new piece they were rehearsing for the annual concert.

Josh moved the next trolley out to the entrance. Rachel kept weeding.

She'd been proud of that song. When she sang, she was free to fly up to the clouds and soar over valleys, more like a bird than a fourteen-year-old Proverbs 31 woman-in-training. Free of corset-like clothes. Free of rules. Free of expectations. Free to be herself. Gloriously uninhibited.

There'd only been one blip on her horizon. Stirling. His name made her want to spit. He'd spotted her on the walk to school, and after a few months of watching, he'd approached and asked her out. Some girls might have been flattered, but he gave her the creeps. He hadn't liked being rejected, and he'd turned mean. Sneaky mean. She'd tried everything she could, including walking different routes and walking as part of a group. Getting to school became a scary business made worse by the fact that he had a sister in her class. Things began to go missing. Her lunch ended up on the ground. If she wanted to eat it, she first had to brush off the dirt.

The concert started at eight, but she was supposed to be there fifteen minutes early. Dad was running late, and the streets were crowded with cars. He'd dropped her at the gate, then gone to find a parking spot.

She hadn't even thought about Stirling. Hadn't considered that, as his sister was in the choir, he might be there. What nightmare put her at the gate when he was tying his shoelace behind the post?

"Here's the kid who stole my sister's moment in the spotlight." His voice had raised the hairs at the base of her scalp. She'd looked for escape, but no one was around. He caught her arm and spun her around. "Not so fast, princess." Even now, she remembered the acid gnawing into her stomach and the pain where he almost pulled her arm out of its socket.

"No one takes my sister's glory." This wasn't about his sister. This was about rejecting him.

She'd struggled. "Let me go." Where were her parents?

"Let you go?" He smiled like a tiger about to devour a doe. "Sure."

He released her with a shove. She staggered back, tripped over the garden edging, and fell into a rose bush.

He loped off as her parents walked through the gate.

"What on earth are you doing there?" Dad looked all around. What had he to worry about?

Mum hurried over and held out her hand. "What happened?"

Rachel's hands were covered in dirt, and long strands of hair dangled from her French braid. Her father held the rose branches out of the way, and she scrambled up, but there were holes in the knees of her stockings. She was in no state to stand in the spotlights and sing.

"We only left you five minutes, and look at you."

Rachel couldn't help it. She'd cried. Did her father think rose bush diving was her preferred sport?

Mum had taken her gently by the elbow. "What happened?"

Her explanation about Stirling had been a flop.

"What kind of girl angers someone she doesn't know?" Dad didn't mention the Proverbs 31 woman, but it didn't matter. That model of perfection would never have any enemies. She was far too nice. Probably Miss Popular, along with her other perfections.

It was no use explaining, Dad didn't accept excuses. His enemies never confronted him. They left. It was simpler.

Her mother found an empty bathroom, redid her hair, cleaned off the dirt and blood, and sponged off her uniform. And wonder of wonders, pulled a fresh pair of stockings out of her handbag. "You're not going to believe this, but I spotted a pair of your stockings on the floor as we headed out the door and stuffed them into my handbag."

Maybe there was some use in being a Proverbs 31 woman after all.

They'd made it to the concert and the song was sung, but the bird never soared. How could it, in front of her father's frown and the animosity of Stirling and his sister? Most of the audience would have considered it adequate, but the choir mistress only gave a brief nod when she'd finished. They'd both known it should have been different.

Rachel used her sleeve to mop her forehead. She'd never sung a solo again.

"Are you okay, Miss Rachel? You look sad."

She'd forgotten Josh was even there. "I'm remembering something."

"Do you have a broken wing?"

"What do you mean?"

Josh stopped weeding. "Mr Dirk says that everybody has a broken wing of some sort."

"What was your broken wing?"

"I was all trembly and afraid of other people thinking me stupid."

"But you're not now?"

His smile was as bright as a car headlight. "Nope. Jesus made me strong and courageous." He grinned at her. "Is Jesus your friend?"

Oh no. Couldn't she escape Jesus anywhere?

Josh was waiting for her answer, eyes shining. She wanted to swear, but something stopped her. It would be like kicking the faithful family pet.

"No. I don't think Jesus wants to be my friend."

He came around the workbench and patted her shoulder. "Oh Miss Rachel, he wants to be everyone's friend."

"I've been too bad for him to want to be my friend."

Josh rubbed his ear, spreading dirt across it. "Mr Dirk says no one is ever too bad to be Jesus's friend. He died for bad people."

Whenever Josh said the word Jesus, her skin crawled. How could she change topic? "How did you get a job here?"

"Oh, that was Mr Dirk answering Mum's prayer."

Not again.

"I was driving Mum up the wall. She tried to find me lots of jobs, but they always wanted me to do tests." He shivered dramatically. "Tests give me the heebie-jeebies. Yes, the heebie-jeebies. I tried, I really did, but no one wanted me." He picked up another pot. "But Mum didn't give up. She asked the whole church to pray about it, and a week later, Mr Dirk asked us to come here."

"And he didn't give you a test."

"No. He just asked what I liked doing. Then he showed me what to do." Josh looked around the shed. "I worked for a week, and then Mr Dirk helped me fill out the form so I could get money. I didn't need money, but Mr Dirk said that wouldn't be right. That every worker deserves his wages."

The phrase sounded familiar—Shakespeare or something. Josh was a lucky guy. He'd be easy to exploit, yet here he was, earning his way.

CHAPTER 29

$\mathcal{E}$sther looked at her father over the top of her crossword. As usual, he'd bought two copies of the morning paper, and they were having their monthly competition. It used to be a daily event, and she was out of practice. She didn't want to be sitting here. She wanted to talk to Mum and find out if she'd heard anything from Rachel.

"Esther, I don't enjoy winning if you're not concentrating."

"Sorry, Dad." Esther forced her mind back to the task. It was hard to sit in the same room as her father. What kind of man not only never mentioned his older daughter but forced his wife to do the same? How had he stood up in the pulpit, week after week, with such secrets on his soul?

If she didn't make some effort, her father would start asking probing questions, and she couldn't risk being interrogated. Esther nibbled the end of her pencil. Two down, twelve letters, the formation of a word that phonetically imitates, resembles, or suggests the sound it describes. She knew this one, but how was it spelled? She jotted various spellings on the side of her newspaper. Onamatopea. Onomatopeia. She was still missing a letter. Esther wrote in the letters she was sure of and kept going. Amazingly, her father only beat her by two words.

While they competed, Mum had laid the table under the beach umbrella in the garden. She'd made her famous roast chicken, pine nut, parmesan, and mango salad.

A normal father would have asked Esther how she was coping with ongoing tiredness but for him, she wasn't recovering from cancer. To even admit Esther had ever had cancer was to admit that God hadn't listened to his prayers for healing.

"How's work?" he said. "Any more awards or promotions?"

Work was one of his few safe topics.

"I'm unlikely to ever win 'employee of the year' again. That's once in a lifetime, and the only way to be promoted again would be for me to become head of a department."

"Well, that shouldn't be beyond you."

He never understood her lack of ambition. She loved physio because of the patient contact. Promotion would take that away. "The roles are all filled by perfectly competent people."

"Maybe you should change hospital."

"Dad, I like where I am. I can cycle to work. Besides which, I've been sharing about Jesus with one of the other physios."

William beamed. "That's my girl."

"Why don't you tell us about how that came about?" Mum said, even though she'd heard this all before.

Her father cleared his timetable when Esther came to visit. Did he still hope things between them could get back to their easy pre-cancer camaraderie? He'd been proud of her. Was that how he'd been with Rachel too? Or had they clashed from the beginning?

"Brenda met a patient who talked about Jesus in a natural way and wasn't afraid of dying." Esther couldn't mention Naomi. "It made her curious. Brenda knew I was a Christian and asked me some questions. She was interested enough to agree to meet up with me again."

"And are you still meeting up?" Mum asked.

"We go for a walk once a week and have a good discussion. She asks tons of questions. Even better, she's found three others who want to hear. We're going to start a group this week."

"Are you ever coming back to Victory?" Her father was like a thrush continually dropping a snail to get at the meat inside. When would he accept she wasn't coming back?

"I'm busy at my new church." Last year had taught her to be a master at the indirect answer. "Gina and I run a Bible study group for young workers."

Dad grunted. She shouldn't have said anything. He was still sore she'd refused his offer to come back to Victory to lead the same age group.

The phone rang.

Dad grimaced. "Sorry. Let's hope it's nothing important." He pushed out his chair and went to answer it. Esther and Blanche cleared the first round of plates and brought out cheese and fruit.

Dad returned. "I'm sorry. An elder's mother is dying and requested I go visit her."

Esther kissed his cheek. "It's okay. Mum and I can keep each other entertained." Considering the size of Victory Church, it was impressive how her father had prioritised this meal every month. It might be the closest she would ever get to a 'sorry' from him.

Esther wasn't upset he had to leave. It was obvious Mum had things she wanted to say. About time. Esther had spent the last eighteen months hoping to hear Mum talk about personal things.

Esther cut up a peach and held up half. "Want some?"

Mum held out her hand. "Thanks, honey, and thank you for coming every month. I know it isn't easy."

"I'd never see Dad if I didn't."

"And he appreciates it. Never doubt it. He just doesn't know how to express it."

"We do have a problem expressing things in our family." Her

157

inability to deal with things had been part of the reason for her broken engagement. She'd known there were problems, but she'd ignored them until it was too late.

"I want to apologise. My keeping quiet about Rachel hurt you both," Mum said.

Esther kept silent. Mum so seldom shared anything personal that she wasn't going to interrupt.

"The day that Rachel ran away was the worst day of my life." She looked across at Esther. "Yes, even worse than hearing you had cancer. I was terrified for her safety and that she'd do something stupid." Blanche covered her eyes with her hand. "I wanted to call the police, but—"

Did Mum regret that decision?

"I nearly lost my mind until I heard from Naomi. I didn't dare visit, but I knew she was safe." She reached across to touch Esther. "I had enough to worry about with you. You wandered around like you'd lost an arm. The two of you were close as could be."

"Everyone keeps telling me that, and I don't understand why Rachel doesn't make more effort."

"I don't know either, but there must be some reason."

"If I knew the reason, maybe I could do something about it."

"I've been praying a lot."

Esther blew out a noisy breath. "We've been praying for ages and seeing no progress. When is God going to act?"

"I'm seeing progress. Rachel has gotten in contact, and we're trying to work out how to meet."

Why could Rachel connect with her mother but not her own sister? What had Esther done to deserve such treatment?

"We both agree we should meet on our own first, but the tricky thing is how to do it without your father finding out."

More secrets, but this one made sense. Mum had kept silent all these years at Dad's insistence. He'd never encourage her to see Rachel. He'd see it as some sort of rebellion. As Esther knew from painful and personal experience, when Dad was displeased, he made his displeasure felt.

"Dad is used to us having a meal on Tuesdays. Why don't you meet up with Rachel instead?"

"I'd already thought of that but wasn't sure if you'd agree."

"I'll agree with anything that helps Rachel."

"Do you know how work is going for her?"

"I didn't expect her to last a week, but she seems to love the job."

"Maybe she's inherited Naomi's green thumbs." Blanche cut a slice of cheese. "Has she said anything about her workmates?"

"She's mentioned a guy called Josh who has Down syndrome. Apparently, there are several guys like Josh, and a recovering alcoholic."

"Is her boss a Christian?"

Esther put her finger against her lips. "Don't suggest that to Rachel. She'd run a mile."

Mum stood up, and she and Esther cleared the table and stacked the new dishwasher. It was a chore they'd often done together in the past.

"Mum, are you ever going to come to our place?"

"I'll have to if I'm going to see Rachel."

Esther hugged her. "I'll be praying you have courage."

"Thank you. I'll need it. Watching you stand up to your father last year was an education. I know this is the right thing to do, but I'm afraid of what your father will do if he finds out."

He'd thrown Esther out of home for disagreeing with him. Surely he wouldn't do that to his wife?

CHAPTER 30

"*R*achel, would you help me hang out the laundry?" Esther asked, laundry basket on her hip.

Was this another plot to spend more time together? Maybe, but it would be rude to say no, as half the load was her work clothes.

Rachel put a bookmark in her page. The fastest way to deal with her sister was to help, otherwise she ended up feeling guilty. This living-with-other-people thing wasn't at all like living alone. She'd had to move all her things over here last week because she couldn't afford to pay for a place she wasn't living in.

Esther headed out the door with the basket and Rachel followed. They said not a word. Halfway through, Esther stopped and leaned forward, palms on thighs.

"What's wrong with you?" Rachel said.

"I'll be fine. I get tired easily."

"You're not even thirty yet."

"My tiredness has nothing to do with age."

Was Esther's enigmatic comment her way of fishing for a conversation? Too bad. Rachel had no intention of playing along. It was best they remain strangers. If she questioned Esther, then

Esther would ask questions too. Rachel didn't want that. There were too many smelly bones she didn't want dug up.

The silence stretched between them. Why did Esther have so many expectations? Rachel stuffed down the sigh in her throat.

"Look at you," Rachel said. "Your life is peaches and cream."

"More like rotten peaches and sour cream. Not that you'd care."

Rachel snorted. How could Miss Perfect understand pain? Rachel had no patience for petty sorrows. She turned to go back to the house.

Esther grabbed her. "Don't you walk away from me."

Rachel brushed her off. "Why not?"

"You can't lock me out forever."

"Watch me." Rachel stomped towards the house, leaving Esther to bring in the empty basket.

*E*sther plopped down cross-legged on the grass. *Lord, what are you doing?* A few tears dropped onto her bare knee. *It's like there's barbed wire, electric fences, Dobermans, and big Keep Out signs around Rachel's heart.*

Esther clasped her knees to her chest. Would Rachel ever soften? Was there any hope that they could ever be sisters?

Esther lurched to her feet. She'd phone Gina. She had to talk to someone or she'd burst.

*E*sther got into Gina's car. "Thanks for coming at such short notice."

"It was obvious you were upset but too tired to drive. I brought salad rolls and fruit." Gina turned the ignition. "Where do you want to go?"

"Why don't we drive two blocks over to the view of the bush?"

Esther leaned back against the headrest and closed her eyes. *Lord, help. I don't understand why I'm feeling miserable and can't pray properly.*

Gina parked and then reached into the basket on the back seat and pulled out two large salad rolls.

"I'm sorry, Gina. I only see you when I need your prayers. I haven't been the friend you deserve."

"Rubbish. We see each other twice a week and you call."

"But it's normally about church-related stuff."

Gina swallowed a mouthful. "Don't be so hard on yourself. I know you're just keeping your head above water. I've already been praying a lot for you. What do you especially need prayers for?"

"Rachel." Esther sighed. The one word swept her a maelstrom of emotion. Anger and pity. Frustration and tenderness. She'd been tempted to move out and ignore Rachel like she had ignored them, but she couldn't do it. Rachel was her sister. Even more, Rachel needed Jesus. If only she could be made to see it.

"What about Rachel in particular?"

Where should she start? "I was over the moon when Rachel turned up. All my dreams were coming true, but Rachel doesn't feel the same way. Sometimes she seems to hate my presence."

"So her arrival stirred up lots of emotions?"

"I was spitting mad that I knew nothing about Rachel and that everyone, even Gran, had kept it from me." Esther clenched her jaw. "I've resolved most of that now, but I still want to pound my fists against my father's chest."

Gina munched on her bread roll, scattering a shower of crumbs. "Back to Rachel—it sounds like she had some sort of breakdown."

"Probably. I didn't think she'd stick around after our second blow-up."

"Tell me about it."

Gina had always been a good listener. Why couldn't she talk to Rachel like this?

"You describe Rachel as hard, but I wonder if her hardness is a protective shell."

"I hadn't thought of that." Rachel couldn't be entirely hardened if she'd come home. Rachel might not hug Gran, but she was always careful not to hurt her. She'd also been angry on their mother's behalf that day in the park. "You might be right. She's kind to Gran and has a real affection for a guy at work with Down syndrome. It's only me she has a problem with."

"Have you any idea why?"

"She views me as living a perfect life."

Gina whistled through her teeth. "Haven't you told her about everything that happened last year?"

"I haven't had a chance. I tried this morning and she shut me down." Esther dashed the back of her hand across her eyes. "I don't understand why she won't talk to me. And I don't understand why God doesn't do something to change her. When is he going to act?"

Gina was silent while she handed Esther some fruit. "Can I ask you a question?"

"There's no need to ask permission."

"My question is somewhat unusual."

Esther twisted around to see Gina.

"Have you been struggling to pray?"

Esther raised an eyebrow. "How did you know?"

"It was something that came into my mind."

Fear beat its wings within the walls of Esther's stomach.

"The whole time you've been speaking, you've told me how Rachel needs to change. You say you're not angry anymore, but I can see and hear anger. And you're frustrated at God's slowness to change Rachel. Are you sure it's only Rachel who needs to change?"

Scalding tears welled in Esther's eyes, and a sob broke free.

"God seldom does things the way I want," Gina said. "Usually he changes me first, and it's nearly always uncomfortable."

Esther clutched her knees to her chest. Was this what Joy had been trying to say? Esther had been focused on fixing Rachel to make her easier to live with, instead of listening to what God wanted from her. No wonder her prayers had ricocheted off the ceiling.

Gina made no sound. It was like Esther was alone. Just her and God. Minutes passed.

She'd been like Sarah. Not waiting for God's timing or solutions, but pushing her own agenda. Jumping in and assuming she knew best. Why did she think God needed her help?

Esther cried harder. What arrogance.

Gina handed her a stack of tissues.

She'd always been scornful of the Israelites in the Old Testament, how they kept forgetting God after they'd seen dozens of miracles. Yet how was she any different? She'd learned to trust God last year but here she was having to relearn the same lesson. It was easy to say 'God can be trusted', but not so easy when he didn't do things the way she wanted. She wanted family harmony, and she wanted it yesterday. Perhaps God had other plans or was running to a different timetable.

Esther reached over and touched Gina's arm. "Thank you for daring to ask those questions. You're right. I'm the one who needs to change. I need to stop telling God how he should work, and trust him to do it. And I need to love Rachel instead of pushing her to change."

"Phew." Gina wiped her forehead like she was in a melodramatic movie. "I was scared I might have overstepped the mark."

"Thank you for having the courage to tell me the truth and to point me towards Jesus." Esther grinned. "I think I might be able to pray now."

They packed their lunch things away, and Esther picked up

some crumbs and threw them out the window. Then they bowed their heads.

"Dearest Jesus," Esther said. "I'm sorry for not trusting you. I'm sorry for pushing you to do things my way. Help me not to be a Sarah or a Martha. Help me to not treat you like you're my servant. Thank you for giving Gina wisdom to speak to me. Thank you for being patient with me. Help me to be patient with Rachel."

Esther prayed for another minute, then Gina prayed.

"Lord Jesus, thank you for being our loving heavenly Father and for looking into every nook and cranny of our hearts. Lord, we can't do that, and we have no idea what is in Rachel's heart. We ask you to have mercy on all of Esther's family. Do the heart surgery you specialise in and bring them together."

They liked to pray short prayers and alternate back and forth. It helped them concentrate.

"Lord, it might be that I have to accept that Rachel can't hear your good news from me," Esther said. "If you can't use me for whatever reason, help me to be faithful in prayer and faithful in loving Rachel. Bring other Christians into her life who can share with her in a way that gets under her defences. Break through that brittle coating."

Praying with Gina always energised her own prayer life. Without others, believers were like a single coal. It wasn't long until the heat was gone but together, one person's passion ignited the rest.

Gina started the car. "You know, as we prayed, I became convinced our prayers are already on the way to being answered."

"I can't wait," Esther said.

"But don't forget, God seldom answers in the way we'd expect."

CHAPTER 31

$\mathcal{R}$achel didn't emerge from her room until three o'clock. She'd heard Esther leave the house ages ago.

Naomi called from the kitchen, "I've put the kettle on. Come and sit with me on the verandah for a while."

Gran had sharp hearing. She'd probably heard the tiff in the garden. Esther was easy to brush off, but she couldn't do the same with Gran. Not to the one person who had cared for her when she'd first run away. It hadn't been a lack of care that had made her run again. Gran couldn't help it that the word Jesus gave Rachel the shakes. And the word had echoed around her grandmother's home.

Rachel looked out into the back garden. "The laundry will be dry. Why don't I bring that in first."

"Thanks, honey."

Honey. When men had said the word, it meant they wanted something. When Gran said it, the sweetness warmed her deep inside. There was no judgement. Only love. Love she didn't deserve. Would it still be there if she ever dared to open her heart?

The pegs landed with clicks in the peg bucket. Rachel buried her face in the clean, sunshiny sheets. She'd occasionally been tempted to tell her grandmother what had happened over the last decades, but what if she destroyed what they already had? To be thrown out of the only place she was truly at home would send her crashing back into nightmare-land. If that happened, would she be able to resist the siren call to end it all?

Naomi believed that tea and a piece of cake was a cure-all. She might be right.

"I heard you and Esther this morning."

Time to get chewed out, but Naomi could be trusted to do it nicely. There wasn't a mean bone in her body.

"I thought you might have." Rachel held up her hand. "Before you say anything else, I have assumed things about Esther. I feel terrible for judging her when I hate her doing the same thing to me."

"Are you ready to hear what has been happening to Esther in the past fifteen months?"

Did she have a choice?

Naomi shifted in her seat. "This time last year I hadn't even met Esther."

Why was she not surprised Dad had hung onto his anger? Contempt curdled in her gut.

"Up until June last year, Esther did have a peaches-and-cream life. She was due to get married at the end of August."

"Who was the guy?" Why had she opened her big mouth? Once Esther became real, she'd be hard to keep out of her heart. And no one must see into her heart.

"Nick was the youth worker at Victory. Your father's protégé."

Rachel snorted. Exactly the kind of guy Esther would cosy up with. What happened to Nick? Had he died, or fallen for someone else? It was a puzzle, because even if Esther annoyed Rachel, others would view her as a catch on most counts.

"Esther discovered I was alive while they were planning the wedding. Your father refused to let her invite me."

So her father still ruled the roost. She had lots of regrets, but leaving him was not one of them.

"At the end of June, Esther discovered she had breast cancer."

"I didn't know," Rachel muttered.

"You're not very observant. She had a mastectomy."

Rachel's hands flew to her chest. Esther's baggy clothes had puzzled her. Blanche's daughter should have better dress sense. Rachel's head told her to button her lips and escape, but her heart wanted to know more. "How did Esther end up here?"

"I'll have to back up a bit. Have you kept up with your father's doings?"

Rachel shuddered. "I've tried to block him out of my head."

"Well, if you had turned on your radio or read the local newspapers, you'd find it hard to avoid him. Victory Church is several times bigger than when you left. Your father has a reputation for healing."

Rachel wanted to laugh, but Naomi would be horrified. Serve him right to have a daughter with cancer.

"William rounded up the elders and anointed Esther with oil. People fasted and prayed, and everyone was sure that the cancer would disappear in a puff of smoke."

"Obviously it didn't."

"No, and Esther was under pressure to confess sin or a lack of faith."

Rachel raised her eyebrows. So she hadn't been the only one to be hectored by their father. Esther hadn't mentioned anything—not that she'd given Esther the opportunity to say anything. Rachel had keeping-conversation-to-the-superficial down to a fine art.

"Esther went into surgery full of doubts and questions, which weren't helped by William distancing himself from her and Nick following suit."

"Because she was one of his failures?" Rachel's chest tightened like it was being crushed in a vice. She knew all too well what it felt like to be considered a failure by her father. She'd never met his exacting standards either.

"Your mother was supportive ..."

"But she wouldn't have dared to stand up to Dad."

Naomi shook her head. "Your sister didn't find it easy to either."

But she must have eventually found some courage somewhere. "What happened? Did she run away too?"

"No, she stood up to him and was thrown out."

Her sister had more gumption than she'd thought.

"Esther met someone who challenged everything she believed about the Bible."

Rachel clamped her teeth together. Why couldn't anyone leave God out of it?

"Esther discovered that the Jesus of the Bible was nothing like the Jesus your father proclaimed."

Rachel didn't put her hands over her ears, but she stared out into the garden. She did not want to hear about Jesus but the last sentence reverberated in the echo chamber of her mind.

The Jesus of the Bible was nothing like the Jesus your father proclaimed.

Could her grandmother's words be true? No. She didn't want to consider the possibility. She wasn't going to be tricked into thinking about Jesus. Her stomach ached. How much more would she have to sit through?

"When Esther tried to raise issues with your father, he closed her down."

Her father had never been able to cope with questions. He took them as personal criticism. Their clashes, when Rachel was a teenager, had been like the endless bombardment on the Somme. Painful and pointless.

Naomi cupped her hand around the cosy-covered teapot. "It's still hot. Do you want another cup?"

"No, thanks." Rachel wanted to be out of here before she began to care.

"The more Esther read the Bible, the more she changed. The more she changed, the more difficulties she had with William and Nick. Nick was too loyal to William to think for himself."

Rachel shifted in her seat.

"Apparently Nick never coped with Esther's diagnosis, but Esther doesn't put all the blame on him."

How like a man. Bailing when the going got tough. Not that she was any better.

"How did Esther end up here?"

"The broken engagement forced Esther into the conversation she'd avoided having with your father about how different his teaching was to the Bible."

Rachel ground her teeth.

"He gave her an ultimatum." Naomi's voice trembled. "Back down or leave. Esther left. I invited her to stay here, and she's been here ever since."

Rachel was nowhere near being a cancer expert, but it sounded serious. Time to change the subject.

"Gran, I've arranged to meet Mum on my own first. It will be easier that way."

She and her mother needed a quiet, private spot to reconnect without the others meddling or trying to 'help.' "Could Mum come here the Tuesday after next?"

Naomi scanned her face. "Are you sure you're ready?"

"No." She'd never be ready, but it was this or run again, and she was done with running for the moment. "But I can't put it off forever."

Naomi wriggled forward. Rachel would have helped her stand, but Esther insisted that Naomi stand independently. Esther was the physio—presumably she knew what she was talking about.

Naomi made it to her feet. "Don't know what I'd have done without your sister since my fall."

Rachel reached down to pick up the cups and plates, but Naomi put out her hand to stop her.

"I know you and Esther have had your difficulties since you came, but I'd like you to make a greater effort. She's worth knowing."

Rachel swallowed. "I'd already decided to make more of an effort."

Her grandmother smiled. "After all, you adored her when she was young."

Rachel's mind flashed to Esther as a toddler, twirling and laughing in the beam of sunshine. So alive.

Vomit rushed into her throat. She covered her mouth and rushed for the bathroom.

CHAPTER 32

*R*achel and Dirk headed for the greenhouses. In the last few weeks at the nursery, she'd mastered weeding and repotting with Josh and how to strike cuttings with Ray. Now Dirk wanted to teach her to graft fruit trees.

"How do you like working with Josh?" Dirk asked.

"He's great. Completely uncomplicated."

"People thought I was mad when I hired him, but now they envy me. He's nearly always happy, never complains, and works like a champion."

"And you didn't stop at one guy like him."

Dirk laughed. "Having Josh here opened my eyes. Others his age are mostly sitting at home and worrying their parents. Here, they grow in confidence and get a real sense of accomplishment. Josh even helps at church. Sam and Dave haven't got the capacity of Josh, but they're strong as Clydesdales and just as patient and cheerful. I'm lucky to have them."

How had she managed to get a boss like this? He was like all the best teachers Rachel had ever had and an uncle all rolled into one.

"When the other nurseries saw how my trio worked out, they

started asking me to find more guys. We trained them here first." Dirk opened the shed door. "After you."

Once inside, he opened a drawer and took out two rolls of green and yellow striped tape, then took two pairs of secateurs and two box cutters off the wall.

Before long, they headed out into the work area. "I'll do the first few while you watch, then we'll do some together. You'll catch on quickly. Let me know if I'm giving too much information."

The bench was already covered in lemon trees about fifty centimetres high. What looked like twigs were laid out to one side.

"We're going to graft lime onto a lemon rootstock. First, put the lemon in front of you. Find a healthy-looking branch and cut it off, like this." He snipped with his secateurs. "Now, take one of the lime cuttings. They're pre-prepared to ensure three to five buds on the twig."

"And someone has removed all the leaves?"

"That way the energy of the plant concentrates on taking the graft." He angled the twig. "Now take your box cutter and make one smooth cut from here to the end. Then turn it over and cut the other side to match exactly."

Dirk made it look easy.

"You mustn't touch the cut surfaces. I usually put the twig between my lips. Don't you dare laugh—it's the easiest way to do it."

Rachel giggled.

His eye twinkled as he inserted the lime twig in the cut he'd made. "Take your time. When it's in the right place, take the binding tape and wrap it a few centimetres above and below the graft." He tore off the tape. "We'll do two grafts on each plant in case one fails."

"Is there any reason for the colour of the tape?"

"Different colours for different grafted fruits."

She was learning something new every week.

"Watch me do another two, and then I'll help you do a few."

Rachel only had to do five before Dirk pronounced her ready to go it alone.

He was relaxing to work with. No unnecessary talk, although perhaps he was keeping quiet for her sake, not his own. Did he sense she wasn't in the mood for idle chatter? Had he somehow read her secrets? She laughed to herself. How? He wasn't a magician, just a wise man.

They worked quietly together for a couple of hours.

"Time for a break," Dirk said. "It's easy to get absorbed and forget to drink."

She stretched. "Grafting is a sort of miracle."

"Yes, it is." He smiled. "A cutting able to produce its own original kind of fruit even though the sap flowing through it is from a different plant."

"Hmm," Rachel said. "That is strange, isn't it? Somehow the lime twig knows to produce limes, not lemons."

They sat down and had a drink.

"But one thing with these grafts is that the cutting has to be healthy and alive," Dirk said. "You can't graft dead branches in."

Dirk was an unusual boss. He did administration, but he also gave each worker personal training. It was almost as if he valued everyone. Why was that?

"I was a dead branch when I was nineteen, but then I was grafted into the best rootstock of all. Now I've been producing fruit for many years."

Was he teasing her? She stood and went back to work. Dirk talked about broken wings. Maybe he was a man who liked to talk in riddles. He was too good a teacher to say random things but Rachel wasn't going to ask him. She'd try to solve the riddle first.

"*G*ood morning, Rachel. We finished the lemon-lime grafting yesterday. Are you ready to do some lemon-lemonade grafts?"

"I'm game." The first weeks here, she'd been sore most days, but her fitness had improved. It helped that she'd been fit before her collapse.

"Pick up some plain yellow tape and prepare the tools, and I'll meet you down there."

Dirk had the cuttings and lemon trees ready for her.

"Why two kinds of lemons on one tree?"

"Lemonade lemons are less tart and can be eaten in sections like an orange. They're popular nowadays. A good nurseryman keeps up with current fads."

They worked in quietness for an hour.

"Was what you said about the dead branch yesterday a sort of riddle?" Rachel asked.

"I prefer to think of it as a parable. Do you know what parables are?"

"Stories with meanings?"

"That's right. Jesus talked about farmers and trees and banquets to teach spiritual truth."

Unbelievable. Another Christian but she'd asked the question and she couldn't back down now. She'd let him get it off his chest and avoid further conversations.

Dirk finished off another graft. "Would you like me to explain?"

"Okay," she mumbled.

She wasn't about to tell him the whole truth. Every time she thought about her father, she wanted to punch something. She shivered. Had he noticed her reaction? "I had religious studies and chapel at school."

"Do you remember who the main character usually is in a parable?"

"Was it a king or a father?"

"Correct, and who did he represent?"

"God, I suppose."

He finished another graft. "In my parable, the rootstock represents God. He is the Creator and source of all life. Originally, Adam and Eve were like branches. Their life and strength came from God."

Rachel kept wrapping the binding tape.

"But when Adam and Eve chose to rebel against God, their branch was cut off from the rootstock. A branch stays green for the first few days after it's cut, but what will happen if it's not grafted somewhere?"

"It'll dry out and die."

"That was Adam and Eve's situation. They might have thought everything was fine, but they were on the way to death from the instant they declared their independence. Now every human being is born already dead in spiritual terms."

She couldn't keep quiet. "I've never understood that—why their choice wrecked it for everyone else."

"Smarter people than I have debated that. Somehow their choice and its results were passed down from generation to generation, like a defective gene or some sort of infection." Dirk snipped off the lemon branch. "Maybe God knew that even if every generation had a new start, we'd still all choose to reject God. I certainly did."

Rachel wiped her slick palms on her overalls. How was it possible that Dirk and her father both followed Jesus? They were nothing alike. "You mentioned yesterday that you were a dead branch that got grafted in."

He took her statement as a question.

"My parents were traditional Afrikaner Christians. Old-fashioned and strict, and I wanted nothing to do with what they believed."

Maybe they had something in common after all.

"I wanted to be popular. Lots of the kids went to church—that's what middle-class South Africans did—but they were into every kind of mischief outside church. By eighteen, I was in danger of making all sorts of stupid decisions." He ripped off the binding tape. "But God was gracious. He sent along a beautiful woman I wanted to impress. The only problem was that she loved Jesus with her whole heart, and the only way to get near to her was to attend church." He chuckled. "But I didn't deceive her. She knew I talked big about Jesus but didn't really follow him."

"Did you get the girl?"

"Not for some years. Even though she kept rejecting me, her family were wonderful. They answered all my objections and loved me to the foot of the cross. No one was more shocked than I was when my dead branch was grafted back into God's rootstock."

If Rachel busied herself with the grafting, maybe he'd keep quiet.

It almost worked.

"I've never regretted my decision to follow Jesus. The man you see today is vastly different to the old me. Like the grafts, Jesus's life flows in us and allows us to produce the fruit we were created to bear."

It might have worked for him, but she couldn't see Jesus welcoming her. What did she have to offer?

CHAPTER 33

On Tuesday, Esther hurried home from work. She busied herself tidying the front living room so she could keep an eye on the driveway. Would Mum show up? Esther was anticipating an evening awkward with hidden undercurrents and long pauses. She could rely on Blanche and Naomi to make an effort. Rachel was less predictable.

Mum's Audi pulled into the driveway, but she remained in the front seat for an age before emerging from the car. She must have sensed Esther watching her, because she gave a sketchy wave as she moved towards the front door. Her clenched left hand relaxed as she crossed the threshold. Had she been expecting to be zapped by a divine bolt of disapproval?

Naomi kissed her cheek. "So good to see you again, Blanche."

Blanche teared up and hugged Naomi. Was she shocked to see her mother-in-law so frail? They hadn't seen each other for nearly forty years.

"Esther and I will finish preparing the meal while you talk to Rachel. She's in the sunroom."

Blanche put her hand to her head. "Silly me. I've gone and left the flowers in the back of the car."

Returning, Blanche handed Naomi an exquisite bunch of orchids. "To apologise for my lack of courage and to tell you how glad I am to see you again."

Naomi gave her another big hug.

Rachel had been wise to meet their mother alone first. Esther knew they had met, because she had given up her Tuesday night dinner with her mum to make it happen although, unsurprisingly, Rachel hadn't said anything to Esther about how it had gone. Two emotional meetings at one time might have been too much, even for someone as composed as her mother.

Esther followed Naomi to the kitchen. She still had to carve the lamb and make the gravy. She'd already laid the table with Gran's best dishes and cutlery, and decorated it with silver candlesticks with elegant blue candles, and foliage from the garden. She and Gran had debated whether to make an even bigger deal of the evening but decided this was not the time for elaborate welcome home dinners.

Esther had been at peace ever since her talk with Gina. She was going to trust that God would work. Her prayers were back to normal, and she loved praying again with Gran, Gina, and Joy. Next time she met with Mum, she planned to ask her if they could pray together. What other hope did their family have?

Once the gravy was made, Esther carried everything into the dining room. Then she stuck her head into the sunroom. "Dinner's ready."

"How lovely everything looks," Blanche said.

Esther came to a new respect for both her mother and grandmother as they passed the dishes around and kept up a steady stream of polite chatter. Manners had been pounded into them, and the training proved its worth. What with "Rachel, please pass the salt," and "Esther, would you like some of this delicious gravy," they got through the first difficult twenty minutes.

Naomi let them finish most of the first course before turning the conversation to more serious matters.

"It's to be expected this first time together will be hard going. After all, some of us are virtually strangers." She looked around at each woman. "We all want this to work. However, we've been estranged so long we've forgotten how to connect." She beamed across at her daughter-in-law. "Blanche, welcome. I hope this will be the first of many visits."

Blanche smiled back. "Thank you for your gracious welcome."

"Esther and I have come up with a sort of get-to-know-you series of questions to help us."

Rachel shifted in her seat.

Would she participate?

"None of the questions are difficult or too serious," Naomi said. She lifted the foliage around the central candlestick and removed an envelope. Opening it, she took out the coloured cards inside it. "Should we take two each, then take turns asking them?"

She handed the cards first to Rachel. Rachel read the questions and chose two before passing them to her mother.

What a relief. Would Rachel answer any of the questions? She'd still said almost nothing about her private life.

Naomi was in charge during this visit because Rachel responded best to her. Rachel had made more of an effort since the day hanging out the washing. Had Naomi asked her to? Their conversations were still more strangers-on-a-train chit-chat than the heart-to-heart conversation of sisters, but anything was better than nothing. Wasn't it?

"Beach, mountains, or city lights?" Naomi asked.

"Mountains," Esther said. So did Naomi.

"City lights," Blanche said.

"Beach," Rachel said.

Things were off to a good start.

"This one is a little harder," Naomi said. "If money wasn't an issue, where would you like to travel to?"

Thinking about their answers gave them time to finish off the first course to the last skerrick of gravy.

"I've never had the chance to travel," Blanche said. "But I'd love to see the castles and museums of Europe. Especially some of the art and needlework."

"While you're in the museums," Esther said, "I'd be hiking or cycling in Europe's national parks."

"I think I've missed my chance," Naomi said. "I always wanted to travel on the Siberian railway and go to eastern Europe and Switzerland."

That was something Esther hadn't known about her grandmother.

"It's the Pacific islands for me. I'd like to learn to scuba dive." Rachel answered last but at least she was participating.

They answered another four questions before Esther and Rachel got up and cleared the dirty dishes. Activity covered their lack of conversation. They were like rusty cogs, jammed tight from years of misuse. Now they were being forced to move with many creaks and groans.

When Naomi had first mentioned the conversation cards, Esther had wondered if it was childish, but she stopped worrying when she heard the buzz of conversation. Rachel willingly answered these kinds of questions, and there was something about clutching a card that relaxed everyone.

Each question applied a drop of grease to the rusty cogs. There had even been moments of conversational hum. Would there ever be a heart-to-heart?

Rachel carried in the fruit salad and Esther brought the Greek yoghurt. Perfect harmony on the surface, but what bubbled beneath? Rachel never looked her in the eyes. Why did she always feel Rachel couldn't wait to get away from her?

Lord, please help us. Give us back the years that were stolen from us.

Everyone served themselves dessert and ate. Naomi still hadn't brought out the one card that went a little deeper. Would she decide to use it or not? Esther prayed.

"Thank you for coming, Blanche. I can't tell you how good it has been to talk again."

Blanche reached across for her mother-in-law's hand. If only her mum had had the courage to stay in touch all these years. Maybe Esther could have had a grandmother during her childhood instead of believing all her grandparents were dead.

"I have one last question to ask," Naomi said. "Then we'll move to the sunroom for tea and coffee. Here it is, can each of us share one happy memory?"

Rachel crossed her arms across her chest. Oh dear. Had this question stepped over some invisible boundary?

Esther jumped in to share a memory. Mum and Gran did their best, but it was as if a dense fog swirled around them.

Esther moved to clear the table to give Rachel the freedom not to answer, but she wasn't fast enough.

"What about you, Rachel?" Mum said.

Hadn't she sensed Rachel's anxiety? Or was she trying to be fair and give everyone an opportunity to talk?

Rachel looked down at her empty bowl. "My life hasn't had much happiness," she whispered.

A kaleidoscope of butterflies took off in Esther's stomach. There was a long pause.

"I've done things I'm not proud of."

Another drawn-out pause.

Rachel pushed her chair back and lurched to her feet. "I can't do this." And she rushed out the door.

CHAPTER 34

*T*here was a note on the door of Rachel's work locker.

BEFORE YOU START THIS MORNING, COME TO THE FRONT DESK.

Had she done something wrong? Rachel pulled her hair up into a ponytail and went to find out.

"The boss has had a heart attack," Colin said.

A heart attack? A tight band constricted Rachel's chest. Was she about to embarrass herself by bursting into tears? Why was it that every time she was happy something happened to make her life fall apart? She'd never had a boss like Dirk. Someone who treated his workers like family, finding out their strengths and encouraging them to use them. Last week he'd even asked her opinions about the front entrance display.

Was she about to lose her job? Colin was good at sales and relating to customers, but he wasn't manager material.

"They think some of his arteries are blocked," Colin said. "They'll probably need to do surgery."

Esther would know the possibilities.

"Would you be willing to be on weeding all week with Josh, and check that Sam and Dave are okay?"

"Sure, they're easy to work with." Rachel headed out the door and high-fived Josh. "Come on, buddy. You and I are working together."

Josh took her arm. "Good. I like working with you, and I like you calling me buddy."

"We are buddies. You taught me how to weed and repot when I didn't have any idea what I was doing."

"You do now."

She winked at him. "That's because you're a good teacher."

He puffed out his chest like she'd given him a gold medal. His simple enthusiasm warmed her down to her toes. Josh's likes and dislikes weren't based on things others valued. He reacted to kindness and patience, not beauty or brains or status. There was no need to pretend to be someone she wasn't. He'd see right through that.

They got to work.

"Where's Mr Dirk?" Josh asked a few hours later. "He usually comes to say hello."

So Colin hadn't told Josh. "He's sick today."

"How long is he going to be sick for?"

"I don't know."

Josh looked at her as though to check whether she was hiding things. "Is he real sick?"

"Yes, buddy, he is."

Her heart beat pulsed in her ears. Dirk was the glue keeping them together. They mustn't lose him.

"I hope not." If Colin hadn't told Josh about Dirk, then he probably hadn't told Sam or Dave either. Was he holding out on her as well? "I tell you what. I'll go and visit him this evening and tell you tomorrow."

"Will he have surgery?" Josh weeded another pot. "Mum went into hospital for surgery and was better afterwards."

"Colin said that the doctors are talking about it."

"What will they do to him?"

Rachel didn't want to scare him. "Josh, do you remember when the sprinkler systems stopped working?"

"Course I do. All the plants started to wilt."

"The boss looked at all the pipes. What was he looking for?"

"To see if any of them were gummed up."

"That's what they'll probably do to Mr Dirk. The pipes in his heart might be blocked ..."

"And the doctors will unblock them and make them flow again," Josh said.

"Something like that."

At the end of the day, as they were packing up their tools, Josh looked at her. "You tell Mr Dirk me and my mum will be praying for him to get better real soon."

"I'll do that, buddy." She patted his shoulder.

"You won't forget, will you?"

"No, I won't forget." How could she forget such sincerity? She used to believe in prayer once. Back when she'd been a kid, before she'd learned to hate her father and his god.

---

*W*hen Rachel got to the hospital, Dirk was half sitting and half lying in the bed.

"Rachel." He struggled to roll over. "I didn't expect to see you."

"The guys at work were worried." Rachel flushed.

"Could you wind up the end of the bed for me?"

Rachel fumbled around and worked it out. "How's that?"

"Better, thanks." Dirk put on his glasses. "Now I can see you better. How are you managing?"

"Are you sure we should be talking about work?"

"I won't tell if you won't," he said in a stage whisper. "My wife should be back any moment."

Rachel hadn't met his wife.

"She's gone to phone our son."

Son? She hadn't known he had a son.

"He works at a big accountancy firm in Perth. If I have surgery, it will be several months until I get back to work."

The pulse in her neck throbbed. Even if the business stayed open, how would they manage without him?

A woman came back in, and Dirk smiled. "Meet my better half. Norma, this is Rachel."

"The Rachel from work?" Norma looked at Dirk and something passed between them.

Why was Mrs Klopper behaving as if there was some special significance to her name?

Mrs Klopper was chatty and asked all sorts of questions about Rachel's family. She answered as best she could without saying too much. Dirk listened, saying nothing. He was the kind of guy who read between the lines. What was he reading between hers?

The nurse popped her head around the curtain, "End of visiting hours. Mr Klopper needs his rest."

Rachel said her goodbyes and headed out the door.

"Have you told her yet?" Mrs Klopper said as Rachel closed the door behind her.

Told her? What was there to tell?

CHAPTER 35

*R*achel and Josh visited Dirk once his surgery was done and he'd started rehabilitation.

"Me, me," Josh said as he pushed the lift button.

Did Josh get out and about? She'd have to invite him to visit Gran and Esther. They'd love him.

"You go in first."

Josh tiptoed into the room and peeked around the curtain. "Surprise, Mr Dirk. Surprise."

"Josh, you are a surprise. The best kind," Dirk said. "You didn't come on your own, did you?"

"Miss Rachel brought me." Josh beckoned to her.

They weren't the only guests. Mrs Klopper was there, and a man about Rachel's age or a little younger. He got up out of his seat immediately and offered it to her. Josh held the heavy fruit basket towards Dirk.

"I'll take that," the younger man said. "Dad's not supposed to lift anything yet." He put it on the side table.

So that's who he was.

Josh insisted on shaking hands. "Has he come to help at the nursery, Mr Dirk?"

Dirk smiled. "Pete's come for a month. He'll have to decide if he'll stay longer."

"Dad has been trying to get me interested in the nursery for years." Pete grinned at his father. "There was no need to go to such lengths to get me here."

"Well, you never accepted my other invitations."

The easy banter made Rachel relax. It looked like Pete would continue the family feel of the nursery. If he hadn't, she'd have been tempted to leave. The nursery wouldn't be the same without Dirk. Hopefully he'd be back soon and feistier than ever.

"Josh," Pete said, "Dad says you're the weeding and potting expert. Will you teach me?"

Josh grew five centimetres. "Of course. I taught Miss Rachel."

Rachel doubted Pete had been called in to weed. Maybe all was not lost.

"Pete will concentrate on the business side, and Colin will stay on the front sales desk," Dirk said.

"What about me and Sam and Dave?"

"Are you happy to stay where you are, Josh? Those weeds will keep growing whether I'm there or not."

"Yes, sir." Josh's heels clicked together and he saluted.

"And what about Rachel?" Pete said.

"Are you happy encouraging the trio of guys and striking cuttings? There isn't any more grafting to do."

"I'm more than happy working with Josh."

"Although, I had been considering something else for you."

She gnawed the inside of her cheek.

"I've been watching you rearranging pots here and there."

She'd hoped he wouldn't notice, but when something was out of place, she couldn't help putting it in a more advantageous spot.

"Everything you've rearranged has started selling better."

Rachel released the breath she'd been holding.

"Design isn't my strong point, and it's not Colin's either."

"And it's definitely not mine," Pete said.

"Would you be willing to work with Pete to tackle the front display?"

Rachel covered her mouth with her hand, but not before she'd smiled the kind of smile she remembered smiling when she'd been in the school choir.

"I knew there were some smiles hidden in there somewhere. If I had known how to coax them out, I would have handed off my worst job ages ago. Do you think you can do it?"

Rachel nodded. Weeding, potting, and grafting were satisfying, but design? That made her heart sing. How often would they want a new display? How long would she have to do it, and what was the budget?

"You look like you are bursting with questions. Pete and Norma, why don't you go with Josh and get him a chocolate bar from the machine in the foyer."

"We can get you one too, boss."

"I'm afraid I'm not allowed chocolate bars any more, but you can enjoy one for me."

Rachel and Dirk settled down to plan. He might not be a designer, but he knew business and could recognise good ideas.

"You've probably been critiquing the display area ever since you arrived."

Rachel blushed. "I noticed it the day I came to apply for the job, and I doodle ideas on the weekend."

"And you didn't say anything?"

"I don't have a degree or anything, and I didn't think you'd let me loose." Rachel cleared her throat. "I never expected to get the job in the first place. My interview was perfunctory. It was like you'd already decided to give me the job before you looked at my references."

"I didn't offer you the job because of your work background."

How bizarre and not very flattering. She'd have been offered the job if she had one arm and three heads.

"I offered you the job because of your car."

What did he mean? It wasn't as if she drove a limited-edition antique. There was nothing remarkable about her car.

"I recognised the number plate."

Could he be some sort of stalker? He'd never made her uncomfortable.

"Sorry. I think the anaesthesia must have scrambled my mind. Could you hand me my glass of water? It's behind the fruit basket."

Rachel passed him the glass.

"My wife and I had been praying for the owner of that car for weeks. When I saw it, I came rushing in to find you."

Stranger and stranger.

"Let me start from the beginning. In August, my wife and I were coming back from a holiday up the coast. As we came around a corner, there was a car right on the edge of the cliff."

Rachel blanched. Impossible. It couldn't have been the Kloppers.

"When I got out of the car, you were in no state to change the tyre."

She'd thought his voice sounded familiar.

"You were crying hard, and we were worried."

Was that why she hadn't recognised him? Her memory of those few hours was muddled. When she had looked at the man it was through the shimmer of tears and shame. What kind of coincidence would lead her here? Hundreds of kilometres from the flat tyre on the mountain.

"Following you down that mountain, the make, model, colour, and licence plate were imprinted onto my eyeballs. I couldn't mistake your car."

"I don't understand. Why did you help me that day? Why did you pay for my room?"

Dirk took a sip of water. "We always wondered about your flat tyre. Something wasn't right. Had you intended to drive off that cliff?"

"Yes." Rachel hung her head and let her hair swing down to cover her face. "That was the plan."

He sighed. "Why would a beautiful woman, with life ahead of her, want to drive off a cliff?"

Rachel wanted to run from the room, but if she ran from this man, she'd run from everyone. Here was someone who was safe, who wouldn't judge, wouldn't condemn. She strained to hear if the others were returning.

"I'll ring the nurse and ask her to delay the others."

Could the man read her heart as well as he interpreted her silence?

She looked out the window. How much of her past did she dare to share? She was nowhere near ready to share it all.

"Okay, she's gone now. Don't be afraid."

Rachel peeked at him. He looked how a father should look. Gentle and sad and ready to listen. She took a deep breath.

"I did intend to drive off the cliff." Rachel detached herself from what she was saying. Like she floated above the woman who'd had nightmares and decided to end it all.

"I was already going pretty fast when I aimed the car towards the edge, but I chose a corner where I wouldn't take anyone else with me." She didn't want Dirk to think more badly of her than he ought. "I put my hand on the horn and closed my eyes as I hit the accelerator."

"How did you end up where you did?"

"I have no idea. I expected to hit the rail and it would be all over. Then I could sleep forever."

Dirk shuddered.

"There was a loud bang, and the car spun around. When I finally dared to open my eyes, the car was where you saw it. Lined up as though I'd parked it out of harm's way."

"The only explanation I can see is that a miracle happened."

Rachel squirmed. "I don't believe in miracles."

"Have you got a better explanation? Cars don't have punctures to conveniently save a life. Your car should have flipped or crashed through the barrier."

He had a point, but she must not let the possibility of a miracle enter her mind. Where would she be if she started believing in miracles? The only things holding her together were her job and her independence. And her family. She'd admit that some of them were worth living for.

"I know you don't like admitting the possibility of miracles, but it makes sense given the evidence." Dirk ticked off on his fingers. "One, the puncture. Two, the way the car was parked. Three, the fact that my wife and I were on the road that day. We'd intended to set off an hour earlier but were delayed by a phone call. We shouldn't have been on the road at precisely the right moment to help you."

Rachel stared at him. A miracle? Why couldn't she come up with a better explanation? And she hadn't even mentioned handstand man. Dirk was going to jump all over that incident.

She didn't want it to be a miracle.

Because if it was a miracle, then the God she hated not only listened to her, he cared. She couldn't handle anyone caring. Caring made people vulnerable. It took away their freedom, and freedom was all Rachel had left.

He looked over his glasses at her. "And four, you came to my nursery looking for a job. If I hadn't been out, I wouldn't have seen and recognised your car."

Rachel could think of another coincidence. She was going to keep using that term. Any other term meant trouble. She wouldn't have still been on the nursery premises if it hadn't had a café and if she hadn't been exhausted from her job search. She seldom had afternoon tea, but that day she had. That's the only reason she was still there when Dirk returned.

What was going on? If this truly was a series of miracles, then what did God want from her?

Men never did anything nice without some ulterior motive.

What did God have in mind?

CHAPTER 36

*E*veryone said recovering from chemo took months and sometimes years. Esther had good days and bad days, but she shouldn't need another shower after merely unlocking her bike and pushing it towards the front gate. Was the humidity especially high this morning? Or was there some other reason she was dragging herself along as if wet concrete clung to her shoes?

Esther swung a leaden leg over the bike seat and started pedalling. One kilometre into her ride her chest was heaving.

Come on, push the pedal.

Again.

Push.

This was the kind of self-talk she'd used when climbing a mountain, but she was cycling on the flat.

Ahead was a slight slope she could coast down. Riders she'd normally fly past overtook her. Esther turned the final corner, wobbled, and almost fell off. She wasn't going to make the last two hundred metres. She lurched off her bike. Sweat ran down her body in rivulets and dripped off her nose. Her breath came with ragged gasps. She leaned over and clutched the bicycle seat before taking one slower breath. Then another.

Her heart raced at the speed of a cheetah in full pursuit. It pulsed in her ears.

Breathe in, one-two-three, she coached herself.

Breathe out, three-two-one.

Her heartbeat was slowing, but it was still well above normal. She took a deep breath. There was a sharp stab of pain in her back. Could she have pneumonia?

Esther pushed the bike the rest of the way to work, walking like a centuries-old tortoise. She dropped her bike lock key four times before successfully locking up.

As she passed the reception desk to clock in for the day, Sue shot out of her office. "Esther, you look dead tired. What's wrong?"

"Terrible shortness of breath," Esther panted. "Could barely ride. Had to walk ... the last part."

Sue went quiet for far too long. "Anything else?"

"Sharp pain in my back ... when I take a deep breath."

"We'd better ring your specialist and see what he says."

An icy hand crushed Esther's heart. "Planning to avoid ... for a day."

"I don't think you'd better. Let's hope you've simply twisted something." Sue touched her on her shoulder. "Do you want to make the call or shall I?"

Tears were too close to the surface. "Would you? I'm afraid I'll ... howl like a baby."

Sue indicated the treatment table in the far corner. "Why don't you lie down." It wasn't a question. She pulled the curtain to give Esther privacy and went off to make the call.

Esther sank onto the bed and closed her eyes. Being a physiotherapist could be a curse. She couldn't help considering all the possibilities. Her stomach churned with fear, spiralling into a whirlpool. She was going to throw up if she didn't gain control.

Lord, help. Give me strength to cope with whatever the day brings.

Way too soon, Sue was back with her handbag over her shoulder. "Dr Webster has phoned ahead to order the tests. I'll drive you down there."

"Sue, you've got ... enough to do."

Sue rummaged in her handbag for her car keys. "I'd never forgive myself if you collapsed on the way. A few minutes ago, I thought I'd have to carry you over my shoulder to accident and emergency."

Esther was too weary to argue. At the clinic she was zapped with x-rays and jabbed with needles. The doctor asked her to wait, and she could hear him phoning in his office. Eventually, he called her in. "Dr Webster wants to talk to you."

Esther took the phone, her hand shaking.

"Paul Webster here," the familiar voice said in a brisk tone. "Look, you have fluid in your lungs and you need to go into hospital. Are you still happy with your own hospital?"

"More than happy." Her voice was more wheeze than words.

"You'll be in for two nights, and I've given you a booking with us the morning after. We'll do our best to have you home before Christmas."

Esther rang Sue, who drove back to collect her and stayed by her side until she was admitted. "I'll pop in at lunchtime to check you're alright," she said. "Don't worry about anything."

Draining the fluid was more scary than painful. The doctor explained the process, administered local anaesthetic, and inserted a drainage tube.

"Whatever you do, don't raise the bottle above your waist level or the fluid will drain the wrong way. Then you'll feel even worse," he said as he tidied his gear.

Any worse would not be pleasant.

"The more you rest, the faster you'll be out of here." It sounded like the well-used cliché it was. "We'll x-ray you each day to check your progress."

Gran and Mum didn't know what was happening. Could she phone without breaking down?

Esther only teared up once with each call. Gran would ring Joy and Gina and get the church prayer chain into action.

Sue popped in during lunch. "I've put you on leave until the New Year. Please do rest. We want you fighting fit."

"Feel like I'm ... letting you down."

"Nonsense. You more than pay your way. Now, someone gave me a message for you. Who was it?" She tapped her finger on the side of her head. "It was somewhat enigmatic. Ah, yes, from Matt. Something about don't worry about the story group—he'd prepare for tomorrow. Does that make any sense to you?"

"We've been learning Bible stories once a week. Matt will do ..." She wheezed. "... the next one."

"I know you're exhausted, but I have to ask. Are you serious about there being a group?"

Wasn't this just like God? Esther had been praying for more than a year for an opportunity to speak with Sue, and it came when she felt like death. *Lord, give me your strength.*

"They each heard one story and loved it," she said between breaths. "Wanted more ... I had no time to meet one-to-one." She sucked in another breath. "Group is better anyway ... better discussion."

"Well, I never," Sue said. "Maybe I'd better hear one for myself." She held up her hand. "Once you're better, of course. In the New Year, I'll ask you for dinner."

"I'll look forward to it."

*N*aomi arrived, bringing Esther's Bible, a shawl, and some flowers from the garden—a breath of home. "Honey, how are you feeling?"

Esther gestured towards the bottle. "It's gross but not painful." She paused to catch her breath. "Tiring to talk. Have to be here until my lung reinflates."

"Can I ring Rachel from here?"

"Can you wait?" Esther wheezed. She was in no mood to have Rachel coming because she felt obligated. "I'll see Dr Webster on Friday morning … for the bad news."

"You think it is bad news then?"

Naomi waited while she took a few more breaths.

"I think the cancer is back."

Naomi winced. "Are you scared?"

"Yes." The single word conveyed little of what she truly felt, but she wasn't up to thinking. It was enough effort to take one tight breath after another. "Less than a twelve-month gap … news can't be good." Her heart pounded in her chest and her palms slicked. Did patients ever completely crack up and start screaming in fear?

Lord, you've promised to be with me. I need you now. Remind me you're in control.

A promise she loved leapt into her mind. 'I will never leave you, nor forsake you.' Her heart rate settled towards normal. *Yes, Lord. You knew about this day before I was born. Help me to be ready for whatever is ahead.* A tear trickled down her cheek. *If you're going to take me through the darkest valley of all, you'll be there, holding my hand no matter how dark the shadows. Thank you.*

Naomi leaned forward. "Shall we pray?"

"You pray," Esther whispered. "Not sure I can manage."

Naomi held her hand, her grip strong as though she was trying to pass her strength through to Esther. "Dearest heavenly Father, we need you. Esther doesn't want to be here, and we don't want her here. We don't know what you're doing, but we trust you. Help us to focus on you, not the situation. Take away our fear and worry. In your name and for your glory, Amen."

Esther's stomach fluttered. How was Rachel going to handle this? After the recent dinner, Rachel was making an effort to talk to her. There were still many drawn-out pauses and false starts, but it was heaps better than before. Would their fragile progress be destroyed? Cancer had proved too much for her relationship with Nick. Would it prove too much for Rachel?

CHAPTER 37

*E*sther walked straight from hospital discharge to Dr Webster's clinic. She had to stop twice on the way to catch her breath. Why had she refused a wheelchair?

Dr Webster greeted her too heartily. "I was hoping we wouldn't see you again apart from your routine check-ups."

"But you suspected you might?"

"I was afraid we would. Your first round was a serious one."

He'd never hidden the complexities of her original diagnosis. The Bible was filled with miracles, so why couldn't she have been one of them? But she'd spent her last months running ahead of God and trying to force him to do her will. She wasn't going to do it again.

God had promised he'd be with her, and she was going to believe him. No matter what.

Esther swallowed. "Please, please put me out of my misery. What are we dealing with?"

His shoulders slumped. "The cancer is back."

Esther's stomach dropped like she was on a rollercoaster and her palms prickled with sweat. Shouldn't this be easier the second time? Dr Webster was saying something about spots on the liver and lung metastases, but she wasn't sure. Her mind seemed disconnected.

"Is this it?" She couldn't yet bring herself to say the word. Death.

Dr Webster avoided her eyes.

Metastases. Double whammy. Double enemy.

She needed more. More details to help her prepare herself for the coming journey. The kind of journey you only ever made once and usually later in life. Much later. She shivered again. Why hadn't she brought her jacket instead of leaving it with Michelle in reception?

"Please tell me the truth." Esther took a deep breath and sat up straight. She wasn't alone. Her companion had walked a far harder road to the Cross. The pain in her stomach lessened. "I'm not nearly as scared as your average person. I know where I'm going and who I'm going with."

"What a pity all our patients aren't your brand of Christian." His mouth twitched up at the corners but didn't get as far as a laugh. Perhaps he didn't feel it was appropriate. "It makes my job easier."

How could she continue this conversation? No ideas. Her mind was sluggish, drugged by shock.

"I'm recommending a different type of chemo."

Nausea surged. Not chemo. Not again. Her hair finally looked normal. Even pretty.

"It's designed to stop the cancer cells reproducing."

Esther sighed. "In other words, it's designed to buy time."

Dr Webster squared his shoulders like a boxer. "We hope for more than that."

Was he as grateful as she was to be talking business again?

"And if I don't take it?"

"Now you're pushing me into a corner."

"It's my life," Esther said. "How long might I have without it?"

He still avoided her eyes. "Prognosis is a tricky thing."

Knowing how long would help her plan and prioritise. "If I was your friend, not your patient, would you be willing to predict how long I have to finish things off here?"

"Under twelve months without treatment."

Esther's mouth went dry, and she clasped her hands together to stop them shaking. Twelve months or less. So little time. So little time to enjoy her new-found grandma. So little time for things to be resolved between herself and Rachel. So little time to finish all she wanted to do. Would her family ever be reconciled? Twelve months wasn't long for God to bring about the needed transformation.

Dr Webster was still speaking. His voice was muffled, like someone speaking through thick fog. "We need to find which chemicals your particular cancer responds to."

"So my body is going to be a chemistry lab." Her words sounded brittle, even to herself. "Am I to come here for treatment?"

"No. This type isn't given intravenously. It comes in a pill form. Morning and evening for fourteen days, then rest for seven."

Dr Webster sounded decisive and positive, as if they were discussing a minor medical problem instead of life and death.

"You'll come in again after the first round, and we'll see how you're responding before continuing the process."

It all sounded easy, but would her body agree? "What are the side effects?"

"Hair loss is minimal."

Her mouth lifted to one side. "Delighted." And she was. One piece of good news, but there were still layers of shock. Layers of dealing with issues and implications.

He handed her a pamphlet. "This lists all the possible side effects."

Esther scanned the list and grunted. Great. Diarrhoea and vomiting. "What's this hand-foot syndrome?"

"It's a possible side effect. Numbness, tingling, and dry skin."

It didn't sound like fun. "Is there anything I can do about it?"

"Sister O'Reilly is the expert. She'll tell you which moisturisers and methods are recommended. The dangerous thing with this chemo is that it interferes with other medications. No vaccinations, no aspirin. Nothing at all, not even vitamins."

Mum had wanted her to take vitamins, but she'd insisted all vitamins came from fruit and vegetables.

"Any medications can cause bleeding. You must contact us immediately with any fever or bleeding, or go to accident and emergency. Any other questions?"

"I'm sure I'll think of more later."

"I'm sending you to do the base-level blood tests now, before Sister O'Reilly gives you the first round of pills. You'll also need to book your next appointment, three weeks from now."

The last two days, she'd poured out her heart in prayer. It helped prepare her for the likely diagnosis. All she wanted to do now was to use her time wisely. For eternal purposes. Purposes that mattered.

Lord, give me an opportunity to talk. Maybe she should make one, but she hesitated to try. Somehow it still bothered her to appear a fool in front of Dr Webster. Maybe it was something to do with him being a doctor. Then she remembered—twelve months. Did it matter? Theirs didn't look like being a long-term association.

Esther opened her mouth. "Did you ever get around to reading Luke?"

He didn't miss a beat. He should be used to her by now. "I've kept putting it off, but if Jesus explains you, then I should make the time."

Her fear had gone, as it always did once she'd obeyed the Holy

Spirit's urging. "It does explain me. Read it with an open mind and look at the evidence."

"What evidence?"

He'd probably let her say three sentences. *Let them be the right ones.* "The Bible claims to be a historical document. Treat it like one. We should ask if the stories are like myths, or the result of eyewitness testimony? Does archaeology or any other historical research support or disprove it?"

Dr Webster held up his hands in mock surrender. "Okay, okay. I'll read it to keep you happy."

"Don't read it to make me happy. If it's true, you're gambling with something important." Rob and Dr Webster were the same. She had to slip truth alongside each joke and hope it slid under their defences. "As it looks like I'll be exiting this life earlier than planned, I'm not willing to gamble with my eternity."

"We'll aim to give you a good Christmas."

The man was a smooth sidestepper. "Will you take holidays? Anyone in your job must need a mental break."

"I de-stress by diving."

For the first seconds she had no idea how to respond, but every time she sent up a *help* the words were there. "How can you dive and not see the magnificence of a designer?"

Dr Webster winked. "I'll be praising the complex evolution."

"I admire anyone with the blind faith to believe in evolution. The evidence for design is stronger."

He raised his hands again. "I give up. I promise to read Luke, if only to get you off my back."

Esther laughed. "If you prepare three tough questions for me, it'll give me something to look forward to but I don't promise I'll be able to answer them."

"Fair enough," he said. "I'll ask you how you've weathered treatment and you can ask me how I've weathered Luke."

Thank you, Lord, for giving me the words I needed once I dared to open my mouth.

The man was beginning to thaw. She, Gina, and Joy had been praying since her first follow-up appointment. Praying he'd melt. Praying he'd be filled with life-giving water instead of chunks of ice.

CHAPTER 38

*E*sther slumped in the back seat while Blanche drove. Once home she headed straight for bed. She had to hold Blanche's arm because her legs wobbled like they'd been deboned.

"Have you seen Rachel?"

"I believe she's working back late. Planning a new display or something."

Really? Or was Rachel using any excuse to avoid her?

Mum pressed her arm. "Be patient. She's cut up, but she'll come right."

Cut up. They were all cut up. "Maybe it's a good sign. I don't think she would have cared a month ago."

"Rachel's always cared, but she's been afraid to let herself show it. Indifference is her way of coping."

Yes, but they still didn't have any idea what Rachel was coping with. What had led to her breakdown, if that was what it was?

"We'll have a lot to pray about."

Hearing Mum talking about prayer was a comfort, and Esther needed all the comfort she could get. Rachel's avoidance wasn't unanticipated. Esther wanted to hide away and hibernate herself. As if by avoiding she could deny the truth.

*T*wo days later, Esther drove home to talk to her father. She gripped the steering wheel. *Lord, this conversation terrifies me. Give me courage.*

This was her second cancer diagnosis, so she could be more objective. The physical responses were the same, but some things had changed. This time she knew talking about cancer robbed it of the power to paralyse her. She'd already experienced one round of God's presence with her in the shadows. The shadows were darker now, but God hadn't changed. The darker the shadows, the more God's light could shine forth.

If only her father would learn these things. Troubles were not to be denied. Troubles were to be embraced as the means God uses to mature his children. To refine gold.

For once, her Dad made it easy. She'd barely sat down when he said, "Are you sure you should be here? You look like you're coming down with a bad case of something."

"I wish it were the flu, but it's not."

He clicked his pen. "What's wrong?"

"I've been in hospital with a pleural effusion."

His eyes glazed over. He'd never been good with medical terms. Probably thinking about his next appointment. Well, first he had one with her.

"Dad." Esther leaned forward and put her hand on his shoulder. "The cancer's back."

His head snapped back like she'd slapped him. "How is that possible after all the treatment you've had?"

If only volume of treatment equalled effectiveness. "My first round of cancer was serious, so there was always a high risk it would come back. That's why Nick broke off the engagement." The betrayal still occasionally gnawed at her like a toothache. "He couldn't handle living with uncertainty."

"I can see why he was concerned."

When would her father learn to tread gently instead of trampling all over the sensitive parts of her heart?

"What are you going to do?"

Not that again. Not fasting and anointing and prayer morning, noon, and night.

"I'm going to listen to the doctors God has given me and trust that God knows what he's doing." If God healed her, good. If he chose not to, then she wasn't going to waste anything along the way.

Dad got up. "I'll get the prayer chain into action."

Would he mention her name, or would the prayer point be for some anonymous woman, so he could feel he was doing something without her cancer reflecting on his reputation?

Déjà vu. Why did she always hope her father had changed? He had no desire to change. To do so, he'd have to admit that his ministry was built on the wrong foundations. That looked like it would need a tsunami-sized event. Her first round of cancer hadn't done it. Looks like round two wouldn't either.

Family harmony. Was it too much to desire?

Lord, I'm not going to give up praying. You love my family. I made a mess of things before, and I'll wait for your timing. But Lord, make it soon, for Dad's sake.

Had her father ever loved her? Maybe he'd never said so, but she could remember plenty of good times.

"Dad, there's no need to spring into action. We haven't had time to talk recently. We used to have lots to talk about."

He grunted.

"You were always a great help with my history and English assignments."

"Well, they're subjects that interest me."

His education had been outstanding and it showed. He was never at a loss for conversation. It was part of the reason for his success. He could talk to almost anyone. "Do you remember all the museums we've been to? Art for Mum, history for you, and science for me."

"Mmm."

No money had been spared. She'd only had to show an interest in something and she'd be whisked off to a concert or a play. And holidays. They'd had glamorous holidays.

They reminisced for the next hour. She had more to be thankful for than most. Last year's events had clouded over many of the golden times. Her father spelled love 'g-i-f-t' or 'o-p-p-o-r-t-u-n-i-t-y.' That didn't make it any less real. Had he been as generous with Rachel? What had made her run away? And was Rachel ever going to tell them?

---

*E*sther and Naomi had invited Blanche over for her weekly meal and coaxed Rachel out of her room.

"I thought the conversation starter questions might rescue us again," Gran said once they'd served themselves. "Esther told me the worst thing about cancer was that people had no idea what to say, but we need to be able to talk about it."

Would Rachel stay or bolt? She had a multitude of issues and seemed no closer to letting Jesus deal with them.

Naomi put a small pile of cards and two pens in the centre of the table. "This time the cards are blank for you to write your own questions."

They all scrawled a question or two.

"I'll go first," Mum said. "Last time you didn't tell anyone you had cancer until you knew for certain. Why are you doing things differently now?"

"Last time I didn't want to stress anyone in case it was a false alarm. Maybe I was also in denial. I didn't believe William Macdonald's daughter would truly have cancer." Esther laughed. "This time, I know I need support."

They covered a few more questions. Rachel barely said anything, but Mum and Gran kept the conversation flowing.

So this was what it was like to be a fly, eavesdropping on people's private thoughts.

"What were the most helpful things people did during your treatment?" Naomi asked.

"That's easy. The best ones were you and Gina. You talked about other things besides cancer. I want to laugh and have fun. Mum, do you remember the day at the wig shop?"

"Do I ever. It was hilarious. I still have the photos." She rifled through her bag and passed the photos over.

When Gran had first suggested discussing cancer, Esther had worried it was too heavy a topic. But if getting their feelings out in the open helped the others treat her normally instead of like a fragile crystal ornament, it was worth it.

Miracle of miracles. Even Rachel laughed at the photos.

"What was the hardest thing during the six months of treatment?" Mum asked. "For me it was William's refusal to talk about it. I had no one to talk to."

"Sorry, Mum. I didn't think enough about how my leaving would impact you."

"Coming here feels like I'm sneaking off to do something I shouldn't." Mum looked at Rachel. "But if the choice is between seeing you both or not, then it's easy."

How could one family have this many problems? Dad might forgive his second daughter for coming here, but what would he do when he found out about Rachel?

"I felt powerless to help Esther cope with the side effects of treatment," Naomi said. "I often wished it was me with the cancer. I'm old. I've lived my life."

People did struggle with a young person having cancer. They wanted a reason, and many of their reasons were wrong. Esther wouldn't be responsible for her actions if one more person suggested it must be some sin or her lack of faith. Hanging around with non-Christians was easier. They didn't attempt to find spiritual reasons for her situation.

The group had gone quiet.

Lord, help me share something that will draw Rachel closer to you.

"Apart from the surgery and side effects of chemo, the hardest thing was the clash between my beliefs and my situation. I believed what Dad said from the pulpit. I believed cancer was a spiritual test. If I prayed hard enough and did the right things, I'd pass with flying colours. In the end, it was *not* being healed that forced me to meet Jesus."

Rachel looked down at her plate.

Would she and Rachel ever get to talk properly together?

Esther helped Mum clear the main meal and bring in the fruit platter. They sat down again.

"We've come up with two more questions," Rachel said.

Gran must have talked to Rachel while they were out of the room. She was the only one who could coerce Rachel to do anything.

"Okay. What are they?"

"What did you learn as a result of the cancer?"

"If Esther hadn't had cancer, I wouldn't be here," Mum said. "Esther's example inspired me to have courage."

The changes Esther had seen in Mum were a miracle in themselves. From a distant vision of motherly perfection to the flesh and blood woman here with them. Had their father noticed, or was Mum only more alive when she was with them?

She must invite Mum over this weekend. She'd love Joy and Gina.

Rachel pointed her chin towards Esther. Was that a tear in her eye?

"I could write a book," Esther said. "You'll have to kick me under the table when you've had enough."

Rachel laughed. "Count me in." Her laugh, such a rare sound even if it sounded a little forced.

"I've met many cancer patients," Esther said. "I've seen people angry and bitter and terrified. I've seen people in denial or full of complaints. That could have been me."

Was Rachel listening?

"Jesus cares more about us trusting him than making our life all hunky-dory. Cancer helped me grow in trust. Trust that Jesus cares about the small details. Trust that he can use me to encourage others even when I feel blah. One of last year's highlights was seeing Anna come to know Jesus before she died. In the end, she died beautifully."

"I don't see how death can be beautiful," Rachel said.

It did sound strange. "The death wasn't beautiful in physical terms, but God took Anna's fear away." Esther gulped. "There are many reasons to be afraid. Sickness or weakness or embarrassment. No one wants their last days to be yuck. I need you to help me enjoy the time I have left."

Mum started crying. Esther grasped her hand.

Esther wanted it to be years, but what if that wasn't God's plan? Would she still praise him if it was only months?

CHAPTER 39

*R*achel put the jug of iced tea and five glasses on a tray, and walked out to the verandah. Mum, Gran, Esther, and a Chinese woman were gathered in a quartet of rattan chairs in the shade, while someone Esther's age perched on a stool.

The garden was in its full summer glory. Flowers spilled out of baskets, pots, and barrels, a profusion of colour, scent, and poetry. Bees wobbled drunkenly from flower to flower. Rachel allowed herself to be introduced to the newcomers—the Joy and Gina that Esther was forever talking about.

Once the introductions were done, Rachel mumbled excuses and escaped to her bedroom. She lay down and opened a book.

Mum now visited every week. They'd negotiated the dangerous shoals of emotion that threatened to shipwreck them and were through to the calmer waters on the other side. Learning to relate less as mother and daughter and more as two contemporaries.

The sound of laughter came through Rachel's closed door. Esther had fantasised about having an older sister yet didn't see what she already had. Sisters come in all ages and races, and sisterhood was more than a matter of blood.

Someone else laughed. What was she doing shut up in her room? All the fun was on the verandah. Yet out there, all she'd get was Jesus, Jesus, Jesus. What was it about Jesus that made a group of women want to talk about him? And what was there to laugh about? There hadn't been much laughter at Victory. Professional music, oceans of it. Sermons that allowed her father to pontificate. Pious prayers that had no substance. Plenty of cardboard smiles, but not laughter.

Nowadays, Rachel was surrounded by Christians. They were completely different to those she remembered as a teenager. She actually liked them.

Ever since she was fifteen, she'd stood separate. On the outside looking in. Taking what she wanted from life and avoiding the rest. She'd avoided entanglements. Avoided bearing other's burdens. Avoided the mess and obligations and ... *joy*.

Joy? Where had that thought come from?

Rachel opened her door. Now she could hear the others more clearly. Like the excited chatter of rainbow lorikeets on the bush outside her window in the morning. Had she misjudged Esther? The others seemed to love her. Why was it that she and Esther brought out the worst in each other? Her heart pained. Had she missed out on something precious by locking Esther out? Could the two of them start again?

What if she crept out and sat behind the curtain at the French doors? If it wasn't her thing, she could slip away without anyone knowing.

Rachel placed her book on the floor and ghosted out in time to hear Esther say, "You know what a blessing Joy has been to me. I've asked her to tell us a story to let you hear a professional."

"I'm not a professional, but I've had years of practice." Joy's slight accent made her voice easy enough to differentiate. There was a pause. What was Joy doing? The disadvantage of only listening was that Rachel couldn't see anyone's expressions or actions.

"I don't know why I'm telling this particular story from Daniel, but I've learned to trust God's urging."

Joy gave some quick historical background—who the Babylonians were, and how Daniel and his friends ended up in Babylon. Rachel vaguely remembered Daniel's name. Something to do with a lion's den.

"God had given Daniel a special ability to interpret dreams. The first dream he interpreted related to a gigantic statue. The king remembered the dream but ignored its meaning."

Presumably everyone else knew what the statue was about. Here she was again on the outside, straining to understand. Was there any point in staying?

"King Nebuchadnezzar built an enormous gold statue, twenty-five metres high. Then he called together all his officials and said, 'When you hear music playing, you are to fall down and worship. If you don't, you will be thrown into a fiery furnace.'"

Rachel was swept back to ancient Babylon. There was no way she'd leave now. Joy's voice was an instrument, highlighting every important word and nuance.

"But some of the officials came to the King and said, 'Oh King, live forever, there are three Jewish men who pay no attention to you. They worship neither your gods nor the statue you have set up.'"

"Nebuchadnezzar summoned Shadrach, Meshach, and Abednego. 'Is it true you don't worship my gods or the image of gold I've set up? I'll give you another chance. If you bow down, you're safe, but if you do not, you will be thrown into the furnace. And then what god could rescue you?'"

Rachel leaned forward.

"The three men replied, 'Oh king, we do not need to defend ourselves in this matter. If we are thrown into the fire, our God is able to rescue us but even if he does not, we will never worship your gods.'"

Why had she never heard about these guys when she was a kid? It would have kept her attention.

"The furnace was so hot that, when the soldiers shoved the three men into the flames, the soldiers dropped down dead."

What? Where was God? Rachel had been certain he'd dash to the rescue of such faithful followers. Her father loved to talk about last-second rescues. No wonder she'd never heard this from him. It was a bit of a downer.

"Suddenly, Nebuchadnezzar leapt to his feet. 'Didn't we throw three men into the flames? How come I now see four men walking about, and the fourth looks like a son of the gods?'"

Now that was more like it. If this had been a movie, the king's words would have been the cue for stirring music.

"Approaching the furnace, the king cried out, 'Shadrach, Meshach, and Abednego, servants of the Most High God, come out!'"

Rachel held her breath.

"When the three men came out, everyone gathered around them. The ropes had burned but nothing else. Their hair wasn't burned. Their skin wasn't burned. Their clothes weren't burned. In fact, they were untouched. Not even the smell of smoke was on them."

No smell of smoke? How was that even possible?

"Then Nebuchadnezzar said, 'Praise be to the god of Shadrach, Meshach, and Abednego, for he has sent his angel and rescued his servants. They preferred to die rather than worship any god but their own. Anyone in my kingdom who speaks against their god will be cut into pieces and his house turned to rubble, for no other god can save in this way.'"

A fly buzzed in the hush. Someone swatted it, jolting Rachel back into the twentieth century. Rachel had heard Esther prattle on about stories with Naomi. Was this what she meant? Was this what she was doing with her workmates?

"The best way to get the story into our hearts," Joy said, "is to listen to it more than once. Help me fill in the blanks." Joy led the women through the story again, line by line, asking simple 'what happened next?' questions. Rachel had no problem identifying the different voices.

When they'd finished, Joy said, "Is anyone willing to retell the whole thing, as much as they remember?"

Mum wouldn't speak up. Would it be Esther or Gina?

"You do it, Esther," Gina said. "You're best at it."

Rachel's mind galloped ahead of Esther's storytelling. She smirked when she remembered two things Esther forgot.

There was a burst of chatter from the group. Was that it? Was no one going to ask anything at all? Her mind had enough questions to fill a junk shed, but there was no way she was going to poke her head out from behind the curtain and let people know she was there. They'd be too excited to see her.

Joy cleared her throat. "Esther, why don't you lead us in the usual questions."

Esther had talked a lot about Joy. Met her once a week or something like that.

"What do we learn about people from this story?" Esther asked.

"People are often stubborn."

Comments flew around, and Rachel wasn't clear who said what.

"Slow learners."

Was that true of herself? What if she dared to tell Esther why she always reacted against her? It wasn't Esther's fault that memories of her as a child had become tangled up with the nightmare of her own lost child. Lost. No, her child hadn't been lost. Rachel blinked back her tears and concentrated again.

"Some people are short fused—always blowing up when they don't get their way."

"Nebuchadnezzar tried to force people to follow him. 'Do as I say or else I'll wipe you out.' Many people are like that, although, perhaps in more subtle ways." That sounded like Gina.

Rachel's chest tightened. What was it about this group that made her wish she was out there with them? A longing swept across her heart. A longing like the thirst for an oasis in the Sahara. A longing for home. Rachel shivered as though a cool breeze caressed her skin.

"Let's think about the three young men," Joy said. "They chose to stand up to the king and die, but what other choices did they have?"

Rachel could think of a few, but what would the others say? Everyone had choices. She'd had choices with her baby, but she'd drowned her conscience and refused to go back to her grandmother. She'd been too stubborn, too proud, too foolish.

"Most people would have bowed," Mum said. "If it was me, I'd have placated my conscience by saying, 'It's only my body bowing, not my heart.'"

How had her mother placated her conscience when her teenage daughter ran away? Why hadn't the police come looking for her? It wasn't as if she'd run far.

Naomi chuckled. "They could have murdered the king or committed suicide or fled to a neighbouring country."

Rachel stifled a laugh. Naomi had said exactly what she'd been thinking.

"Could they have claimed sickness?" Gina asked. "Simply avoided turning up in the first place?"

"Good thoughts," Joy said. "What can we learn about these men from what they chose to do?"

There was silence. It was hard to sit here and not make a noise. To not give in to the urge to join them.

Gina answered first. "Honouring God was more important than their own lives."

Rachel bent at her waist, straining to hear. She must not bump the curtain and alert them to her presence.

"They're sharing their faith to the last moment," her mother added.

"They know that although God has the power to save, he doesn't always do so," Esther said. "This resonates with me. God had the power to heal my cancer, but he didn't choose to."

If only Rachel could ask her question. God delayed saving them until after they were thrown in the fire. Why did he do that?

Her mother's voice interrupted Rachel's ponderings. "Are we allowed to ask questions, Joy?"

"Certainly."

"I don't understand why God saves them when they're fully prepared to die."

Good on you, Mum.

The quietness was broken by the sound of a kookaburra cackling in the garden.

"Do you think it might be for the sake of Nebuchadnezzar?" Gina said.

Rachel's forehead brushed the curtain, and it swayed. Did anyone notice?

"God rescues them, not for their sake but for the sake of those who don't yet know him," Esther said.

Her mother's question generated others.

"After that stimulating discussion, why don't we praise God together?" Joy said.

Oh. Why were they stopping now? Just when things were interesting. Who would have thought she'd ever listen to a Bible story and find it fascinating? It was even relevant to some people. Not to her, of course. She was a long way from believing.

No, it was more like she was a long way from trusting. She'd believed as a little kid, but she'd rejected the god her father proclaimed. The god of Daniel and his friends seemed to be a different god altogether.

CHAPTER 40

"Come on, Miss Rachel." Josh tugged at her arm. "I've been potting all morning while you've been working on the display."

"Do you like it?"

He stuck his tongue out of the corner of his mouth. "Yes. You're better at it than the boss. I think Mr Pete will be happy."

Pete had settled in without causing any ripples. It helped that he used to spend his school holidays working at the nursery. Like his father, he rotated round the sections getting to know his team. He and Sam had spent the morning doing Rachel's grunt work. The display area now featured more than fifty pots of flowers. The wow factor came from a tinkling waterfall surrounded by maidenhair ferns.

"Hurry up." Josh said. "I like working with you."

It had been forever since someone had liked her just for her. Josh reminded her of Esther when she'd been a toddler. Always happy to see her and wanting someone to play with. Always uncomplicated.

Rachel's breath caught in her throat. What kind of God would allow Esther to be dangerously ill?

Josh had filled several trolleys already. "Look, I'm way ahead of you."

Rachel laughed. "You always will be. You're the champion of this." She set to work running her knife over the bottom of the pot to cut off the roots and then eased the plant out. "Do you want to do the whole process yourself, or work together doing half the task each?"

"You do the first part, and I'll put them in the new pot." He'd given her the easy task.

They were soon in a rhythm. Part of the satisfaction of working here was how soon they got to see results. It wouldn't be long until they'd repotted one hundred plants. The physical demands of the job had taken some adjustment, but she didn't regret the career change.

The one problem with the job was the amount of time for thinking. And thinking was not something she wanted to do. Not when Esther was fighting the alien invaders in her body. Already in her lungs and liver. Rachel's legs quivered. Right into the core of Esther's body. Her sister seemed cheerful and determined to keep working, but for how much longer? Was her cheerfulness another sort of denial? Would Esther still trust God if he allowed her to die?

"Why did you sigh?" Josh asked. "Are you sad?"

She hadn't realised she'd sighed out loud. Trust Josh to ask. He was sensitive to her moods.

"Yes, I'm sad."

He came around the bench and gave her a hug. "Why are you sad?"

"My sister, Esther, is sick."

"Real sick or only a little sick?"

"Real sick, Josh."

His brow wrinkled. "Sick-enough-to-die sick?"

Dying. That was exactly what she'd wanted to avoid thinking about. Avoiding Esther had seemed the better choice to shield herself from coming pain. Had she made the wrong choice? Esther was her sister. Her new-found sister. Esther couldn't die. How were they ever to become real sisters if she died? Icy fingers tinkled down Rachel's spine.

Never. Esther must not die.

Josh put his big, dirt-covered hand on her arm. "Does your sister know Jesus?"

If anyone else had asked this question, Rachel would have snapped at them, but this was Josh. She could no more be annoyed with him than with the questions Esther used to ask when she was a cuddly toddler. Rachel nodded and the first tear trickled down her cheek. Was she crying because of Esther's cancer, or because Esther had something she didn't have? Something she couldn't understand?

"Then Esther will be okay," Josh said. "If she dies, she'll go straight to be with Jesus."

Oh, to have his confidence. "How do you know that?"

He pursed his lips. Had she asked a question that was beyond him? Did he believe because he'd believe anything that anyone told him?

"I believe because Jesus says so. He rose from the dead, and he said we would as well. He said he was getting heaven ready for us."

What use was this? He'd parroted the words he'd been taught. He believed because Jesus said it, because he trusted Jesus. Well, she didn't trust Jesus. Jesus was her father's god, and any god of her father's wasn't worth knowing.

Rachel patted Josh's knee. "It's okay. I'm glad you believe in Jesus, but the problem is, I don't." She grabbed her knife and sliced across the roots at the bottom of the next pot.

"Why don't you believe in my Jesus?"

My Jesus. She'd perfected the way to cut Christians dead when they brought up Jesus, but she couldn't do it to Josh. Not to Josh who thought of Jesus as his Jesus. It would be like stabbing him with the knife in her hand.

"I do know ..." Rachel hesitated. "I do know Jesus existed two thousand years ago. His followers said he did miracles and he died on the cross." She believed those few historical facts, but little more. It would have been easy to fool the people in that unscientific age.

"He did do miracles," Josh said. "He walked on water and calmed a storm."

"Could the calming of the storm have been a coincidence? Could walking on water have been walking on a sandbar hidden out of their sight?"

Josh stuck out his chin. "Peter walked on water too."

True, and another sandbar was one coincidence too far. And it would have had to have been a sandbar with a big pit in the middle. Otherwise why would Peter have thought he was drowning? Rachel savagely pulled the plant out of the pot.

"Gently, Rachel. You'll break the plant." Josh looked at her again. "Jesus made blind people see and helped people who couldn't walk to walk again."

Could some of them have had emotional reasons why they couldn't see or walk?

"Jesus forgave sin. Everyone knows only God can do that."

Rachel had blocked these things out of her head years ago. Who would have thought they'd still be there? Now she remembered the whole story. It wasn't fair. Could she never escape her past?

"And Jesus raised the dead."

Josh was unstoppable. She had to risk hurting him if only to get him to shut up.

"The twelve-year-old girl might not have died. Even Jesus said she was only asleep." There was a horrible metallic taste in her mouth. Hurting Josh was no fun.

Josh chuckled. "There was a man called Lazarus who had been dead four days."

That was harder. The bandages alone would have been suffocating. "Maybe he wasn't dead after all. Maybe he revived in the tomb. He was in a cave tomb—there could have been air in there."

"You are silly." He giggled. "You can tell when someone is dead." He looked towards the floor.

"Look here." He picked up something and brought it across to her. "I'm not clever, but I know that fly is dead." He dropped it on the counter. Its legs stuck up in the air.

Rachel had no intention of giving in and no longer worried about hurting him. Josh was as resilient as the plants he dealt with every day. "Okay. What about Jesus' resurrection?"

"When Jesus came alive again?"

"Why do you believe he rose from the dead?"

Josh repotted another plant and patted around the base of it. His lips moved but no sound came out. Was he rehearsing an answer? "A lot of people saw Jesus after he came alive again." He stopped. "Lots of women. All the disciples. Those two blokes walking back to their town." He rubbed his nose, adding a streak of dirt. "It had a funny name."

"Emmaus." Once again she'd remembered something she'd thought buried.

"They didn't imagine Jesus to come back to life. Jesus showed them by getting them to touch him and feel the nail holes, and eating and other stuff." Josh peered at her. "You know what? I think you don't want to believe. Maybe you're afraid."

Rachel's knife slipped across the bottom of the pot. For someone who claimed not to be smart, he was certainly perceptive. The last thing she wanted to do was believe in Jesus. To believe in someone who demanded the same standards of perfection her father had. She'd endured them until the only choice was either to buckle and be crushed, or run. Why did she feel breathless, as though the crushing had happened anyway?

"Mr Dirk says we all have broken wings. I wonder what yours is?"

What was it about this guy? He skewered her under a microscope, ready for his diagnosis.

He tapped another pot to settle the soil and muttered, "What lies does Miss Rachel believe?"

Who was he talking to? Was he praying for what to say, or was he praying for her? A tingle went down her spine. Who would think she was worth praying for?

I do.

Where had that thought come from? Her whole body prickled with goosebumps, like a cool breeze loaded with the scent of flowers had blown across her wet skin.

"You know." Josh looked sternly at her. "You should go and talk to Mr Dirk. He's cleverer than me at listening to God. Had more practice. He can help you work out what is true." He finished another pot. "Yes. That's what you should do."

She wouldn't dare. It was one thing talking to Josh. He wasn't the rejecting kind. But Dirk? He was the boss. He had power over her future. Sharing her past would give him a hold over her.

What are you scared of?

Rachel shivered. She was scared of being seen for who she was. Empty. Worthless. Orphaned.

The last word startled her. She had a grandmother and sister. She had both her parents, even if she never intended to see one of them again.

CHAPTER 41

$\mathcal{T}$he first round of the new chemo had all the side effects of a placebo. The next round hit Esther hard. By Thursday morning, Esther couldn't stand her discomfort any more. She went to see Dr Webster.

"Rough week?"

Esther groaned. "I've been throwing up every day, and this hand-foot syndrome means I keep dropping things and can't sleep."

"We need to drop the dose." Dr Webster scribbled in the notes.

Did a drop in dose also mean a drop in effectiveness? "I hope it helps. I haven't even been able to manage half days at work and I'm considering resigning."

Dr Webster peered at her over his reading glasses. "That's a major step."

"I've been praying, and it seems the best option for both the department and myself."

Dr Webster didn't even flinch at what he usually considered 'religious talk.'

"My colleagues are carrying me, and they shouldn't have to. I need my energy to battle cancer. If, one day, I need another job, God is more than able to provide one."

"I admire your faith."

He always accused her of unreasoned faith. Esther grinned cheekily. "It's not a blind faith, for God has never let me down. Not once."

Esther had spent hours in prayer since the return of her cancer. Praying for all the people she still wanted to talk about Jesus with. Praying about her future. Praying about how to use whatever time she had left. She was also getting her business affairs in order.

"I had another thing I wanted to ask you, but I don't know if it's your role."

His eyes flicked to the clock behind her head. "I've got time."

"I want to know about palliative care."

He didn't blink. "What do you want to know?"

"You're not denying I might need it."

"No, but palliative care isn't the only option. You can stay at home and be nursed there."

Being at home among familiar things sounded tempting. "I don't think it would work. Gran would be willing, but she's in her eighties and she's already emotionally supporting my mother and sister. Dad's no use. He still denies I'm sick."

"Is this one of those things you pray about?"

Did he finally raise a spiritual topic on his own?

"It certainly is. Prayer reminds me God is in control, and that keeps me thankful."

He smoothed his eyebrow. "I don't pretend to understand you."

The radical nature of the biblical worldview had only become apparent when she'd started sharing it with everyone. It had generated laughter, sometimes concealed and sometimes not. It had generated ridicule and jokes, usually from the men. It had generated anger and rejection. Seldom had it generated joyous acceptance. Her own sister thought her mad.

"The more I read the Bible, the more I see things from God's point of view."

"Was that an unsubtle way of finding out if I did what I promised?"

Esther laughed. "Perhaps." How exciting. The long-prayed-for melt seemed to be well underway.

"Don't die of shock, but during my holiday I finished the second book you gave me, and I've read up to Exodus chapter eighteen. I know you suggested I read Luke, but reading from the beginning made more sense to me."

Why was it that, despite praying, she still doubted God would work? As if people's freedom of choice was stronger than God's love for them.

"You're about to hit some tough stuff—lots of laws. What about finishing to the ten commandments, then skip to Luke. If you develop a deeper interest, you can read the other chunks of history later."

"I'll keep reading as long as you keep hanging in there," Dr Webster said.

"It's a deal." They solemnly shook on it.

Esther changed the topic. Saying less often kept people thirsting for more. "Back to palliative care. How do I know when I'm ready?"

"I'll let you know, but I continue to hope you won't need it."

She'd never have guessed he'd become human. Was it just with her, or were other people noticing changes? "I hope so as well, but I want to be prepared. Investigating my choices now will make it easier later."

He stood up and opened a drawer in his filing cabinet. "If only all our clients were like you." He flipped through the hanging files. "We've got plenty of brochures on the choices in this area."

"Do you have one for the place across the street? Being there would be the most convenient for my friends, family, and workmates."

He came back and handed her a few different brochures. "Don't let all this talk make you lose hope."

Esther looked directly at him. "What I hope in is never going to fail."

CHAPTER 42

*R*achel had crept out of the house at daybreak. During the summer months, the non-sales staff were allowed to come in early to work in the cool of the morning. She could have left at three each day, but she hadn't told her family. It was easier to pretend she had loads of overtime.

Today, Rachel clocked off at three. She had an appointment. An appointment she'd dithered about for days.

The Kloppers only lived through the back fence of the nursery, but it was further by road. Rachel parked her car next to the curb and clutched the steering wheel. What if talking to Dirk made things worse?

Rat-a-tat-tat.

Rachel jumped.

"My husband says come in. The kettle's on."

It was too late to change her mind. Rachel grabbed her purse, locked the car, and followed Mrs Klopper into the house. All houses have a distinct feel. Her apartment had been a temporary residence, like a hermit crab's shell. Her parents' home had been formal and stylish, but soulless. Naomi's place enveloped her in warmth. This house was filled with elegant carvings of African animals and a couple of gallery-quality oil paintings. Outwardly, the house was totally unlike Gran's place, but there was something similar. A clean, wholesome, family-feel. A house that had been lived in. Loved in.

Dirk was sitting in the lounge looking out the big front window. "I shouldn't sit here. I can see the weeds." He chuckled. "A bad advertisement for the nursery."

"You know Pete would do it if you asked him." Mrs Klopper arrived with the teapot.

"He's got more than enough to do and some big decisions to make."

Rachel pricked up her ears.

"Milk and sugar?"

She'd have preferred coffee. "Just milk, thanks."

"The specialist is pleased at my progress but doesn't think I should have the burden of the business. Pete needs to make up his mind whether to move over here or not."

Pete as boss? Pete was a younger version of Dirk in many ways, but there was a vast difference between standing in for someone and being the boss. Would he keep on guys like Josh? The place wouldn't be the same without them. Klopper's wasn't a business. It was a family.

"We're all praying about it."

So Pete was a Christian too? Why did that make her feel depressed?

"There's a lot he'd have to wrap up in Perth. Resign from work, sell his house, and buy a new one here."

"And what about his family?" There. Rachel had asked the question. She examined her tea as if reading the tea leaves.

"He'll tell you more if he wants to, but I'll tell you what I told the trio. I didn't want them bursting with questions." Dirk pointed at the photo wall she'd briefly glimpsed in the hallway. "We took some of the photos down before Pete came. His wife died the year before last."

Died? How? And what was there about the death that meant the photos needed to be taken down? There was no point asking. If Dirk said it wasn't his right to share, he meant it. Perhaps that was why she'd come today. He had both wisdom and discretion, rare qualities in today's world.

Dirk watched her over the rim of his tea cup. What did he see? The beautiful blonde others saw? Or the wreck with the broken wing? The nightmares had returned after Esther's diagnosis. How long would it be until driving off the cliff again felt like a sensible choice?

Dirk and Norma exchanged a look.

"Rachel, I have to walk twice a day. Would you be willing to accompany me?"

"Okay. I'll grab my water bottle and hat from the car and slap on some sunscreen."

They set off at a steady pace.

"I'll take you on my usual loop. It keeps me away from the nursery."

"Do you miss it?"

"Yes, but visitors like Josh help."

Rachel couldn't help it. She smiled.

"You should smile more often. Josh makes me smile too. I was sure you'd get along with him."

"He's sort of soothing." Like an ice-cold lemon, lime, and bitters. "Does your wife usually walk with you?"

"Usually, but I told her not to come today."

So that was what the look had meant. Did Dirk sense she wanted to talk to him? Probably. Would he help make sense of the tangled threads of her life? Threads that threatened to strangle her.

Dirk kept walking. Rachel followed, content not to pay attention to where she was going. The road was lined with trees. A lawnmower hummed in the distance.

The road began to wind upwards. "Don't worry. The doctor says hills are a good workout."

Could he read her mind? She both hoped so and hoped not. It might make things easier if he could. There was so much she was ashamed of. Her choices had coated her heart in muddy sludge.

They came to the top of the road. It swept around in a circle, and Dirk led her over towards the edge and leaned on the back of a bench. She could see back down to the trees in the nursery. Beyond that were more trees and more houses and more nurseries. In the distance was the smudgy blue of the mountains.

"Beautiful, isn't it? I never get tired of this view. I come up here to pray. It helps clear my mind." He turned to her. "But you didn't come to drink tea and walk with me, did you?"

Rachel shook her head. "I wanted to tell you about what led me to the cliff edge."

He patted the back of the bench. "Well, let's sit a while. Why don't you start by telling me about your family?"

She told him about her parents and schooling. "For Dad, everything was always about his reputation. If I got dirty or started giggling or did anything that he didn't approve of, he told me I'd never be a Proverbs 31 woman. I hated that woman." The venom in her voice shocked her. Why couldn't she laugh it off?

"And you never questioned your father's interpretation of the Bible?"

"I was a child and he was the big-shot preacher. It never occurred to me he could be wrong."

"Did you ever look up the passage for yourself?"

"No."

"It's important to look at the context of Bible passages people manipulate for their own ends."

If only she'd met Dirk or someone like him earlier. She'd never considered her father might manipulate the Bible, not when he sounded so sure of himself.

Dirk was silent. Was he regretting his decision to let her talk?

"I'm praying about what is best."

There he was, reading her mind again. It was uncanny. It might be downright creepy with someone else, but Dirk prayed because he cared.

"I think you should tell me everything first."

How much of everything should she tell him? Her head urged her to keep quiet, but her heart urged her to spill everything. Dirk was safe. If she closed her heart today, she'd regret it forever.

She took a deep breath to still her racing heart and started right back with her decision to run away from her parents, then her grandmother. How naive she'd been. She'd had no idea how hard it would be to rent a place. No idea how many people were paid the minimum wage but expected to work more hours. No idea how expensive it was to live on your own. She'd believed her good, if truncated education, would get her a decent job.

Dirk remained silent. This must be why Roman Catholics went to confession. Pouring out her soul was soothing.

Rachel's hands sweated as she talked about the abortion. She didn't sugar-coat anything. If Dirk despised her, then so be it. She was tired of keeping secrets. What good had keeping secrets ever done her?

"That's why I planned to drive off the cliff. Life didn't seem worth living any more. I was tired of not sleeping, tired of night-mares, tired of constantly feeling guilty. And tired of trying to struggle on alone."

"There is one last thing you haven't told me. Why did you go back to your grandmother's?"

Trust him not to miss the one gap. Even now, the way she'd tested God that day at David Jones sounded unbelievable. She told him the story.

Dirk didn't laugh out loud. Didn't gasp. Didn't tell her not to be ridiculous.

"I told you God loves you. He's done the equivalent of writing across the sky to get your attention."

Rachel slid her hands under her thighs. "Even if I accepted that the puncture, meeting you, the handstand man, and my applying for a job at your nursery were caused by God, I don't understand why. I'm not worthy of his attention."

Dirk turned to look at her and smiled a smile of such sweetness that tears sprang into her eyes. "That's the whole point. None of us are worthy of his attention."

"You seem a wonderful sort of man."

"Seem is the operative word. How can I illustrate it?" He rubbed his ear. "It's like in a war. It doesn't matter if you have a new gun that can kill a lot of people or an old gun that can only kill one or two. Or even if you're the cook and never kill anyone. If the other side captures any of you, you're labelled 'enemy'." He coughed. "It's not the volume of our sin, but whose side we're on."

Rachel pictured the situation he'd described. "It doesn't seem right to me. How could someone like a Hitler be forgiven?"

"God doesn't think of things like an accountant. He thinks of things like a father."

Her guts turned to water. "And I react negatively whenever I think about anyone being like a father."

"Having listened to your story, I think you've been searching for a father all your life."

"I. Don't. Need. A. Father."

Dirk grunted. "I thought the same. The problem is that, like me, you looked in the wrong places and for the wrong sort of father."

Rachel wiped her palms on her trousers.

"My father wasn't an easy man to love. Boer farmers are tough. They have to be." Dirk grimaced. "I didn't love him, but I respected him. I didn't dare not respect him, but I longed for closeness."

Maybe the longings of a boy in South Africa weren't too different to the longings of a girl in Sydney.

"The situation wasn't helped by the way the church and my father used the Bible. Their God was a distant, terrifying judge. The kind of God who only the people at the top of the pack could appreciate. A God who was useful for keeping the weak in line. I wanted nothing to do with him."

More experiences in common.

"I only had two choices. Toe the line or become a prodigal." He winked. "At the time, becoming a prodigal sounded more fun. Stupid me. I wasted a lot of time before my father-in-law showed me I was running from a false god. The God of the Bible was nothing like my father had led me to believe. He was a God of grace through and through."

"Grace —I've hated that word." Rachel frowned. "Perhaps I've been wrong about grace."

"Most of us are wrong about grace. I had to see grace demonstrated before I finally understood it." He looked across at her. "Lots of people think it's a weak word. Something wishy-washy. If they understood grace, they'd know it's as strong as steel." He stared off towards the Blue Mountains. "I said I was a prodigal. Do you remember the story?"

She nodded.

"The son had to sink to the level of feeding pigs before he woke up. I never got that low, but who knows how low I'd have gone if God hadn't stepped in and allowed me to meet Norma."

How low would Rachel have sunk if the old lady hadn't overlooked her age and rented her that first room? Or if there'd been no job at the fish and chip shop? The first boss hadn't been generous, but he hadn't asked for anything inappropriate either. Other runaways weren't so lucky.

Lucky?

Maybe it hadn't been luck. If Dirk was to be believed, it was a loving God caring for her.

"The father demonstrates grace. No matter how badly his sons treated him, he was there waiting to forgive them and welcome them home. Do you remember what the father said when the younger son says he's no longer worthy to be called his father's son?"

No longer worthy. Strange that he would use those words. Naomi's love always made her feel unworthy.

"Kill the best calf, pull out the best robe," Dirk said. "My son who was lost is now found; who was dead is now alive."

It was like someone had plucked a sweet note on a guitar string. The music reverberated through the chambers of her heart.

"That's the father I serve. The God who called me home many years ago. Jesus specifically identified the father in this parable as the heavenly Father. He's a father who is beyond our wildest imaginings. He never says, 'I told you so.'"

She remembered that.

"The father sees his son and runs. Runs, not walks, to welcome him home."

Rachel stared at the horizon.

Home. That was where the handstand man had told her to go. She'd been sure he'd meant Naomi's place, but maybe he'd meant something deeper. Something more permanent. Home to a heavenly Father. Was that what she'd been missing all these years?

"Was this the first time you've told anyone your whole story?"

"Yes."

"You need to tell your family."

She shivered. Impossible. Naomi maybe, but Mum? Esther? Impossible.

"Secrets have a way of building high walls between people."

How did he know what life had been like at her grandmother's?

"Promise me you'll think about it? I'll be praying. I know it won't be easy, but they need to know."

They would be the toughest words she'd ever had to say. The delicate relationship she had with her sister might not survive her revelations but time could be short. What if trying and failing was better than never trying at all?

CHAPTER 43

*E*sther felt odd. Weak and lethargic, as though all her blood had drained out of her body overnight. She staggered to the bathroom and threw up. Grabbing the door frame, she hauled herself upright. Something was wrong with her eyes. Black spots danced across her vision. Two lamps instead of one, two plants by the window, and two Bibles beside her bed. The multicoloured book spines in her bookcase merged, making her queasy.

How hard could it be to take the four steps to the bed? Esther launched herself away from the door frame. Bad idea. She fell, hitting her head on the way down. There was now a ringing in her ears. Fear clutched her with icy claws and twisted her gut. What was happening? This wasn't on the list of side effects.

"Rachel." Her voice came out as a tiny squeak. Then she remembered she'd heard Rachel leave for work hours before. Would her grandmother hear her?

Esther took a bigger breath, willing her voice to be strong. "Gran."

What if Gran was already out on the verandah? She closed her eyes. She couldn't crawl, but could she roll across the floor towards the door?

At the door, she prayed for strength and called again. "Gran."

Slow footsteps came up the hall.

Naomi gasped. "Esther, what's happened?"

"Don't know." It was an effort to speak. "Dizzy. Seeing double. Fell over."

Gran clutched the doorpost. "Is it a side effect of the drugs?"

Esther squeezed her eyes shut. Could she avoid throwing up all over the carpet? "Can you help me back to bed?"

"I'm going to ring your mother."

Even thinking about moving left Esther exhausted. "I'll stay here. Lying down should be safe enough."

Gran came back promptly, hands fluttering. "We need to take you to hospital. Your mum will be here as fast as she can."

How many more hospital trips would she have to make? Couldn't she lie in bed, eyes closed, and let life drift by for a few days?

"Lie there and tell me what to pack."

Between them, they filled a small backpack with clothes and toiletries. Esther crawled onto a sturdy chair, and Naomi helped her dress. She stuffed her arms in the openings Naomi held ready.

"Gran, I'm going to need a bucket."

A car tooted and Esther allowed herself to be led outside.

It was yet another morning of tests. Blood and a full body scan. Usually the technicians were full of laughs, but today there were no smiles, no jokes, no excess words. A heaviness settled over Esther, a gloom of impending disaster. Surely it couldn't be any more bad news? She was having chemo to buy her time beyond twelve months. This was way too soon.

Eventually, Esther was shunted into a side room to rest. She allowed the whispers to lull her into a doze.

She was jerked out of sleep when Dr Webster came in, his

mouth a hard, straight line. This could only mean one thing. Things were bad. Really bad.

"It's not a drug reaction, is it?" Esther said. "Has the cancer metastasised to my brain?"

"There are disadvantages to having a medical background."

Was that a tremor she heard in his voice? Esther attempted a joke, striving for control. "You mean we ... we scare ourselves by imagining the worst."

"Not this time," he said. His voice was gentle, so gentle she almost missed the next words. "This *is* the worst."

This was it. The death sentence. No hope remaining, no false platitudes, no time. She'd expected fear. She'd expected tears. She'd expected rebellion against the thought.

What she hadn't expected was peace.

God had been preparing her for weeks. Holding her in his almighty hand. This was why she'd felt the urging to complete the tasks on her mind. They were almost done. When the final summons came, she'd be ready.

"How long?"

"It's variable, but with your diagnosis, I was worried from the start."

"You didn't show it."

"I've trained myself not to. It's my job to give people hope."

Was that another quaver in Paul's voice? When had she stopped thinking of him as Dr Webster and started thinking of him as Paul? He had indeed become human. "You've never discouraged me. Should I be going to palliative care now?"

"You'll be better at home unless you begin to have more symptoms."

So there would be more symptoms. Weren't the ones she had more than enough? "What's possible?"

He was silent, as though debating with himself whether to tell the truth. He stared at the floor. "More falls, paralysis, seizures, or headaches."

"Not a fun future."

"No."

This truthfulness was obviously hard for him. How could she let him know she felt a peace she'd never experienced before? He'd probably interpret it as denial, but it was in a different category altogether.

"What did the scans show?"

He avoided her eyes.

"I want to know. It helps me prepare."

"Your body is not responding to treatment."

Did he normally look so ravaged at such news? If so, his job must be hell.

"The scan showed multiple metastases in the brain, and your lungs and liver have deteriorated. There are also suspicious spots on some of your bones. We could look further at those."

"It sounds like a waste of resources to do more tests and treatment. I'll talk to my family, and we'll pray about it."

"I envy you your family."

What aspect of her family was he envying? The fact that they did things together? "God has done miracles." She'd nearly said 'miracles have been happening', but she wasn't willing to deny God his glory. Miracles didn't happen in the abstract. They were instigated by the master of miracles.

"I knew you'd credit God." Dr Webster's voice cracked. "Most people would look at you and conclude your God was either a figment of your imagination or didn't care."

Was this 'most people's' opinion or his own?

"If I didn't believe he cared, I'd have given up long ago. I'm thankful for these last twelve months."

Paul raised one eyebrow. "Sometimes I can't decide if you're nuts or if I want what you have."

"If this is nuts, it's a great state to be in. If the choice is between thankfulness or bitterness, I've made the right choice. I'd hate to go through this without Jesus."

"You almost sound excited."

"You know, I think I am. God made a sublime world the first time. Picture it at the dawn of creation. No plastic. No pollution. No deforestation." A joy oozed through her. "The hiker in me starts leaping in anticipation. God's kingdom will be a million times better than anything you or I could dream up." Esther stretched her arms wide. "No, a trillion, trillion times better. I'll have a body that can't hurt or fall or break."

Paul cleared his throat. "What proof do you have of all this?"

Most doctors would have left her to her delusions at a time like this. *Lord, help.* "What proof would I need?"

"I'm not sure what proof I'd accept." Paul scratched his nose.

"I'd want a heap of trustworthy eyewitnesses," Esther said. "I'd not be willing to gamble eternity on anything less."

Was it only a few hours ago that she could barely function? "Actually, I've got even better proof. I have a man raised from the dead and this man never told a lie."

Paul's gaze seemed to pierce her heart. Was he trying to discern if she was a liar or a madwoman? "I presume you mean Jesus. I'm not sure I fully accept the Bible as history."

So the book she'd given him hadn't completely dealt with this issue. Not unexpected. A lifetime of scepticism doesn't vanish overnight.

"Jesus told his disciples several times that he'd rise from the dead, but they were still caught out. They weren't idiots. They knew dead men don't walk out of the tomb themselves."

Thank you, Lord, for the strength to talk. "When Jesus appeared to them after the resurrection, he had to give them all kinds of proofs he wasn't a ghost. He encouraged them to touch him, and he ate fish in front of them. To make quite, quite sure, he allowed five hundred people to see him."

"They might all have been wrong."

"Come on P ... Dr Webster." She'd almost called him by his first name. "How do you get five hundred people to have a mass hallucination in different places? How do you get five hundred people to agree to lie and not one of them ever changes their testimony? And how do you explain the disciples going from cringing in fear to being willing to go to prison and die for Jesus? Their transformation only makes sense if they were convinced Jesus had risen from the dead."

"I haven't read the parts you mention yet."

"Where are you up to?"

"Halfway through Luke."

She'd thought he'd be further along by now.

"I ended up reading Joshua, Judges, and Samuel first."

He was taking the reading seriously. "Keep reading Luke, then jump to Acts. Acts will show you what it cost people to believe Jesus rose from the dead. It wasn't all a bed of roses."

"I still find it incredible that an intelligent, modern woman believes all this stuff about miracles and virgin births."

At last he was bringing his objections out into the open. "You're amazed? I'm amazed at scientists who refuse to believe in a creative designer and prefer to believe in random chance. That takes more faith than I have." She clenched her fists. "Everything depends on our assumptions. Some people assume God doesn't exist and start from there. I assume the opposite."

Had she said too much? There was no point hammering at the door of a locked mind. Paul's hands on the bed rail were relaxed.

"I look at Jesus and ask who he was. His generation knew he was claiming to be God. They wanted to kill him for it."

"There are people in mental homes who think they're God."

Paul's objection wasn't original and it was one she'd prepared for.

"It doesn't take long to discount their claim and diagnose their problem. John's Gospel contains more of Jesus's claims. It's shocking and startling, unless it's true. Good questions to ask would be, who does Jesus think he is? What proof is there to back up his claims? Come on, put on your scientist's glasses and look at the other possibilities. Was Jesus mad? Was he a megalomaniac? Was he a liar? Follow the evidence."

"You're determined to make me work."

"But think about the benefits. If you decide it's all rubbish, then you have a rebuttal for every other Christian who ever bothers you."

Paul guffawed. "Now that gives me strong motivation to complete the job. A lifetime's excuse to silence Christians." He glanced at his watch. "I'd better head home."

"If you visit all your patients, you must be exhausted."

Did she detect the tiniest of blushes?

"This visit was two percent business and the rest as a friend."

Esther lay there, totally drained but exhilarated. All through the conversation it had been obvious that the Holy Spirit was giving her the words she needed. *Oh Lord, I need the same help to speak to Rachel.* Would she respond well or was she more like their father than she'd like to admit?

Did it matter?

Esther's responsibility was to do what Jesus wanted, even if everything exploded in her face.

CHAPTER 44

*R*achel put the key in the front door and walked inside. All was quiet. Much too quiet.

"Gran? Esther? Are you here?" Her voice rang out. No answer. Had something happened to Gran? Why hadn't they called her?

She put her bag down inside the front door and searched the house. The note was on the kitchen table.

ESTHER HAD A FALL.

Rachel's stomach cramped. Esther, not Gran.

DIZZY AND NAUSEOUS. YOUR MUM AND I HAVE TAKEN HER TO HOSPITAL.

Had she left things too late?

Adrenalin coursed through her. She drove as fast as she dared. What if Esther was already past talking? What if she died believing Rachel hated her? *God, if you're there and really care, don't let Esther die.*

The room reeked of disinfectant. Rachel wrinkled her nose.

"Sorry about the smell," Esther said. "We've had a hectic few hours, what with my vomiting and falling."

Rachel's eyes widened. "Are you okay?"

"Nothing broken." Esther ran her right hand down her left arm. "But I'll have another set of bruises."

Naomi was seated in the corner. Gran being here was okay—she wasn't the shockable kind.

"Pull a chair over, Rachel. I need to talk to you."

Rachel obeyed.

"Closer," Esther said. "I've spent all morning knowing I must say sorry while I still can." She grabbed Rachel's arm. "I've been a total idiot. Angry at you for not living up to my fantasies. Angry at Mum and Dad for keeping quiet about you."

"Some of your anger was justified."

"Maybe towards Mum and Dad, but not towards you. You didn't need to fulfil my fantasy about what a sister should be."

And she hadn't been anything like a normal sister. It wasn't Esther's fault that her eyes jerked Rachel back into her nightmares. Things had been different once. Back when she'd cuddled her baby sister and vowed to protect her and be her hero. In the end, she hadn't been a hero to anyone.

"There must be reasons for the way you react to me. Like you hate the sight of me—"

Was this the lead-in for her own confessions?

"—but nothing excused my attitude to you. My desire for harmony wasn't wrong, but I went about it the wrong way." A tear trickled down Esther's cheek. "Joy and Gina helped me to see what I was doing. I was playing God. I rushed ahead of his timing and tried to manipulate the situation. I'm sorry. Especially for making things worse for you."

Rachel clamped her lips together. She would never get through what she needed to say if she cried now. "Thanks," she mumbled. She stared at the wall.

Esther kept quiet. Probably praying. It used to irritate Rachel, but she needed all the prayer she could get.

"I had a long talk to Dirk this afternoon, and he suggested I tell you my story." She swallowed. "All of it, if I can manage." Her heart pounded in her chest.

"Would it be okay if I moved a little closer?" Naomi asked.

Rachel got up to help move the big armchair.

"You've been patient with my silence, but you must let me talk without interrupting or I'll break down. I was ten when you were born, Esther." Rachel looked directly at her sister for the first time. "You're almost a stranger to me now, but I adored you back then."

Esther's eyebrows rose. No wonder. It wasn't as if Rachel had ever given any indication of adoration.

"But even my love for you wasn't enough. I hated the pressure of being William B. Macdonald's daughter. I hated having to look like a doll and behave like one too. I hated being urged to 'be a Proverbs 31 woman and think about our reputation.'" Rachel mimicked and mocked the words that had almost destroyed her. "Of course, when Dad said 'our' reputation, I knew he meant his reputation. It went on day and night, like a dripping tap. What I hated most was when he used the Bible to manipulate me. Why couldn't he be honest enough to see he was using God to get his own way?"

Rachel twisted her hands in her lap. "As a young teenager, it felt like the whole church was against me. And if the church was against me, I figured God must be as well. How can someone fight the creator of the universe? I tried, but the more Dad used the Bible, the more I hated his god. It got so bad that I felt physically sick when I was dragged to church."

Rachel swallowed the bile in her throat. Gran and Esther were listening quietly as she'd asked. Did they have any idea how hard this was for her? And these were the less traumatic parts of the story.

"I was in a terrible state when I arrived at Gran's. Maybe it would have been easier if you had been an ogre. You were too kind. I wasn't ready for your Jesus after an overdose of Dad's."

Gran wiped her already damp cheeks.

"Now I'm older, I see the dilemma you were in. You didn't want to leave me alone, but it felt to me like you were in the same game as Dad."

"I'm sorry. I didn't see how badly you were hurting," Naomi said.

"Gran, only a total fool would run away from you. When a teenager runs away, they're in terrible danger." Rachel shuddered. "In some ways, I was lucky."

Gran would say luck had nothing to do with it. Having lived here all these months it wouldn't surprise her to discover Gran had almost worn her knees out praying.

Rachel kept her head down. "I didn't end up in the worst kind of mess, but only because someone found me first." She looked up. "Esther, don't cry."

"I can't help it, hearing the pain you have gone through."

Rachel swallowed and her eyes filled with tears. Pain had deadened her heart, but what was it about kindness? Kindness could crack a heart of stone.

"I felt worse whenever a relationship ended. My whole life was about pleasing men." She flushed. "So pathetic for a modern woman."

"I waited and waited for you to come home," Naomi said, voice trembling.

Rachel covered her face with her hands. "I wanted to come, but I didn't deserve you."

Could she even do this? Could she say the words that might push them further apart?

"Is there something more?" Naomi's voice was a gentle whisper.

Rachel squirmed and stared at her feet. "I can't tell you."

"Don't be afraid," Naomi said.

The empathy overwhelmed her. Head down, Rachel hugged her arms around her body. Naomi murmured endearments like she was talking to a toddler.

Oh, if only she could bask in the comfort without saying any more. They still liked her. Now. Would they still treat her this way after she told the whole story? It had been hard enough already. Surely she'd said enough.

But Dirk would ask. He'd reminded her she couldn't hide from family. Not if she wanted to walk the road to freedom. Right now, freedom sounded the best gift in the world.

"We'll love you no matter what you did." Esther's eyes were full of pain and compassion.

Rachel gulped. Her nightmare was back. The child's accusing eyes. The chant. Murderer. Murderer. Murderer. She moaned and rocked backwards and forwards.

Esther gripped her arm tighter.

"Too much." Rachel rocked and moaned. "It's too much."

"What's too much, dear?" Naomi said.

"You are." Rachel moaned again. "I don't deserve your kindness. If you knew what I did, you'd throw me out." Rocking, rocking, rocking. "Have nothing to do with me. You wouldn't treat me, like a beloved ... family member."

Esther shuffled down the bed and enveloped her in a hug. "You are a beloved family member."

Rachel cried harder. "Oh nooo. You wouldn't say that if you knew. I shouldn't have come home. I'm dirty. No use to anyone."

Words tumbled out of her mouth. Endless repetitions of unworthiness. Endless repetitions of private torment. Pus and pain and gunk, washed with a deluge of cleansing tears.

At last, she hiccupped to a stop. "Sorry about all that."

"Don't be sorry," Naomi said. "It sounded like it needed to come out."

"Gran." Rachel used the heel of her hand to wipe her nose. "I don't think I can bear to sit in the same room with you."

Esther handed over two tissues. "We want you to. It's where you belong."

"But I don't feel like I belong."

Naomi stood up, placed her hand under Rachel's chin and angled her head up. "Listen here, young lady. You need to listen to the truth instead of lies. You are part of this family. And you belong here, no matter what you've done. You're stuck with us."

"You might change your mind when you hear the rest."

"Nothing will make me change my mind," Gran said.

Maybe Gran would accept her, but would Esther? Would this final revelation be the last straw?

"Come on. Out with what's bothering you."

Was she going to throw up all over Esther's knees? Her secret blocked her throat, choking her.

Esther's lips moved. Was she praying?

"I ..." She swallowed as the contents of her stomach rose in her throat. "I killed my baby."

Esther clenched her fists.

"I killed a defenceless human being because I didn't want to lose my job." She put her forehead on her hands. Her whole body quivered. A wave of sorrow engulfed her and dragged her down.

Long moments passed. She could hear Esther crying too. Rachel didn't dare to raise her head and look at Esther.

Esther blew her nose. "Thank you for trusting us with your pain. I knew something was crushing you, but I didn't know what."

Rachel sniffed. "I never could explain it to people. Maybe it's the way I was raised, but I never could see this like others do."

"Dearie," Gran said. "I'm pleased this wasn't something you could shrug off. That would indicate someone without conscience and without humanity."

Rachel finally dared to raise her head. Esther was looking at her with eyes full of tears. She leaned forward and hugged Rachel.

"I'm terribly sorry for all you've gone through."

Rachel hugged her back. How was it possible that she was being treated like this? How could she have misjudged Esther to this extent?

"I used to fantasise about coming back to Gran's, but I never dared."

"Oh, I wish you'd come." Naomi stroked Rachel's hand.

"Sometimes I came and stood outside."

"Why did you come back?" Naomi asked.

"One of my friends had a miscarriage. I think it triggered the nightmares I used to get after the abortion." She looked at Esther again. "In the nightmares, my child would be running away. Then she'd turn and accuse me of being a murderer." She shivered. "Somehow my child would merge with my early memories of you. At the end, it was always your eyes accusing me."

Esther gave a tremulous smile. "No wonder you never looked at me. I'm sorry I didn't understand."

"It wasn't your fault." Rachel cleared her throat. "Gran, in my mind, my early memories of Esther were like a string of pearls. Beautiful memories that hurt to think about. I kept those pearls of memory locked in a mental drawer."

Gran's eyes widened. "So that's why you went deathly pale when I gave you the pearl necklace all those years ago."

"It was a trigger for things I wanted to forget." Rachel sighed. "Eventually, my nightmares pushed me over the edge."

Esther twisted her hands in her lap.

"But even at suicide, I was a failure."

"Oh, Rachel," Esther said.

Rachel's stomach churned. This was harder than she'd believed possible, but it needed to all come out. She told them all about Dirk and ended with the story of what had happened her final day at David Jones. "A stranger told me to go home. My feet seemed to bring me to your door of their own accord." Rachel sniffed. "I'm not sure how long I lay there. Maybe I hoped to absorb some of your love through my skin. I never intended you to find me. The first knock was an accident. The second time, I barely brushed my fingers against the screen."

"I wouldn't have heard you if I hadn't been unable to sleep," Esther said. "I doubt that was an accident."

Rachel used to get irritated at any mention of God, but things were different now.

"I will never forget that light coming on as long as I live. When you threw your arms around me, I knew I was where I wanted to be."

Naomi and Esther grasped her hands.

"Yes," Esther said with a thousand-watt smile. "You were home."

CHAPTER 45

*E*sther was at home for five days. On the sixth, she woke with a headache—an inadequate word for the throbbing monster trying to claw its way out of her head. Its titanium talons had a stranglehold around her head and neck, an only-morphine-will-help kind of headache. With frightening swiftness, she found herself in the palliative care ward. The first dose of morphine temporarily tamed the monster to a kitten, but slowed her mind to a sloth-like pace.

Mum arrived an hour later, looking ten years older. Esther smiled a weak welcome. Mum sat down and took Esther's hand.

"I've cancelled all my appointments to be here. Would that be a help or a hindrance?"

"The best kind of help. Gina has driven Gran home to get my pyjamas and toiletries." Esther smiled. One corner of her mouth dragged. "And the blue teapot. It will make this place seem more homelike."

"I'm sorry our home hasn't been yours lately."

Esther squeezed Mum's hand. It was easier than talking.

Mum teared up and fumbled in her handbag for a handkerchief. Heart-rending to watch her family battle with grief.

"How is Dad going to handle you being here?"

Blanche blew her nose. "He'll have to lump it. My mind is made up."

"Can you write a note for me, asking him to come? I can't bear the thought of not seeing him again."

They composed the note together. The headache had stolen Esther's eyesight to the point she could no longer read.

"I'll make sure he reads it at lunch," Mum said. "I've been praying for him constantly."

"Gran has prayed for forty years. Sometimes I wish God would knock some sense into Dad."

"It took thirty-plus years for Nebuchadnezzar."

"You've been reading Daniel." The mother that Esther had known up to last year would never have presumed she had anything worthwhile to say about the Bible.

"Who would have thought I could learn from someone who lived two and a half thousand years ago?"

Esther yawned. "Sorry. The medication makes me sleepy."

Mum stood up and smoothed out her wrinkled skirt. "I'll head home and prepare your father's lunch, and do my best to get him to come this afternoon."

"If he does come, can you take any visitors away? There's no way he'll talk in front of anyone else."

---

*E*sther opened her eyes. Rachel was draped over a chair in the corner, Naomi was quietly knitting, and Mum was back. No Dad. She hadn't expected he'd come, but she'd prayed he would. How could he live with himself if he missed his chance to say goodbye?

Mum pulled over a chair and laid her hand on Esther's blanket-covered leg. "I've had an eventful few hours."

"I wouldn't have thought lunch with Dad would be eventful."

"Then you'd be wrong." Blanche heaved an enormous sigh. "I think I've been thrown out."

"What do you mean?" Rachel's feet hit the floor as she sat bolt upright.

"I delivered Esther's note. During our subsequent conversation, I said things that should have been said decades ago."

My goodness. What had given their conflict-phobic mother this courage?

Rachel snorted. "I assume he didn't take that well."

"I've been ignoring my conscience for years." Blanche looked first at Rachel, then at Esther and Naomi. "My childhood was full of conflict. As a result, I condoned things I shouldn't have condoned." She sobbed. Broken sobs like she was choking on jagged glass.

Esther reached out her hand. "Mum, you don't have to go on."

"Don't stop me, Esther." Blanche turned to Rachel. "This should have been said long ago. I'm sorry I wasn't a good mother to you."

"I had no objections to you as a mother."

Blanche thumped the bed. "Don't let me get away with it. A mother should protect her children, and I didn't protect you." She sniffed loudly.

Mum wasn't a sniffer. She was usually a blow-her-nose-on-an-elegant-handkerchief kind of lady.

"The day we discovered you'd gone was the worst day of my life. Any normal mother would have called the police. I'm sorry I kept silent."

What would life have been like if Mum had spoken up? Would she and Rachel have grown up as sisters instead of strangers?

"My inaction sanctioned your father's views and deprived both of you of a sister. How could I have been so cruel?"

Finally. Mum was figuring out her views on submission were twisted. What had brought about the change?

Tears shimmered in Rachel's eyes. "I wish you'd had more courage, but I understand how scary Dad can be." She came over and put both hands on her mother's shoulders. "Thank you for apologising, but I don't think I would have stayed, no matter what you did."

Naomi asked, "Does William know about Rachel? About me?"

"He does now. He was furious." Blanche blew her nose. "But the final straw was my determination to prioritise being here."

Naomi looked around at each of them. "Praise God the four of us are reconciled. It's a miracle I never thought I'd see." She touched Blanche's shoulder. "You're most welcome to stay with us."

Gran was amazing. Her heart was big enough to welcome them all, and now it looked like she needed to.

Esther took a deep breath. Thinking about Dad drained her strength.

"Sorry, everyone. I'd love to talk more but I need a nap. Can you come back this evening?"

"Could you cope with us praying before we go?" Mum asked.

Mum had never initiated prayer with anyone. Peculiar for a pastor's wife.

"Dear Jesus, thank you for forcing me to deal with things I was avoiding. Thank you that you never leave us alone." Blanche swallowed loudly. "We ask—oh Lord, that's too small a word—we beg for mercy, for William. Please, oh please ..."

Lord, help the changes in Mum to impact Rachel. She needs you desperately.

"From our human point of view, nothing can change William, but you changed Nebuchadnezzar. Please do the same again. Save William as you've saved us. Amen."

Esther's eyes were bright with unshed tears. "I'm excited about the changes in you, but I'm curious about one thing. What gave you the courage to speak to Dad?"

"I think it was Shadrach, Meshach, and Abednego. If they could choose a fiery furnace, then surely I could confront my own husband."

CHAPTER 46

"*R*achel, would you help me out of bed and into the armchair? I'm sick of being in bed."

Rachel looked up from the magazine she was reading. "Sure."

Esther moved with the slow movements of someone decades older. Rachel grasped her hand and offered a supporting arm.

"Ouch," Esther said. "I can feel that fall already. I'll be black and blue tomorrow. Sorry to be so helpless, but my feet are cold. My slippers are in the bottom of the cupboard."

Rachel went around to fetch them. How humiliating this must be for Esther. A few months ago, she'd been cycling to work. Now, getting out of bed tired her. Tears leaked out of Rachel's eyes. She swiped the back of her hand across her eyes. *Esther's God, I have no idea what you're doing or why you are making your faithful follower suffer like this. It doesn't seem fair.*

"You okay, Rachel? There's nothing exciting in the bottom of my cupboard."

Sprung. She couldn't even cry in peace. Rachel straightened up and sniffed. "Finding this a challenge."

"That's understandable. It isn't what any of us wants."

"I don't understand why your God, if he truly cares, would allow this to happen to you."

"That was exactly my question last year."

"How did you battle through it?" Esther had explained before, but Rachel still didn't get it. If anyone else said what Esther said, she'd have accused them of being in denial.

"I'll answer if you pass me my slippers."

Rachel looked down. They were still in her hand. She knelt and let Esther slip her feet into the warm, woolly slippers that would normally be used in the depths of winter. Not the back end of summer. Rachel's heart clenched.

"Pull up a seat and I'll try to explain." Esther pulled her shawl off the back of the chair and wrapped it around herself.

"All humans are self-centred and assume God's job is to make our life rosy. That's why I was angry I had cancer at all. God didn't seem to be upholding his end of the bargain."

Rachel had always thought her own anger was only directed at her father, since she refused to think about God at all. But now it was obvious she'd also been angry with God. Angry that he hadn't protected her from her father's demands. Angry she'd had to struggle on her own. Angry she'd lost her child and suffered night-mares. Yet could God be held responsible for her choices?

"It was only when I examined my assumptions that I realised the problem wasn't God. It was me." Esther snuggled further into her shawl. "Jesus was upfront about the cost of following him. He promised a steep, narrow way with lots of persecution and satanic opposition. I don't know whether Satan is directly linked to my cancer, but I do know God has used it to mature me and bless others."

"What do you mean?"

"There are many people I've been able to tell about Jesus because of my cancer. Before cancer, I never even considered talking to others outside the church."

It wasn't long ago that Rachel wouldn't have allowed Esther to talk about Jesus at all, but the subject no longer felt threatening. More like something she wanted to understand. At the very least, it would allow her to understand Naomi, Blanche, and Esther.

Rachel rubbed her chin. "I've been curious about something, but I'm afraid my question might offend you."

"I won't be offended."

"You worked in a hospital. Have you ever been tempted to … you know, tempted to end your suffering?"

Esther swallowed. "You mean, steal enough drugs for an overdose?"

"Something like that." Had she asked too personal a question?

Esther shifted in her seat. "If I did, it would be like I was saying to God, 'You don't know what you're doing.' Like I presumed to know more than he did about the timing of my death. What if God still has work for me to do? People for me to talk to?"

"Maybe I'm one of them."

"I'm hoping so. If I'd taken the easy way out, we might not be having this conversation."

Rachel stared at the toes of her shoes. "I'm not a prize as a sister."

Esther leaned forward and touched Rachel's cheek. "I'm happy with the sister God gave me."

"You weren't happy about it before."

Esther gave a lopsided grin. "Yeah, well, I had false expectations about you too. Now I appreciate what I have."

Rachel snorted. "Sometimes I think you and Gran are too good to be true."

"Do you understand why?"

Rachel shook her head.

"It's because we understand that God has forgiven us. The forgiveness we've received, we pass on to others."

"Your God is totally different to Dad's."

"His god is a monstrosity." Esther shuddered. "Don't trash the real because you encountered the fake."

"I know I want whatever you and Gran have, but I also know I'm not worthy of it."

"No, you're not."

Rachel's stomach churned.

"Whoops. That came out all wrong. No one is worthy of Jesus's love. Not me, not Gran, not anyone."

Esther and Gran were squeaky clean compared to her. "You've never done much to be ashamed of."

"Don't you think that's one of people's problems? That we consider some sins worse than others?"

"Don't I know it." Rachel cringed as she pictured the accusing eyes and fingers of her nightmares. "Adultery and abortion always come out on top."

Esther closed her eyes.

"I'm tiring you, aren't I?"

Esther's eyelids flicked open. "Do you think I care if my last breaths are used to help you? I'm praying for wisdom to speak clearly."

"I do confess I listened in the other day."

"Mmm," Esther murmured.

"You knew, did you? I've found Daniel in the Bible and read it, and now I've completed Genesis and half of Exodus." Why did she feel the need to parade her progress in front of Esther? After months of ignoring her she now craved her approval.

"Can I share a story with you?"

Rachel touched Esther's arm. "Don't strain yourself doing it."

"I'll try not to. This story is from John 4. As I tell it, please don't think I'm trying to condemn you or say something about your previous lifestyle. I've chosen this because of what Jesus says, not the kind of woman she is."

Condemn. An interesting choice of word. How did Esther know

she'd laboured under a truckload of condemnation since she was a kid? Would the story make her feel worse?

Esther reached for her glass and took a mouthful of water. "Jesus went to a place outside a town in Samaria and sat down beside a well. It was midday. A woman came along to draw water and was astonished when Jesus spoke to her, because Jews didn't associate with Samaritans. Jesus said, 'If you knew who I was, you would ask me to give you living water.'"

Rachel didn't remember ever hearing this story.

"'You have no bucket and the well is deep,' the woman said. 'How can you say this?'"

"Jesus said, 'If you drink my water, you'll never thirst again.'" Esther stopped and took a sip of water.

"'Give me this water,' the woman said."

"'Go and call your husband,' Jesus replied."

"'I have no husband,' the woman said."

"'You're right when you say you have no husband,' Jesus said. 'You've had five, and you're not married to the man you're living with.'"

Esther took another sip of water. "Rachel, there's more, but I can't remember it accurately. Can you see why I told it?"

"I'm like that woman."

"Not just you. In one way, we're all like that woman."

No. Gran and Esther were nothing like that woman. Nothing like Rachel.

"Why did she have five husbands?"

Rachel's mouth twitched. "Perhaps she had atrocious luck and they all died." She stuck out her tongue. "Just joking. I suspect her heart was empty and she tried to gain security or love." Exactly what Rachel had spent the last twenty years doing.

"And did the woman's methods work?" Esther asked.

"No." And they hadn't worked for her either. She'd tried love and pleasure and ended up feeling cheap. She'd tried hard work and focusing on fitness. All that achieved was ending up limp and useless, like overstretched elastic.

"Why do you think Jesus used the living water analogy with this woman longing for love?"

Rachel slumped back in her chair. Water, wells ... water, refreshing ... water. Wait. Thirst. Was that the link? "Is he promising her that if she comes to know him, she'll never be thirsty for love again?"

Esther nodded. "Like I said, we're all like this woman. We've had empty hearts ever since Adam and Eve rejected God."

Rachel's was certainly empty.

"The woman tried to use relationships to fill the hole in her heart. Some people use money or power."

Tension radiated up her neck. She'd been on an endless mouse wheel of striving.

"All the ways we use are equally useless." Esther scratched her elbow. "Later, Jesus says he is the water. If we have him, then our empty hearts can be filled to overflowing."

Overflowing.

Rachel's heart had been dry for the greater part of forever. What if the thing she'd been running from ... no, not a thing. Jesus.

What if he was the only one who could quench her thirst?

CHAPTER 47

*O*nce she arrived home, Rachel checked that Mum was settled in Esther's room and said goodnight. It was still early enough to do some reading. She'd borrowed the Bible from Gran's bookcase the night after she'd heard about Shadrach and company. A few books plugged the gap. No one seemed to have noticed.

Rachel lay down and snapped on the bedside light. She might be a biblical ignoramus, but she remembered John was in the New Testament. She found it and started reading.

The first paragraphs were dense. Was the whole book going to be this hard? She ploughed on, and the reading got easier towards the end of the first chapter and into the second.

The third chapter was more familiar, and she'd definitely had the verses in the middle quoted at her before. She slowed down and whispered them out loud.

For God so loved the world that he gave his one and only son, that whoever believes in him shall not perish but have

ETERNAL LIFE. FOR GOD DID NOT SEND HIS SON INTO THE WORLD TO CONDEMN THE WORLD ...

She stopped and reread the last phrase.

Why had she always felt condemned? Condemned if she didn't look perfect and behave like a princess. Condemned if she failed to be near the top of her class. Condemned if she did anything that might besmirch her father's reputation. The people at Victory had always seemed to be whispering behind her back. Perhaps she'd been paranoid.

Rachel's head throbbed. Even now she could close her eyes and feel a big finger stabbing at her heart. *You're not worthy. You don't measure up.*

But this verse said Jesus didn't come to condemn. Why had her father made it seem that he and Jesus were pals? Condemning left and right. Condemning morning and night. Condemning summer and autumn, winter and spring.

But Dirk and Josh had never condemned her.

A tear welled up in the corner of her eye. Dirk was like toasted crumpets by a winter fire. He'd tease her about the comparison, but even his teasing would be kind. If she could have chosen a father, she would have chosen Dirk. How different her life might have been. She might have finished school and gone to design college. Perhaps she'd have been married, with children.

Rachel wrapped her arms round her body. How many times had she woken after nightmares, aching with emptiness? Yearning to feel the heavy warmth of a child in her arms. Yearning to bury her nose in silken hair. She moaned. God couldn't be blamed for her pregnancy or what she'd done afterwards. The choices had been hers. She'd thought she had no other choice, but she'd deceived herself. Naomi would never have turned her away.

Rachel filled her lungs with air. She should go to bed, but the Samaritan woman's chapter was next.

She kept reading. And reading. The sleepiness left her.

John was astonishing. She was only snorkelling on the surface. She'd need years to scuba-dive down into the corals and mysteries below. Even if she lived to be a thousand, she'd never reach the deepest depths.

Rachel started reading chapter eight.

WHILE JESUS SAT IN THE TEMPLE COURTS THE TEACHERS OF THE LAW AND PHARISEES BROUGHT IN A WOMAN CAUGHT IN ADULTERY. THEY MADE HER STAND BEFORE THE GROUP AND SAID, 'TEACHER, THIS WOMAN WAS CAUGHT IN THE ACT OF ADULTERY. IN THE LAW, MOSES COMMANDED US TO STONE SUCH A WOMAN. WHAT DO YOU SAY?'

Rachel's stomach heaved. Did people ever change? The self-righteous bunch of hypocrites. Using the woman to put Jesus on the spot. Looking for an excuse to condemn her. Condemn him. Condemnation. Like cats toying with a mouse but this wasn't a mouse. It was a woman. A woman who'd committed adultery. Was this the first time? Did she do it out of love or desperation? Did this woman know, as Rachel did, what it was like to be young and scared and alone?

Questions tumbled in Rachel's mind like shoes in the dryer. What happened to the man who'd been with the woman? Had the morality police let him off? Typical. Letting the woman bear the full force of their condemnation. Did they allow her to dress properly before they dragged her into public?

Would Jesus condemn her too? How could he not?

Rachel traced the verses with a trembling finger.

> *Jesus bent down and wrote on the ground. When they kept questioning him he straightened up and said, 'If anyone of you is without sin, let him be the first to throw a stone at her.'*

How unusual. Rachel read the whole line again to make sure she'd got it right. Then kept reading.

> *Those who heard began to go away one by one, the older ones first until only Jesus was left with the woman. 'Woman, where are they? Has no one condemned you?'*
> *'No one sir,' she said.*

A sob erupted from Rachel, and then another. She grabbed a cushion and stuffed it in her mouth. The last line quivered and blurred. She dashed the back of her hand across her eyes and squinted at the next verse.

> *'Then neither do I condemn you,' Jesus declared. 'Go now and sin no more.'*

The words rang in Rachel's head like the peals of a cathedral bell.
Neither do I condemn you.
Neither do I condemn you.
Something she hadn't felt in years flowed in her heart. Was it hope?

Could Jesus take away her condemnation? Were those who condemned Rachel like the hypocritical religious leaders? Their full-time job was teaching the Bible. If they'd got it wrong, then her father could be wrong.

And if her father was wrong, she could spit on his condemnation. Trample his words underfoot and forget them.

Neither do I condemn you.

It was her and Jesus. In the end, even the hypocrites had been honest enough to walk away. Only Jesus had the authority to judge, and he'd said, 'Neither do I condemn.'

Could the Jesus her father had tried to sell her have been a fake? A cheap, pirated copy of the real thing?

Rachel closed her eyes. The words seemed to dance across a sky in Aurora Borealis shimmers. Not condemned. Purple and green and pink. Not condemned. Her blood pulsed and she wanted to caper around her room, but it wasn't going to happen. She'd scare Mum and Gran into a stroke. They'd had enough of falling and stresses and strains. They didn't need a flakey daughter as well.

Not condemned.

Rachel's head whirled. Was that joy surging in her heart? Had she ever experienced joy since she'd run away? Back then, joy had been a tiny hand in hers. Joy had been butterfly kisses and Esther's absolute trust in her. How could she have lost that?

Rachel sat up and scooted back against the headboard. Not condemned. Could it be true? Why hadn't anyone told her? She hugged her body. Even if they hadn't said the words directly, Gran, Mum, Josh, and Dirk had all demonstrated them. Even Esther. But she hadn't been able to interpret their words. She'd blocked them out.

What had she been afraid of? Had she been afraid to admit she'd been wasting her life? That all her endless strivings had been pointless? Worse than pointless. Destructive. Had she been like this woman? Afraid to look up? Afraid to discover that Jesus was no different to the hypocrites.

What perverseness had made her flee from Jesus? Flee from the one person who offers the desires of every heart?

Tears slipped down Rachel's cheek. She used her sleeve to wipe them.

No condemnation.

Hadn't there been other verses about condemnation earlier? She scanned the chapter before. Nope. Back another chapter. Not there either. She skimmed chapter five. The word leapt out at her.

I TELL YOU THE TRUTH, WHOEVER HEARS MY WORD AND BELIEVES HIM WHO SENT ME HAS ETERNAL LIFE AND WILL NOT BE CONDEMNED; HE HAS CROSSED OVER FROM DEATH TO LIFE.

She read the verse through several times, emphasising a different word each time. Whispering the words aloud. Rolling them over her tongue as though to taste all their subtle flavours.

Here was the way to stop feeling condemned. No, more than just a feeling. To stop *being* condemned. Jesus, the judge of the universe, was willing to declare her 'not condemned' as he'd done for the woman in chapter eight. And the woman at the well in Samaria. Jesus cared.

Jesus cared for her. How could he? Dirk said God was like the Prodigal Son's father. These pages showed it to be true. Josh had been astounded that anyone would not be a Christian. Was that because he grasped the Father's love? Yet she'd sneered at his simplistic understanding of life. What a fool she'd been. Josh saw more clearly than she ever had.

Rachel had thought she was trapped on a mouse wheel when it was only her stubborn pride keeping her there. She should have looked up and seen the love shining in Jesus's eyes. Love that took him to the Cross for her.

Rachel hugged her knees more tightly.

What choice did she have? How could anyone do anything but fall on their face before this Jesus and say yes, yes, yes?

What was it that chapter three had said?

FOR GOD SO LOVED THE WORLD THAT HE GAVE HIS ONE AND ONLY SON, THAT WHOEVER BELIEVES IN HIM SHALL NOT PERISH BUT HAVE ETERNAL LIFE.

She'd been blind. The sun had always been there. Unchanging and warm. She'd allowed clouds of anger and bitterness to get in the way. How foolish.

Home. That is what she'd been seeking and it had never been far from her. Jesus had been waiting.

Esther had described cancer as the fire that purified the gold. Could her nightmares have been the means God used to catch her attention? Dirk said God had done miracle after miracle for her, showing he cared and had plans for her life.

Rachel shivered. Sheer bliss. Jesus loved her. He cared. He'd always cared, and now he wanted to call her his beloved daughter.

Tingles ran up and down her spine.

She was home. At last, she was home.

CHAPTER 48

*I*t took Rachel three days to organise her surprise. Would Esther be well enough to participate? Timing was tight. The palliative care nurses had promised Esther would be dressed and in a wheelchair ready to go.

"What's going on?" Esther said. "Are you taking me out into the sunshine for a picnic?"

"We can do that afterwards if you still have energy."

"Well, come on then. Giddy-up."

"Should I give you a whip?" Rachel asked.

Esther laughed then doubled up with a hacking cough. Blanche's knuckles were white on the back of the wheelchair.

They manoeuvred the wheelchair across the road and through the gate.

"Why are we going to the hospital?"

"Patience, patience."

They pushed the chair right through the hospital grounds. "There's nothing back here except the hydrotherapy pool," Esther said.

Rachel imagined Esther's face all scrunched up, trying to guess what was going on.

"I'm not exactly dressed for a swim." Esther checked her watch, now looser than it used to be. "Besides, it's lunchtime. The pool won't even be open."

"It's open."

"I have no idea what you're up to."

Rachel laughed. "That's the whole idea."

She'd told the others what she'd planned. Ringing Sue at the physiotherapy department had been scary. She'd been easy to convince, although it was obvious she couldn't fathom why Rachel thought this was a gift Esther would appreciate.

The automatic doors opened and the smell of chlorine enveloped them in a warm cloud. A lady came forward. "Good to see you, Esther."

"Are you in on this, Sue?"

"Well, someone high up had to sanction your sister's idea. I'll leave it to her to explain." Sue turned to Rachel. "It's all yours. I'll be nearby if you need anything. You've got one hour."

Rachel pushed the wheelchair to one corner of the pool. "Don't worry. I'm not going to shove you in."

"The old me would have loved it."

Rachel put on the brakes and crouched next to Esther. "I told you I became a Christian the other night."

"You couldn't have given me a better gift."

"I'm hoping to top it today."

Esther's eyes widened. "You haven't somehow hidden a boyfriend from me and you're getting married. No, that doesn't make sense. We wouldn't be here."

"Esther, all those drugs must be scrambling your brain. Surely a pool suggests something to you besides swimming."

Esther shook her head again.

"Clue. Jordan River."

"Oh, oh …" Tears ran down Esther's face.

"Yes, I'm going to get baptised while you're still around to watch me. Sorry I can't do a wedding or magically produce a baby, but this will have to do."

"Oh, Rachel." Esther hugged her. "Couldn't be better."

Footsteps clattered across the tiles behind them. Esther turned her head. "Joy, Gina, how come you're here?"

"We asked for an extended lunch break."

The last four guests waited behind Esther's chair. One was a shock to Rachel. A pleasant kind of shock. She flushed and looked at Esther's tear smeared face. "I invited some of my friends to help us celebrate. Let me introduce you."

"Let me guess," Esther said. "You must be Dirk and Mrs Klopper. And you must be Josh, but I'm afraid I have no clue who your fourth guest is."

"This is Pete, Dirk and Norma's son. I have no idea how they've all managed to make it on a Wednesday."

"We told Colin we had urgent business," Pete said. "It's great to finally meet Rachel's family."

Josh jigged up and down. "Rachel said I was part of helping her decide to follow Jesus."

Rachel gripped his arm. "You sure were, buddy."

Josh leaned in and said something in Esther's ear. She beamed at him, her pale face shining with joy. What was he up to? She'd have to ask Esther later.

"We'd better get moving if we have to be out of here by one o'clock," Dirk said. "Rachel, are you ready?"

"I'm wearing my swimsuit and can go in with these clothes. But I haven't done this before. You'd better tell me what to do."

"You're not the only inexperienced one, and you didn't give me much warning. Why don't you and I go into the water, and the others can gather round the edge."

They moved Esther's chair while Pete and Gina collected plastic stools for everyone. Naomi and Blanche sat on either side of Esther.

Rachel accompanied Dirk down the ramp into the pool. They stood out about a metre from the edge in waist-deep water.

"Before we do this, I wanted to say a short something about baptism." Dirk's voice was strong.

Out of the corner of her eye, Rachel could see Sue and two other therapists listening in. She blushed. She mustn't be embarrassed at everyone staring at her. This was something between her and her heavenly Father.

"Baptism is like a death, a birth, and a marriage."

The others chuckled.

"A death because baptism demonstrates that Rachel is dying to her old life. The life she lived for herself. That's why I prefer this kind of baptism. It better shows the death as she goes under water. Then the new life as she rises from the water. So, a second birth. A spiritual rebirth."

So simple. So profound. Rachel had goosebumps all over.

"And a marriage, because baptism is also a day for vows to God," Dirk said. "Rachel, do you promise to follow Jesus for the rest of your life?"

Six months ago, she'd have vomited at the thought.

"Yes, I will as long as he helps me."

"Jesus is more than strong enough. Will you listen to Jesus and obey him?"

"With his help, yes."

"Okay. I'm going to put my hands on your shoulders. The water is deep enough that, if you bend your knees, you'll go right under. When you come up, I've asked Norma to read two verses to bless you. Are you ready?"

Rachel nodded, eyes shining.

"I baptise you, Rachel Macdonald, in the name of the Father and the Son and the Holy Spirit."

Dirk's hands were warm on her shoulders. She took a deep breath, bent her knees, and submerged. For a drawn-out moment, she stayed under the water, then burst out.

"Whoa there." Dirk laughed. "Norma, will you read the blessing?"

"Therefore there is now no condemnation for those who are in Christ Jesus."

Dirk had chosen exactly the right verses. She'd find out later where they were from.

"... because through Christ Jesus the law of the Spirit of Life has set you free from the law of sin and death."

Rachel looked at Esther, Naomi, and Blanche. Three precious women. Her family.

"Gran and I bought you a Bible," Mum said. "You don't have to pretend you're not reading Gran's spare. We've written out the verses that Norma read, and Esther says she wants us to add the others you loved from John's gospel."

"Mum," Esther said, "what time is it?"

"About half past twelve. Why?"

"I know I've been baptised, but I didn't understand what a Christian was in those days. Do you think it would be okay if I was baptised again?"

Rachel choked up. What a God. He was surpassing her gift.

"Do you think it's wise to get wet?"

"Can someone ask Sue if she has any spare hospital robes? If she does, I'll endure the humiliation of being pushed back to palliative care in them."

Gina went to ask.

Sue came over. "Sorry, we ran out this morning, and we won't have any more until after lunch."

"Never mind, Sue," Esther said. "It probably isn't a good idea anyway. I'd have preferred to be dunked, but sprinkling will have to do. Rachel, you need to come up here."

Rachel waded up the ramp, wrung out the worst of the water, and came around to Esther's corner.

"Esther, would you mind if we watched?" Sue indicated the two other therapists.

"Not at all. Come closer and you'll hear better."

Esther indicated the newcomers. "Everyone, this is Brenda and Matt. They're part of the Bible story group. Did you three hear what Dirk said about baptism being like a death, a birth, and a marriage?"

"We didn't miss a thing," Brenda said.

Esther turned to Joy. "Would you pray for me, since you were the one who led me to Jesus?"

"My pleasure. Why don't Gina and the family members link hands and stand around Esther. Is that okay?"

Everyone did as Joy suggested.

"Dear Jesus. This is a special, special day. We've been praying for Rachel for months, and Naomi has been praying for much, much longer. Thank you for answering prayer. Thank you for saving Rachel's life and saving her from despair. Esther wants to be part of this ceremony today and to reaffirm her love for you. Thank you for caring for her and carrying her through the last couple of years. They've been tough—"

"But amazing and joyful as well," Esther cut in.

"Yes, Lord, amazing as well. Please help Esther as she follows you in the next stages of her journey. In Jesus name, Amen."

"Anything to add, Esther?"

"Sorry if my baptism is confusing. I was baptised as a teenager, but I didn't truly know Jesus then. Today, I want to share this special day with my sister." Esther gripped Rachel's hand. "Please pray that I keep my eyes fixed on Jesus. As Josh whispered to me, he's envious of me. I'm going to be seeing Jesus soon, and that's something to celebrate."

Rachel could barely see her sister through a film of tears.

"Okay, ladies," Joy said. "Scoop up some water and put it on Esther's head."

Rachel passed some to Gran. Linked together, they each put their drops of water on Esther. Trickles ran down the sides of her head.

"It's gone in my ears." Esther giggled.

Everyone laughed and several blew their noses.

Esther held her arms up to Rachel. Rachel kneeled and they held each other for a long hug.

"Welcome home, sister," Esther said. "Now you're my sister twice."

CHAPTER 49

"*R*achel, what are you doing here?"

Rachel looked up. Esther was awake but there was something wrong with her voice.

"What do you mean? It's seven thirty. Mum and Gran will be here any moment."

"S-something wrong with my eyes."

An ice block of apprehension slid down Rachel's spine. How much longer would Esther be with them?

Esther rubbed her temple. Her headache must be back. She'd been living on morphine recently.

Footsteps approached and a head Rachel didn't recognise poked around the corner.

"You must be Esther's sister. I'm Dr Webster."

So that was who he was. Esther had talked about him a lot and said they'd be unlikely to ever meet him because he never came to palliative care. Obviously Esther had been wrong.

More footsteps, and the whole crowd arrived. Joy, Gina, Mum, and Gran. But no Dad. Rachel hadn't expected him to come, even though Mum had begged him. Rachel didn't want to meet him, especially not under these circumstances, but she'd have been willing to do it for Esther's sake. What if he never came? Esther would be devastated.

Naomi came and sat next to Esther's bed. "You've had a tough day. What do you want us to do?"

Esther pointed to the envelope on the side table. "Memorial s-service … s-suggestions."

Why was Esther still slurring, and why even worse than before? Was it tiredness or had she had some kind of stroke? Rachel looked at Dr Webster, trapped in the far corner. There were two worry lines between his eyes.

Her grandmother combed the front of Esther's hair. Bless her for her sensitivity. No one likes to be caught in their pyjamas, not looking their best. Should she suggest half of them leave?

Esther gave a lopsided smile. "Welcome, everyone."

Esther rotated her hand. What did she want? Esther repeated the movement and pointed to the end of the bed. Oh, she wanted the end of her bed raised. Rachel stepped forward and did it.

Naomi scanned several pages of instructions and handed them to Blanche. "You've obviously thought hard about this."

Esther nodded again, her movements clearer than her speech. "Important. Last chance to s-share with people."

Blanche looked ready to cry. She leaned over to whisper in Esther's ear. Esther didn't answer.

"Sing or read the Bible or pray?" Blanche asked.

"Favourite s-songs … Bible."

Blanche clapped her hands to gain everyone's attention. "Esther would like each of us to share a favourite song or Bible passage." She glanced at Dr Webster. "But if you don't have something, that's fine."

Dr Webster looked ready to flee.

"As an old person getting near the end of life, I return to these verses again and again." Naomi started them off, her voice soft but confident. She recited the words as though they were old friends. "I heard a loud voice from the throne saying, 'Now the dwelling of God is with men, and he will live with them. They will be his people, and God himself will be with them and be their God.'"

Rachel closed her eyes to absorb the beauty of the words. Esther would soon know their reality.

"He will wipe every tear from their eyes. There will be no more death or mourning or crying or pain, for the old order of things has passed away.'"

Mum pulled a Bible out of her handbag and opened it. She was seldom without it nowadays. "Who shall separate us from the love of Christ? Shall trouble or hardship or persecution or famine or nakedness or danger or sword?" Her finger slid down the page. "For I am convinced, neither death nor life, neither angels nor demons, neither the present nor the future ... neither height nor depth, nor anything else in all creation will be able to separate us from the love of God in Christ Jesus our Lord."

Beautiful words. Just beautiful.

"Such a waste." The words exploded into the quietness, and all the eyes in the room swivelled to look at Dr Webster. He blushed crimson. "I didn't mean to say that out loud."

"Don't you understand yet? My life is about to start." Esther's words were no longer slurred, but clear and strong. "I shall live forever and ever and each day will be more glorious than the one before. Don't pity me. Pity yourselves who have to wait ..."

There was absolute silence in the room. Rachel's heart pounded as though it would leap out of her chest.

Naomi started to sing in a fluting voice. Joy and Gina joined in.

When we've been there ten thousand years, bright shining as the sun. We've no less days to sing God's praise, than when we've first begun.

*W*hat time was it? Rachel rubbed the crick in her neck. Something had woken her. In the distance was the faintest of murmurs. Was it a TV?

Esther had insisted everyone leave, but they'd argued her out of it. Rachel had taken Gran home, then returned. Mum was here as well. Neither wanted to leave Esther alone. Not now. Not when Esther seemed close to the end of her strength.

There was the sound again. A sort of rattle and catch in Esther's breathing. The glow from the hallway allowed her to see Mum's head jerk.

"Mum, do we need to call the doctor?"

"I don't think she's in pain," Mum whispered back. "Why don't we sit for a while?"

They moved a chair to each side of the bed. Rachel put her hand on Esther's and rested her forehead on the edge of the bed. Did Esther know they were here?

She must have fallen asleep again, but suddenly, she was wide awake. Esther's eyes were open.

"We're here, Esther. Mum, and me."

"Good."

The slurring was worse. Esther's breathing laboured, like sandpaper over rough wood.

Rachel stroked Esther's hand. Did it calm her a little?

"Rach."

Were single syllables all Esther had the energy for?

"I'm here."

"For—give him."

"Dad?"

"Ye—ss."

She didn't ask much, this sister of hers.

Esther's chest moved up and down. Mum was crying. She sat down and put Esther's hand against her cheek.

"Tw—i…"

What was she trying to say? Rachel leaned down with her ear near Esther's mouth.

"Tw—ice." Two more breaths. "Sis—ters."

Rachel gulped, and the first tears slid towards her ear.

"S—ee you." Pant, pant. "In mor—ning."

A tiny puff of air touched her cheek.

"No." Rachel shook Esther. "No."

Mum reached across. "Let her go."

"We only just met. I had so much more I wanted to say." Rachel collapsed back onto the chair, striking her funny bone on the way. Pain and pins and needles shot up her arm. Esther wasn't going to feel anything again.

The floodgates opened. She muffled her cries in the mattress. Tears for her sister and the time that they'd lost. Tears for her child. Tears for all her poor choices.

Mum hauled her to her feet and embraced her. They clung to each other for long minutes. She should have been prepared for such a moment, but now the moment had arrived, she wasn't prepared. Nothing could have prepared her. They clung together like survivors on a life raft. Together, but somehow also terribly alone.

Desolate.

CHAPTER 50

*R*achel's back ached with tension as she guided her grandmother up the scuffed and threadbare carpet towards the front row of the church. Their progress was slow because everyone wanted to greet her grandmother.

"Sorry for your loss," another stranger said in low tones. Rachel lost count of how many times she'd heard the words.

It had been a week of numbness and tears. Esther had been right. Death can be beautiful. Rachel's heart was one throbbing bruise, but she would never forget Esther's peace and joy.

Naomi stopped again as another person leaned forward to kiss her cheek. Rachel's throat tightened. If she started crying now, could she stop? Her grandmother was loved. Would these people ever love her like that? She was included in the whispered condolences because she was obviously family, but most of the people were strangers.

The building was packed. If this was her funeral, she doubted there'd be more than ten people present. Someone played hymns on the piano. The mellow sound soothed her.

Rachel spotted Esther's boss halfway down the church aisle. Presumably, the people with her were also physiotherapists.

Naomi straightened up and walked forward once again. Rachel smiled a tight smile towards Mum, looking back at them from the front row. Her pale face was partially hidden under a black hat.

"Mum, do you know any of these other people? What about the lady three rows back?"

Mum glanced over her shoulder. "That's Michelle, the receptionist at the cancer clinic. I also spotted Dr Webster sliding into the back row. Esther would be touched. She prayed a lot for them."

The pianist played a final chord, and a middle-aged man went up to the microphone.

"Welcome everyone, Esther's friends and family. I'm Stuart Olsen, and I pastor this church." He placed a roll of paper on the stand in front of him. "Esther has given me a long list of instructions." He shook out the roll, and it unfurled to touch the floor. There was a twitter of nervous laughter. "Esther thought her idea might make you laugh."

Trust Esther to plan her own funeral.

"We'll keep things as informal as possible. You should have a programme. Esther chose some of her favourite songs, songs that reminded her of the truth she found in the Bible."

He looked up at the listeners and smiled warmly. "She told me there would be people here who weren't yet followers of Jesus. Please feel free not to sing."

Would she ever have Esther's kind of courage to talk to people about Jesus? The whole thing was still new to her.

After the song, Stuart said, "Naomi, Esther's grandmother, will share first followed by Joy, one of Esther's close friends."

Naomi clambered stiffly to her feet, eyes red. The lines on her face were deepened with grief. Her hand shook as she placed a sheet of paper on the stand.

"Esther asked me to tell you her story." She licked her lips. "Since she couldn't be here to tell you herself."

Rachel had questioned whether Gran was up to speaking at Esther's funeral. The first sentence was shaky, but now her voice strengthened.

"Esther grew up assuming she was a Christian. She thought one became a member of God's family by going to church services." Naomi looked up. "It's a good thing it doesn't happen that way, or some of you wouldn't have dared to step into this building."

There was a ripple of laughter.

"She later discovered that you can only be a member of God's family through a second birth. A new start only God himself can give. For Esther, this moment came after she was diagnosed with cancer. Her crisis forced her to re-examine the Bible. She found she'd created a god to suit herself. He was somewhat like a genie in a lamp, granting our every wish."

It was interesting how their father had managed to give each of his daughters different impressions of God. Both were equally false. Rachel had only seen a harsh judge who demanded perfection.

What kept her father away from Esther's deathbed and funeral? Esther had longed to see the whole family reconciled. In the end she had to be content with a partial answer to her prayers. Could she keep praying in heaven, or was prayer only relevant down here?

If only Rachel had become a Christian months ago, she could have asked Esther these questions. Instead, she'd wasted precious time. Years. If only she'd never run away from Gran's place, how different life might have been.

"The God Esther discovered in the Bible was nothing like a genie. Not that he's against happiness, but it isn't his first priority. He wants his wandering children to return home." Naomi spoke for another minute before concluding. "I want to use the time I have left as wisely as Esther did."

Naomi picked up her programme. "We're going to sing *Amazing Grace*. The words are printed out for you. This song was written by a former slave trader who discovered the new life Jesus gives. We sang the final verse to Esther on the night she died."

Rachel sang three lines before she choked up. She grabbed the handkerchief from her pocket and scrubbed her face. Mum and Gran couldn't get through the song either. Instead, they held hands. There was something special about being here together, comforting each other.

After the song, Joy stood up. She wore a traditional Chinese outfit in navy blue.

"My name is Joy Wong." She gave a little bow. "Esther and I met at the cancer clinic. Every time she came in for her chemo we discussed Bible stories. She asked me to share one of her favourites. I'll explain later why she chose it."

Esther knew many Bible stories. Which was her favourite? Rachel didn't even know the answer to this simple question. If only she'd talked to Esther when she first returned to Gran's house, instead of giving her the silent treatment.

"Jesus was born about two thousand years ago. He did numerous miracles and, along the way, made enemies among the religious rulers. Eventually, they crucified him." Joy opened the Bible she held and placed it on the stand beside her. "Two criminals were crucified with Jesus, one on his right and one on his left."

Joy didn't rush. She enunciated every word and painted mind pictures in front of them.

"One of the criminals hurled insults at Jesus. 'Aren't you Christ the Saviour? Save yourself and us.' But the other criminal rebuked the first. 'Don't you fear God, since you are under the identical sentence? We are punished justly, for we are getting what our deeds deserve but this man, Jesus, has done nothing wrong.'"

Rachel could see why Esther loved this story. It contained the heart of the biblical story.

"This second criminal turned to Jesus and said, 'Remember me when you come into your kingdom.' Jesus answered him, 'I tell you the truth, today you will be with me in paradise.'"

Joy picked up the open Bible and closed it.

"Most people presume that if there is a paradise, they're good enough to get into it. Here we have a real criminal. Every religion in the world would be unanimous, '*If* there *is* a Paradise he'd *never* get in.' Yet what does Jesus say to him at the end? 'Today you will be with me in paradise.' How does this man get in? He freely acknowledges he doesn't deserve it."

Rachel bowed her head. For the first time ever, she prayed for those who didn't yet know the truth of this story.

"Esther used to say to me, 'This story proves entry into heaven isn't based on good deeds, because this man never had time to do any.' He couldn't say, 'Hey there'"—Joy waved her hand at the imaginary guards. "'Excuse me. I need to get down from this cross. I've got to be baptised, help the poor, or donate money to the church.' It's too late for this man to do anything." Joy looked up for a long moment. "So why does Jesus accept him?"

That had been one of Rachel's questions. How could Jesus accept someone like her? *Lord, open people's hearts.*

"The first criminal demands Jesus prove his claim to be God. If you save yourself, I'll believe you can save others." Joy slowly built her case and reeled in her listeners. "The paradox is, if Jesus had come down from the Cross, we'd be permanently cut off from God. It wasn't nails that held Jesus on that cross. It was love." Joy gestured to her listeners. "Love for you and me. The Cross was the only way our friendship with God could be restored."

And for so many years Rachel had regarded it as unimportant. *Thank you, Lord, for loving me enough to die for me.*

"The majority of people there that day saw Jesus as a dying failure. Only the second criminal saw a king coming into his kingdom."

That was a new thought. One to ponder when her head was less fuzzy.

"How does the criminal see this? Did he watch and listen to Jesus through his trial? Did he notice Jesus never cursed or screamed against his oppressors? Did he hear him forgiving his enemies?" Joy paused. "The Bible tells us no one can recognise who Jesus is unless God reveals it to them. It happened to Esther as she reread the Bible in her bedroom. It happened to me in a prison cell during the Cultural Revolution in China."

Rachel blinked. She'd done it again. Assumed Joy was someone without a story worth telling. She must ask her about her background.

"Of all the people at the crucifixion, the one who is least likely is the one who is saved. A criminal submits to a new king, and he's no longer condemned."

Joy smiled. "Perhaps Esther is chatting to him right now."

What a delightful thought. Was Esther, even now, twirling in the sunshine of her father's smile? Laughing for joy.

The pearls of memory from Esther's childhood no longer pained her. The sting was gone now she'd brought everything to Jesus. These days her memories were lustrous jewels to linger over.

"I'm going to suggest we repeat the previous song. I hope it will have more meaning for you now."

It did. *Lord, make it more meaningful for others.*

Stuart stood up again. "Okay, it's your turn to speak. How did Esther's life impact yours? I want us to limit ourselves to two minutes each, so more people can share." He indicated a man towards the back. "We have a roving microphone."

Rachel swivelled around and hooked her arm over the back of her seat. She wanted to see who spoke. A man in his forties stood up and took the microphone. "My name is Tony Agosto."

The name was unfamiliar.

"My wife met Esther during chemo."

Oh, she knew who this was. Esther had kept saying she'd meet Anna again soon.

"When Anna ended up in palliative care, she was terrified of dying. Esther gave up her lunch breaks every day and even came in on weekends to tell Bible stories."

That explained why all the staff in the palliative care unit had known Esther.

"Anna came to accept the Jesus of the stories and died at peace." Tony looked towards the family in the front row. "Even though I'd grown up in a church, I didn't understand her peace. After hearing what Esther said at Anna's funeral, I went and read the Bible for myself. Now I'm looking forward to meeting Anna and Esther again one day."

Maybe that was what Esther's last words had meant. She wasn't living in hope that she'd make it through to the next morning. The morning she was speaking of was the new morning in God's kingdom. Rachel wiped her eyes. Esther was making an appointment. It was an appointment Rachel planned to keep.

Several women from the church shared and then another man stood up.

"My name's Rob. Esther was the best person to talk to in the waiting room at the clinic because she was real, not plastic. I was one of her failures. Once I was cancer free, I tried to forget about the things we discussed and dismiss them as irrelevant. I'm willing to admit, I may have been wrong and need to check out what she said. Maybe that's the best way to honour someone who was sincere and—"

Was he struggling to find a word or was he about to cry?

"—winsome. I know that's an old-fashioned word, but it fits Esther. Her sense of humour made even chemo bearable."

Stuart raised his index finger. "Time for one more."

Rachel was about to stand when the last person she expected beat her to it. Dr Webster was the most formally dressed person in the building. He must have respected Esther to be here. His cheeks were slightly flushed.

"Esther intrigued me. Here was someone with a science background who believed in something I labelled 'ridiculous superstition.'" He cleared his throat. "But Esther wasn't ridiculous. In fact, she was level-headed, humorous, and not averse to going on the offensive during a debate. I came to respect her even though I didn't always understand her. I've seen many people face death. It sounds weird, but watching Esther on her last evening was a privilege. Her final words were a confident restatement of her beliefs. I don't pretend to understand why her God would take her away. I don't pretend to understand why she was full of gratitude and never complained. I only know she was radiant with joy at the thought of being with her Jesus."

Rachel curled her arm across her stomach. Missing Esther was a deep ache. It would be hard to go on without her but she would. Nothing must stop her keeping her appointment with Esther in God's new morning.

She was going to wear Gran's pearl necklace and remember Esther. Remember the pearls of the good times and look forward to the times to come.

Stuart said, "Esther knew she was dying, and she spent her last weeks preparing. She wrote dozens of letters. If she has written to you, your first name will be listed on the back of the programme."

Rachel looked down at the programme clasped in her hand. Her name headed the list. She'd save the letter for later. Esther would write as she'd lived. She'd remind her how wonderful Jesus was and urge Rachel to keep trusting him.

Rachel's tears boiled over. If Esther could see the tears streaming down her face, she'd say, 'Rachel, don't cry for me. I'm more alive than I've ever been.'

Esther would be right.

STORYTELLER FRIENDS

• Do you want to receive book updates, latest news and offers? Sign up at http://subscribe.storytellerchristine.com to become a storyteller friend.

Once you're signed up, check your junk mail or the 'promotions' folder (gmail addresses) for the confirmation email. This two-stage process ensures only true 'storyteller friends' can join.

• **Facebook:** As well as a public author page, I also have a VIP group. You need to ask permission to join.

NON-FICTION BY CHRISTINE DILLON

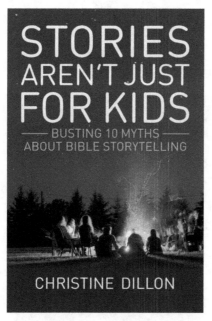

Stories Aren't Just For Kids: Busting 10 Myths About Bible Storytelling (2017). Free to subscribers and packed with testimonies to get you excited about the potential of Bible storytelling.

1-2-1 Discipleship: Helping One Another Grow Spiritually (Christian Focus, Ross-shire, Scotland, 2009).

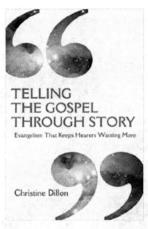

Telling The Gospel Through Story: Evangelism That Keeps Hearers Wanting More (IVP, Downer's Grove, Illinois, 2012).

ENJOYED GRACE IN THE SHADOWS?

Readers often check the reviews before they buy a book. As this book is independently published, the only way it will be 'discovered' by readers is if you get excited about it. Online reviews are one way to do so.

How to write a review – easy as 1-2-3

1. A few sentences about why you liked the book
2. What kinds of people might like the book?
3. Upload the review - the same review can be used on each site. Possible places are Amazon, Goodreads, Bookbub, Kobo and Koorong (for Australians).
4. If you loved the book please also share your review on your personal social media, or feel free to tell others about it in any context.

BIBLE STORYTELLING

This book models Bible storytelling with adults. I was introduced to this method of communicating the good news about Jesus in 2004. At first, I had a lot of prejudices about it. Once I started using storying, I thought it was only to introduce people to Jesus. Later, I discovered it works equally well to teach and train people of any age. Now, it's rare for a day to go by without me telling a Bible story.

• For more resources, please look at the list of my non-fiction books or go to:

www.storyingthescriptures.com
• **Facebook at storyingthescriptures.**

ACKNOWLEDGMENTS

This is now my second published novel. It was easier this time and I am now less a 'reluctant novelist' than for the first.

Again, this novel was a team effort.

Joy Lankshear, thank you for your wonderful cover designs. You are a patient woman. Hopefully this time was less stressful than the last. Thank you for encouraging me to follow Jesus.

I had intended to only have one editor this time (to keep costs down) but both of my editors are so fantastic and have such different gifts, that this book was still double edited. Iola Goulton and Cecily Paterson, it is a privilege to work with you both. Thank you for all that you teach me and for your hard work to make the story shine. Check out Cecily's books for teenage girls.

The advantage of this being the second book is that I'm beginning to gather a team of beta readers (who read the book earlier in the process and make suggestions for big changes) and proofreaders (who read the book after all the editing and look for typos and small issues). Thank you to Rosalyn S, Lizzie R, Kim W, Laura T, Katie D, Candace B, Jane P, Jeannette K, Rebekah D, Jane C, Kristen Y. and Kate B.

Thank you Cecily, Laura and Kristen. Long may we encourage each other. I look forward to more excellent fiction to come (and probably non-fiction as well).

I ran a competition at my book launch to name two secondary characters. Tony K, thank you for the name, 'Alice' and Sue Boddy, 'Peter' is named after your brother.

I collect illustrations to use in evangelism and often don't remember the original source. Thank you to Phillip Jensen, Randy Adams, the late John Chapman and possibly Steve McKerney for any that may have originated with you. If I've missed someone out, sorry. I hope it encourages you that your illustrations are being used to communicate the best news of all.

Finally, a thank you to the unsung heroes, the prayer team. You know who you are and more importantly, Jesus knows who you are. This book has been carried along on a current of prayer that enabled this book to be released less than a year after the previous one.

I mentioned previously that this book contains two miracles based on real stories (so I couldn't be accused of making them up). The mountaintop tyre blowout is how Pauline Hamilton, a former OMF missionary in Taiwan came to Christ. She writes about it in her outstanding autobiography, *To a Different Drum (OMF, 1998)*.

To understand more of the Bible's grand story go to www.story-ingthescriptures.com

Discussion Guide

There is a discussion guide for *Grace in Strange Disguise* and *Grace in the Shadows* available to download from storytellerchristine.com

ABOUT THE AUTHOR

 Christine has worked in Taiwan, with OMF International, since 1999.

It's best not to ask Christine, "Where are you from?" She's a missionary kid who isn't sure if she should say her passport country (Australia) or her Dad's country (New Zealand) or where she's spent most of her life (Asia - Taiwan, Malaysia and the Philippines).

Christine used to be a physiotherapist, but now writes 'storyteller' on airport forms. She spends most of her time either telling Bible stories or training others to do so.

In her spare time, Christine loves all things active – hiking, cycling, swimming, snorkelling. But she also likes reading and genealogical research.

Connect with Christine
www.storytellerchristine.com/

PROLOGUE

11 November 1944
Sydney, Australia

The radio dominated the room. All gleaming wood and intriguing metal dials.

William zeroed in on it, ignoring all the people, desks, and typewriters crammed into his father's office. This was the first time he'd ever been allowed here, although Ian, his older brother, was always welcome.

William reverently stroked one finger across the radio's wooden case.

"Careful son," his father said.

"He won't hurt it, Mr Macdonald." William could hear a smile in the lady's voice. His face warmed and he looked around at the people eating and drinking out of tall glasses. The kind lady offered him the plate of scones. William looked towards his father, who nodded. He took a scone and thanked the lady. Mum always insisted he show good manners.

"Nearly time," said someone at the back of the room. His father pulled out his fob watch and then came forward to switch on the radio. It crackled to life.

"One hundred thousand people packed into Flemington race track today. Good sports and good sorts." The marching music in the background and the way the radio announcer emphasised the words sent reverberations into William's stomach. "The bookmakers' area is seething with punters."

Yesterday he hadn't known what all these words meant, but last night his father had explained what would happen today and had given him strict instructions about how to behave. Being too noisy or behaving like a hooligan would get him sent home.

"Bookmaker." William whispered the word to himself. Dad wasn't a betting man. Said it was a game for mugs but he allowed something called a sweepstake at the office and he'd promised both boys a ticket—against their mother's protests. Dad picked him up, sat him on the edge of one of the desks, and handed him a slip of paper with the number four and one word written on it.

It was a strange word and William didn't know if he could pronounce it correctly, but he knew it must be the name of a horse. S-i-r-i-u-s. He looked over Ian's shoulder and read his horse's name—Peter. Dad said the first three horses would win money—a whole shilling for the winner. William could hardly imagine it. He never won anything. Ian might have been only two years older, but he was bigger and faster and smarter. He always came out on top, and Dad was always there to clap enthusiastically.

"And the ladies," the radio announcer said. "A sea of blue and green, red and pink. Whoops!" The announcer's voice rose. "There goes someone's hat."

Who cared about ladies and their hats? William swung his legs and clipped the side of the desk. His father glared at him over his glasses, and William froze. He mustn't mess up his first visit to Dad's office.

People said his father was a successful man. He supposed Dad was, since he was boss of this office and had a big car and house, but William wished they saw him more. Dad almost always arrived home after William and Ian had eaten. By the time his father finished dinner, William was in bed and only Ian got the chance to talk to him. The weekends weren't much good either for kicking a ball around or getting help with his train set, because Dad spent all his time attending Ian's sports matches, instructing the gardener, or reading the newspaper.

Mum said they were lucky to have Dad home at all. Half the boys at school had fathers away in Europe, fighting.

"They're coming out now. Twenty-three of the nation's finest horses. Look at the sheen on their coats. Look at the way they prance and fight the bit. They know what's coming—Australia's greatest race."

William couldn't control a tiny wriggle. The announcer sounded so excited, and all the adults were motionless, staring at the radio like they didn't want to miss a single word.

"Two miles of speed and glory. Two miles of agony and ecstasy. Two miles to prove who's champion."

The announcer reeled off information about each horse. William glanced down at the paper cradled in his hand. He was only interested in ..."Number four—"

William sat up straight.

"Sirius, ridden by Darby Munro and owned by Reg Turnbull, our very own Chairman of the Victorian Racing Club. Three to one favourite." William's stomach fluttered. The numbers meant nothing, but favourite sounded promising. If only his horse would win.

"Ladies and gentlemen, the 1944 Melbourne Cup is about to begin. May our boys be home from the front to watch the next one." The announcer's voice went sombre for a moment. Dad said the tide of the war had turned, and Hitler would soon be running for cover. Course he would. How could he stand up against the great British Empire and the Americans?

A gunshot sounded, and William jumped in his seat.

"They're off!" The microphone squealed. "A great start to the 1944 Cup."

William had seen last year's race on a newsreel, and he could picture the horses all bunched together.

"Clayton has settled down near the fence."

He didn't care about Clayton. Where was Sirius?

"As they pass the two furlongs post for the first time, Clayton is out front by two or three lengths. In second place is Judith Louise, and Sirius in third place."

Sirius had a chance. William clenched his fist around the slip of paper. *Come on, Sirius.*

"As they come to the third furlong, Sirius is moving up." The commentator's voice sped up. "He's looking in control."

Come on, Sirius.

"Two furlongs from home, and Sirius is still in the lead."

Could he do it? Could he win?

"Sirius now a length and a half in front. Cellini in second and Peter coming up on the outside."

Not Peter. Any horse but Peter.

The commentator's voice rose in a crescendo. "Peter on the outside has thrown out a challenge. He's surging forward."

William squeezed his eyes shut, clenched his jaw, and willed Sirius on. *Go, go.*

"Peter is closing the gap. He's closing the gap."

William wanted to vomit.

"Sirius is being ridden for dear life. Can he hold his lead?"

Come on. Come on. William pounded his fists on his knees. *You have to win.*

"And it's Sirius by a head," the commentator finished, his words breathless. "Peter in second and Cellini third."

William pumped his fist in the air and flashed a smile at his brother. Finally. A win. He jumped off the desk and waved his paper. "Sirius won! He won!"

A whole shilling. What could he do with a whole shilling? Maybe buy the model aeroplane he'd been staring at for weeks in the shop window. Or maybe he'd keep the money and treasure it. He bounced up and down. Today he'd beaten Ian for the first time, and he didn't intend it to be the last. Dad often told them "no one remembers who is second."

Well, Sirius would be remembered, and maybe, just maybe, his father would notice him at last.

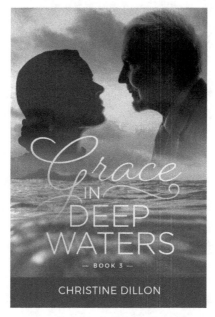

Book 3 in the Grace series

CPSIA information can be obtained
at www.ICGtesting.com
Printed in the USA
LVHW010446211221
706819LV00010B/788